ESCAPE TO THE SUN

ELENA AITKEN

Escape to the Sun

Also by Elena Aitken

Summit of Desire

Summit of Seduction

Summit of Passion

Fighting For Forever

The Springs Collection: Volume 1

The Springs Collection: Volume 2

The Springs Collection: Volume 3

The Springs Complete Collection - Books 1-10

The McCormicks

Love in the Moment

Only for a Moment

One more Moment

In this Moment

From this Moment

Our Perfect Moment

Stand Alone Stories

All We Never Knew

Drawing Free

Sugar Crash

Composing Myself

Betty & Veronica

The Escape Collection

Vegas

Nothing Stays in Vegas

Return to Vegas

His to Tame

His to Seek

Hers for the Season

Bears of Grizzly Ridge: Books 1-4

Bears of Grizzly Ridge: Books 5-8

Halfway Series

Halfway to Nowhere

Halfway in Between

Halfway to Christmas

Chapter One

HEATHER HOLT PICKED her way through the paper bags, empty bottles and...*oh no, was that a used...?* She didn't want to think about what else was under her feet on the crowded dirt road. The man at the airport told her it was Main Street, but it was unlike any main street she'd ever seen. And she'd been living in Central America for five years. It wasn't just the road that was dirty and littered. It was the very air she pulled into her lungs. It was heavy. Heavy with humidity, yes. But more than that. Heavy with the cloying scents of curry and fried foods, some type of blossoming flower that she couldn't pin down and...people. It was a dizzying perfume. One Heather was absolutely certain she didn't want to wear.

She tried to fight the growing sense of desperation. *No. Not desperation.* It was more like a terrifyingly crippling realization that she had nowhere else to go. For better or worse, she would be staying in Bocas Town in the Bocas del Toro archipelago on the west side of Panama. At least for a few months. Even looking through her veil of emotion, Heather feared she'd only seen a small part of the *worse*, and there was definitely no *better* in sight.

It's not as if she was new to the country or the people. But if she hadn't seen it for herself on a map that Bocas Town was part of the Panama she'd come to know and love, there's no way she would have believed it. Not that she'd come to know much of the country, living as a dockmaster's wife at a well-to-do marina just a few hours north of Panama City for the last five years. If she'd had anywhere else to go, she would have gone there.

As it was, all Heather had was a name—Mick. And the name of a bar—the Bitter End—scratched on a piece of napkin. It wasn't much. But it was all she had. She'd make it work.

It's not as if she had a choice.

The more she looked around at the mix of locals, backpackers who wished they were locals, and transplanted North Americans, who likely were some sort of mix of the two, the tighter the knot in her stomach pulled.

"Great idea, Heather." She mumbled the words to herself, but a passerby heard and tried to high-five her. She dodged him, but it didn't deter him any.

"Whatever it was, man, I'm sure it was stellar."

Stellar? It was anything but stellar. It was a gut reaction, last minute, completely foolish, act of a woman out of options. That's exactly what she was. A woman completely and totally out of options.

She'd been worse. And she'd be better, too. Just not today.

Heather straightened her shoulders and hitched her backpack higher on her back. Everything she owned, or at least, everything she wanted to own, was in that pack. She'd only had a few hours' notice when her friends Cass and Archer confirmed that they'd have room for her on their charter sailboat to take her to Bocas del Toro. Not that she needed much more. Everything back at the Shelter Bay Marina was full of memories of a different life. An old life. A life she no longer wanted anything to do with. If she was honest, it was a life she'd never really wanted. At least not with Joe. But it wasn't until he'd had a baby with one of his waitresses that she got the out she'd been looking for.

It didn't make her proud to think that she'd stayed in a loveless relationship because it was *easy*, but it was what it was and she couldn't go back and change it.

No. It was all about looking forward now.

Bocas would most certainly not be the cushy life of Shelter Bay, but that's why she knew it was going to be okay. No. It would be more than okay. She was more than ready for a change and a challenge.

Heather glanced down at the scrap of napkin again as if she hadn't memorized the details days ago, a full five minutes after it was given to her. She owed a lot to her friends, and the connections they had in the islands that had led her to that address on that napkin. What was waiting for her after she checked in with Mick, she couldn't be entirely sure. Although, she hoped her friends were right and it involved a bed-and-breakfast run by a woman who could use some help. More specifically, *her* help. Because that's why Heather was there.

Only a few weeks earlier, when she'd hopped on another charter with Cass and Archer out to the tranquil San Blas Islands, she'd met Josie, an eccentric old woman who, in one afternoon, had changed her life. Heather couldn't even explain it. She wished she could. But ultimately, it didn't matter because Josie had seen that she was lost and broken, and with only a few words, the older woman gave her hope. And at that moment, that hope looked like a beer shack with a broken surfboard hanging over the door, a scrawny mutt curled on the crumbling concrete step, and a crate full of empty bottles sitting next to him. *The Bitter End* was painted in block letters on the surfboard.

She looked at the napkin.

Back to the surfboard. It wasn't what she'd been expecting, that was for sure, but Heather had long ago learned to expect the unexpected. She stepped up, resisting the urge to pet the flea-ridden dog, and reached for the door at the same moment as it opened. The pumping beats of what sounded like Top 40 hits on a steel drum band spilled from the opening; a shirtless, golden brown man who looked as though he could have been riding that surfboard in a different circumstance, appeared. His back to her, the man walked backward down the stairs as he yelled back to someone inside. Instinctively, Heather stepped out of the way, narrowly missing the dog. Or maybe she didn't miss him, judging by the growl beneath her.

The man turned at the sound.

"Hey, Poco." He bent to scratch behind the dog's head. "You all right?"

"Excuse me?"

The man looked up, seeing her for the first time.

He was gorgeous, if you liked the rough around the edges surfer boy type with hard, tight muscles, golden skin, salt-tousled-curling-over-the-ears dirty blond hair, and an attitude to match. She swallowed hard.

"Did you need something?"

She did. She needed a lot of things. And judging by the way her body vibrated into a full-scale heat, he might just have exactly what she needed.

If only she had time for that. Heather cleared her throat. "Mick?"

"Depends." Looking up at her from his squat, his lip curled up in a smile so sinful, in any other instance there was no doubt she'd be in trouble.

Any instance where she didn't need a place to sleep that night. Alone. She narrowed her eyes, fairly certain she wasn't speaking to Mick. "Where can I find him?"

He laughed and straightened. "It's like that, is it?"

"It's like, I need to find Mick." Heather crossed her arms, which only made Surfer Boy laugh again.

"Don't get all twisted up, sugar." He pointed behind him. "You'll find him behind the bar."

Heather twisted to look past the golden muscles in front of her. "This is a bar?"

"Of course. And a hostel. And…" His mouth twisted up in that damned sexy grin again. "Let's just say, this place lives up to its name."

"Its name?" She glanced around but didn't see any other sign telling her where she was.

"The Bitter End."

"What does that mean?"

"It's just like it sounds." Surfer Boy swallowed his laugh so hard he looked as if he might choke. "It's also a nautical term."

She didn't respond, unsure of what any of that meant. What any of it meant.

She didn't realize she was staring at him until he winked at her, flashed a smile that could only mean he came from money, and said, "Mick's inside."

"Right." She shook her head, embarrassed that he probably thought she was checking him out. It wasn't entirely untrue, but even if there was truth to it, she certainly didn't need him thinking that. Heather pulled herself together and squeezed past him through the doorway, careful to avoid both the dog, who'd returned to sleeping, and Surfer Boy, who made no effort to move out of her way.

He smelled like salt, suntan lotion, and sex. She couldn't help but inhale his scent, holding her breath to keep it in just long enough to push out the stench of the street but not long enough for her body to register the effect he had on her.

Too late.

He waited until she finally moved past him to let out his own breath. Damn, he didn't usually go for the fresh-off-the-plane backpacker type. Too young. Too idealistic. Too needy.

But that woman was different. Sure, she had a backpack, and yes, he hadn't seen her around. Bocas Town was a small place, and Ash knew everyone, including—no, *especially*—the ladies. The woman was obviously new to Bocas, she wasn't new to traveling. That much was clear by the slight wear of her clothes, as if they'd been kissed by the sea a few too many times, the scuffs of her pack, and the tan on her skin. He was willing to bet that tan probably didn't have a whole lotta lines if he looked close enough.

And he would be happy to investigate closer.

On any other day, that's exactly what he would be doing.

But not today. "Damn. Hey, Paco?" The dog lifted his head before tucking down again.

Ash shook his head to clear himself of the sight of her long, dark braid, and toned, tanned legs. It didn't totally work.

No. Not today.

He didn't get into town very often these days, and he'd felt the loss of companionship in his arms, as well as his balls. His dick twitched, needing attention. With one more look behind him at the now closed door, Ash shook his head. "Maybe later," he assured himself.

His trips to Bocas Town didn't come as frequently anymore, and although he usually had time to fool around and play for a bit, today he didn't. He'd promised Sherri he'd pick up all her packages, including the new caretaker of her jungle bed-and-breakfast.

He'd somehow become the self-appointed caretaker of Sherri's bed-and-breakfast, and more importantly, of the older woman. She was like an eccentric old aunt who'd taken him in when he was new to Bocas and as lost as anyone else in what could only be described as the *Land of the Misfit Toys.* She'd recognized something in him that he couldn't even see himself. At least, not at the time. Sherri probably didn't even know it, but she'd saved him with the unconditional love she'd had no reason to give him. No reason beyond the fact that Sherri's heart was too big for her own good.

He'd do anything for her. Including missing a primo surf day to take the boat into Bocas Town to pick up anything she needed.

And that's just what he was going to do.

His flip-flops provided a thin barrier protecting him from the street. He hardly noticed anymore. Not that he noticed it much when he'd first come to Bocas four years earlier. The contrast between his ordered, all too clean life back in the States and the tousled mess of Bocas was exactly what he'd been looking for when he'd arrived. After time, as he slowly woke to his new life, the disorder and chaos around him, the pure opposition of his surroundings to his past, gave him comfort. He'd craved something different. Anything.

"Ash. Ash. Señor Ash!" The familiar high-pitched shriek Ash had come to know would be followed by Miguel's toothy grin, made him grin and was just about enough of a distraction for him to forget about the long-legged beauty. Just about.

"Hey, kiddo." Ash turned just in time to catch the small boy before he crashed into his legs. Miguel had the ability to pop out of nowhere and if Ash wasn't careful, he'd take him out. It'd happened before. But only once. As soon as he untangled the kid from his legs, he reached into the pocket of his cargo shorts and handed Miguel the peppermint he'd stashed there.

"*Gracias.*" He unwrapped the candy; it disappeared in an instant. "Help today, Señor Ash?"

"You know it, Miguel."

Ash had sort of adopted the boy—or more likely, it was the other way around—only about a year before on a trip into town. He had a huge order from Sherri that required more than one trip to the boat, where he'd have to leave supplies unsupervised. That was never a good idea in a place like Bocas Town. Not unless you felt like paying for those supplies twice. The second time with a *local tax* attached. That's where Miguel came in. For a small fee, usually the price of a sandwich or a bottle of soda, he'd happily guard anything for Ash. Or carry bags, or pretty much help out with whatever was needed.

As far as Ash was concerned, it was the perfect symbiotic relationship.

"Where we headed?"

Ash pointed up the street. Everything in Bocas Town was within a few streets. It was small, but the town managed to pack in a whole lot of trouble in such a tight space.

"The clinic?"

Ash nodded.

"What ya gettin' there?"

He shrugged. "You know Ms. Sherri. Could be anything." And it could have been. With Sherri's place so far away from town and the clinic—as basic as it was—she liked to have a well-stocked first-aid kit for her guests. Just in case. Not that there'd ever been a case. Nothing more serious than a monkey bite, anyway. "Comin'?"

Ash didn't need to ask. Miguel was right behind him like a crow picking up crumbs. Not for the first time, Ash wondered what Miguel's home life was like.

Or whether he had one at all.

"All right, kid. We have lots on the list today. I'll need all the muscle power you can handle."

Miguel flexed his scrawny arms. His smile was so hopeful, Ash would find him a whole afternoon's worth of work, even if he had to make it up.

The inside of the Bitter End was not at all what Heather expected. Not that she had any idea what to expect. But if it was a bed-and-breakfast she was looking for, the Bitter End was decidedly not that. Just inside the door was a small doorway with numbers labeled on a piece of paper tacked to the wall. She peeked inside and saw two rows of bunkbeds with backpacks, towels, and underwear slung over the frames.

Interesting choice for a bed-and-breakfast.

She followed the pumping music, lulled as if it was the Pied Piper leading her out of town instead of into what could only be described as a pit of pleasure. If your idea of pleasure was lounging around on hammocks and overstuffed chaise chairs, spending your day drinking and smoking all kinds of things. It wasn't hers. But maybe because she got her hard partying days out of her system many years ago. Now, Heather would settle for a good book and a quiet place to enjoy it. Far away from the pounding music.

She took another look around.

She'd signed up to run a bed-and-breakfast. Not a youth hostel. But things were a little foggy in Central America and there were more shades of gray when it came to things like this than there were colors in the rainbow. It wouldn't surprise her if she'd signed up, sight unseen, to spend the next six months slinging drinks to backpackers.

She would have sighed—or more likely, cried—if she thought it would do any good. But Heather had been out in the world long enough to know it wouldn't have any impact on the outcome. Besides, she was up for an adventure if need be. Anything that allowed her to move on.

Which was exactly why she was there and exactly why she was going to keep forcing her smile until finally it stayed put on her face, where it needed to be.

She'd do what she had to.

Especially if it meant staying in Panama and not returning

home to her *I told you he was no good—you should have listened to me and stayed home* mother.

Heather dropped her hand on the plywood but it wasn't necessary. A glass of something red, sweet, and dangerous-looking appeared in front of her.

"Welcome, *chica*."

Heather waved her hand to dismiss the drink. "I didn't order that."

"You didn't have to." The man's grin was toothy, warm and practiced. "It's on me. And you clearly need it. Name's Mick." He didn't offer his hand, a fact Heather was grateful for. It had been a long day, followed by a long week on Cass and Archer's boat, preceded by a long life. At least that's how it felt at that moment. She'd lived a lifetime in the last few months. A life she no longer wanted to live. "Drink, Heather. Then we'll talk."

He left her alone, another fact she was grateful for. She was halfway through the drink that was every bit as sweet as she expected it to be, and only half as strong as she needed, before she realized that he'd known her name.

She finished the drink, and then another that was placed in front of her before the man came back. This time he held out his hand, and she was ready for it. "Nice to meet you, Heather. Welcome to Bocas. Feeling better?"

"Was it that obvious?"

"Nah. You're okay. But Bocas Town can be a bit much the first time. But it's just the town."

That was an understatement. From the moment she left the serenity of Cass and Archer's sailboat, all five senses had been assaulted to the point of complete overload.

"Whatever you put in that drink helped."

"It always does. The rest of Bocas del Toro is…well, paradise," Mick said. "Wait until you get a chance to see it."

"I look forward to it." She slid the glass around the bar top.

"How did you know who I was? Is it so obvious that I don't fit in?"

He laughed. "Sweetheart, you fit in just fine. *Everyone* fits in here. Look around."

She did as she was told and for the first time noticed the mixture of those around her. There were men, women, and people who could only be described as both, all ages and colors in a variety of clothing or in a few cases, not much clothing at all, scattered around the room. The mix was eclectic to be sure, but no one looked out of place.

"Am I right?"

"You are."

"Bocas Town is the Land of the Misfit Toys. Even if you don't belong anywhere else, you will here."

Land of the Misfit Toys. Perfect. She reached for her empty glass.

"How about a water?"

"Probably a better idea," she agreed. Whatever he'd given her had been delicious, but she could see how it could be dangerous. She drank half the bottle of water he placed in front of her before she finally asked, "You seem to have a good handle on things around here. Why do you need me?"

"You?" His eyes danced under the frayed brim of his San Francisco Giants cap. "Oh no, *chica*. I don't need you."

A flicker of panic lit in her chest. No doubt it would have burst into flames had it not been for the two magic red drinks currently flowing through her. "You don't need me?"

If this bed-and-breakfast deal didn't work out, where was she supposed to go? No doubt, Archer and Cass had already moved their boat, *Cassiopeia,* to their next destination. They had paying guests aboard and had only been doing her a favor bringing her to Bocas Town. *Without them, she'd have to—*

"You're thinking." Mick's friendly tenor interrupted the

train of panic that was quickly picking up speed in her brain. "Another drink then?"

Heather shook her head. "No. But if you don't need me, I will need a—"

"*Chica.* I don't need you. But Sherri does."

"Sherri?" The train in her brain slowed slightly. "Who's Sherri?"

"The one who needs you." He wasn't helping. "At Casa del Sol. *Chica,* you didn't think you'd be staying here, did you?"

She could lie. There was no point. "I did."

"And you're glad you're not."

"A little." She laughed. The first real one in a long time. "Okay, a lot."

Mick winked, and the train slowed even more. He had that effect. "Sherri's place is a little piece of paradise. It'll be exactly what you need."

"And what is it I need?"

"I need to tell you?"

There was no point in answering him. He didn't need to tell her anything. At the same time, there was nothing he *could* tell her. How could anyone else possibly see what she needed, when she herself was blind to it?

"Sherri," she said the name again to clarify. "She needs my help?"

Mick nodded. "That's why you're here. I guess Josie wasn't too clear with the details."

There hadn't really been any details. Not that she'd asked for any.

"When I say that Sherri's place is paradise, it's not an exaggeration. It literally is. Or at least the Garden of Eden."

"Then it can't be nearby." She raised her eyebrows and Mick laughed.

"No. It's about a twenty-minute boat ride from here. Cut off from the world. People go there to unplug and hide."

"Hide? From other people?"

"From themselves, *chica*." Mick winked at her.

Perfect.

"So how do I get to Sherri's? She's expecting me?"

"She is. And I'm sure she's just as eager for you to get there as you are. Ash will take you when he gets back."

"Who's Ash and where is he?"

Mick shrugged. "Ash helps Sherri out with things. And honestly, there's no telling what he's gotten up to this afternoon. He probably had a list, but he'll be back by three. He likes to get the boat out there before the sun goes down. You're welcome to wait here. Make yourself comfortable." He pointed to a lounge chair on the deck close to the ocean, away from the business of the bar.

"Thank you." She hoped the weariness didn't show in her eyes, but it was false hope, because there was no way it didn't. She hefted her backpack up and grabbed the water on the bar. Just as she turned away, Mick stopped her.

"*Chica?*"

Heather glanced over her shoulder.

"Welcome to Bocas. You came to the right place."

"For what?"

"For everything."

"I've got what you need right here, Ash."

There was no doubt in Ash's mind that Sara had exactly what he needed in all the right ways, and without a doubt there was no one who filled out scrubs the way she did. His dick twitched just thinking about the curves that the thin piece of pink cotton was concealing. Ash had personal experience with those curves and those experiences were more than enough to deserve a replay. If it weren't for—

"I'm also free tomorrow night for dinner. Rumor has it Oscar got some fresh lobsters this morning."

If it weren't for that.

Sara was a nice girl. Despite the fact that she fell for his moves, she was a smart girl, too. She was in Bocas on some sort of work exchange, which made her dangerous. Because she was not like any of the other women Ash *dated*. Sara wanted more. She wanted Ash to take her out. She wanted to date.

Like all nice girls did.

Ash didn't.

Ash avoided nice girls.

Ash wasn't a nice guy.

"Ah, if only I could, Sara." He ran a hand through his shaggy blond hair and gave her a smile he knew was devastating. "But I have to get back to Casa del Sol. Sherri has a big order and a new manager starting today. She'll need a bit of help getting everything set up and you know how that is."

The girl didn't even bother trying to hide her pout. "Another time?"

"Of course," he lied.

The truth was, Ash could have a lot of fun with Sara if she didn't try to push so hard for a relationship. It was too bad, but there was no way Ash was going there. Not with anyone. *No matter how fun they were. Or how far their legs bent—*

"Ash, did you hear me?"

He hadn't.

"Sorry. My mind drifted."

"I bet it did." The mischief in her eye and the way she licked her lips almost made him change his mind. Almost.

"Behave." Not that she would. "How many boxes did Sherri order for me today?"

"That's what I was telling you. Her order today is quite large. You're going to need help."

"I have Miguel." He pointed to the boy, who'd been

standing by, listening to everything with an interested ear. No doubt, the kid had gotten quite an education hanging out with Ash, despite his efforts to keep things as G-rated as possible when he was around.

"I think you might need more than Miguel for today's load." She shot the boy a doubtful look.

"Two strong men like us?" Ash nudged Miguel and they both flexed comically. "We got this."

Sara rolled her eyes, but he didn't miss the way her eyes traveled over his bare chest. *Damn, he should have found a T-shirt to put on.* Not that it would have stopped her.

"Wait here. I'll get your stuff."

When she returned moments later, wheeling a cart full of boxes and bags, even Ash had to admit it might be a little more than he and Miguel could handle. *What had Sherri ordered this time?* There was more than a few first-aid supplies on that cart. He mentally calculated the size and weight of each box, what each of them could probably handle and in the end, admitted defeat.

"I'll have Miguel bring the cart right back." He put one hand on it and attempted to glide it away from her. But Sara wasn't having it. She held firm, the cart jostling awkwardly between them.

"No can do, Ash." She shook her pretty little head, her mouth pressed into a line. "Clinic property."

He gave her his sexiest smile, but still she didn't relax her grip.

Ash knew when he'd been beat. "Okay, what will it take to let me borrow the cart?"

It was clearly the right question. She opened up; her lips curled into the smile of a woman who knew she was about to get exactly what she wanted. "A date. A real one."

Dammit.

He took a step toward her, reached out and tucked a strand

of hair behind her ear before his fingers drifted across her cheek. "Oh, baby. You know you don't need to bribe me for a date." He leaned in, just enough so she'd feel his breath on her skin.

Just as he knew she would, her body trembled, a sigh escaped her lips, and her hand released the cart. Ash pressed his lips in a gentle, sweet, dismissive kiss and pushed the cart back to Miguel, who started down the street with it long before Sara knew what'd hit her.

Ash was already a few steps away when she called out after him. "Call me about that date."

"I'll have Miguel bring the cart back right away." He blew her a kiss. "Thanks, Sara."

He probably should have felt bad about using the girl's affections for his benefit, but she was a grown woman, and he'd been upfront with her from the beginning. She made her choices; he made his. It wasn't his fault if they didn't line up.

Besides, he didn't have time to dwell on her or the feelings she may or may not be having for him. Feelings that may very well include causing him bodily harm when she realized he had zero intention of taking her on that date. He still had more orders to pick up before he headed back to Casa del Sol and if he didn't hurry, he'd run out of daylight.

"Miguel, can you take this and load it in the boat? I'll meet you there."

"*Sí*, Señor Ash."

"You're a good kid."

The boy beamed and hurried off with the overloaded cart. Ash wished he could do more for the boy. He never asked what Miguel's family life was like, but he had a sneaking suspicion there wasn't much of one.

Ash hurried through the rest of the list Sherri had given him and by the time he returned to the dock outside of the

Bitter End where he'd tied up his boat, Miguel had almost finished up loading the supplies.

"Good job." He patted the kid on the head as he hopped into the boat with a practiced, fluid motion. "Almost ready?"

"*Sí*, Señor Ash. All done." He grabbed the last box and tucked it under the front seat. The boat was full. It would be a slow ride back if he wanted to keep the splash down.

"Good work, Miguel." Ash reached into his back pocket and pulled out a few bills. "You'll get that cart back to Sara for me?"

Miguel nodded. "I'll get the woman now."

"Right. The woman." Ash shook his head. "Wait. The woman?"

"*Sí*, Señor. *La mujer*." His scrawny arm pointed toward the deck of the Bitter End and the same dark-haired beauty who'd tempted Ash to break his self-imposed rules.

Damn.

While he watched, she stood and stretched her arms overhead. Her T-shirt crept up just enough that he knew he'd be able to see a band of sun-kissed skin if he stood close enough.

Double damn.

Chapter Two

HE WAS HER RIDE.

Surfer Boy.

Sexy, sinful, Surfer Boy.

Heather swallowed hard. Even from a distance, her body reacted to him. Her first instinct was to shut it down, but she'd had two of Mick's red drinks, plus a beer, and though she was far from drunk, she was...looser. Besides, she'd been thinking.

Why did she have to shut any thoughts down? She didn't have anyone to report to. She was a free woman. And she could definitely do with a little fun.

No.

She could do with a whole *lot* of fun. It was a rebound thing. *Isn't that how it was supposed to work?* She was expected to fall into bed with some sexy stud, who'd make her forget her cheating ex and the disappointing life she'd left behind. It was a rite of passage. She'd be doing herself a disservice if she didn't pursue it.

"I see you found Ash." Mick appeared at her side. He raised his arm in a wave to Surfer Boy, who was watching them. He waved back.

"Ash?"

"He'll be your taxi driver. He kinda works for Sherri. Taking her supplies and running guests back and forth when she needs it."

"Kinda?"

"I guess so. He never takes any money from her, from what I can tell. But he's always there for her."

"Are they...together?"

Mick laughed. "Nah. It's more like a mother-son relationship. You'll see when you meet Sherri. Although, with Ash you never...nah." Mick dismissed his own thought with a laugh. "You want me to take you over there and introduce you?"

"No." Heather hefted her pack to her back. "I got it. Thanks, Mick. You've been great."

He pulled her into an unexpected but not unwelcome hug. "Whatever you need, *chica*. You know where to find me."

She walked down the dock toward Surfer Boy. Knowing Mick stood behind her, she felt oddly comforted by the older man. Or maybe it was the town itself that gave her comfort? Despite—or maybe because of—the shambles of both the place and the people, in the few hours she'd been in Bocas Town, her initial distaste for the place had disappeared, replaced by a strange sense of belonging. She felt like for the first time she might have found a place where, for whatever reason, everything might be okay.

Surfer Boy watched her pick her way across the broken dock, carefully stepping over the rotted boards and exposed nails. She didn't speak until she stood directly in front of him and his very full boat. "I think you're my ride."

He raised one eyebrow. His smirk said everything he didn't need to. She could feel her face flush. There was a chance it could be mistaken for a sunburn. It was a chance. But not a very good one. *Might as well own it.*

"To Sherri's place."

"Of course." He crossed his arms over his bare chest and for the second time that day, Heather had to force herself not to focus on the tight muscles and golden skin that just begged for her fingers to run over—

"So you'll take me?"

His face split into a sinful smile. "Absolutely."

It wasn't going to be a conversation she'd be able to get out of gracefully. "Then you're just the guy I'm looking for." And he absolutely was. She hadn't realized just how true that was until she closed another foot of distance between them and once more felt her entire body come alive at his nearness.

Damn.

She needed a man.

This man.

They stared at each other for a few moments. *A challenge? Or a request?* It was the boy who pushed between them, carrying a box of something that looked heavy before he jumped down into the boat.

Ash stepped back, ran a hand through his shaggy hair and surveyed his boat. It wasn't much more than a wooden dingy, but longer. Heather was used to riding in similar boats, although the ones at the marina looked to be a little newer and in better shape. Surfer Boy's boat didn't even have a place to sit. Or if it did, it was completely covered in packages. There was nowhere for her to ride.

"Is there room for me in there?"

Ash turned to the boy, who was tucking the box into place. "Miguel? Are we done?"

"Last one, Señor." The boy looked up at his captain with a smile.

Ash shrugged and turned back to her. "I'm sure we can squeeze you in…"

"Heather." She offered her hand. Instead of shaking it, Ash took it and with a quick jerk, pulled her down to the boat. She only stumbled slightly before his arms were around her, bracing her and righting her body against his.

He still held her hand, and as soon as she took a half step backward to put space between them, he brought it to his lips and pressed a kiss on her knuckles. "It's nice to meet you, Heather."

She should be offended, or outraged that he'd manhandle her in such a way. But it wasn't anger that flowed through her veins. She didn't pull back, but let him hold her hand to his mouth and she felt every breath of air as he said, "I'm Ash. And I'll make sure you get out to Sherri's place, even if you have to be on top."

Oh, sweet baby Jesus. If it was possible to spontaneously combust from desire, Heather would be lit up like a Christmas tree. It was all kinds of wrong, and went against everything she'd ever done or stood for as far as a moral code, but as far as she could tell, her morals weren't going to have much of a say in anything when it came to Ash. Because if it came down to it, her body and every single feel-good hormone racing through her at top speed were definitely going to win out.

She slipped her hand from his. "I know who you are."

"You do?" He raised an eyebrow. "My reputation precedes me, I see."

"Maybe it does." She smiled, enjoying the easy flirting. "But Mick told me."

"Don't believe anything." He laughed. "Make yourself comfortable. I'm almost ready to shove off."

Heather looked around and finally decided the only place for her backpack would be on her lap. The little boat was packed well, but her first assessment had been spot on. There wasn't anywhere for her to ride. But she couldn't stand. She picked her way through the packages and found a wooden crate toward the bow that looked as if it might be stable enough to support her. She perched delicately and watched while Ash dug in the pocket of his cargos and handed Miguel something. Judging by the smile on the boy's face, it was likely cash.

"You ready?" Ash hopped into the boat, nimbly making his way to the stern, where he pulled the starter. The engine roared to life.

"Yes." Her voice floated away on the air. There was no way he heard it over the rev of the engine. "Yes," she yelled at the exact moment the engine settled into a low purr. "Yes. I'm ready to go," she said again at a much more reasonable level.

He winked at her and gestured to Miguel to untie them. The moment the boat moved, she shifted on her perch. The fingers of her free hand gripped the crate beneath her while the other struggled to keep hold of her backpack.

"Are you okay up there?"

She nodded. It's not as if she'd never been on a boat before. She had. Once or twice.

After all, she'd spent the last five years living at a marina, surrounded by boats. She'd been on her fair share of yachts of all kinds. Sailboats, and power boats big and small. But small was relative. And she'd never been on a boat quite as small as the one she was on at the moment. Especially one that was as loaded as Ash's. For all intents and purposes, she'd lived a fairly sheltered life at the marina. The life of a dockmaster's wife wasn't all that demanding, and for the most part, Heather sat in the restaurant, visiting with guests from around the world, dreaming about going to those places. She didn't actually participate much as far as the business was concerned.

Ash maneuvered the boat slowly through the docks. Even at the low speed, Heather knew her placement was precarious. Mick had said it was about a twenty-minute boat ride. She scanned the boat again, searching for an alternative.

There wasn't one.

"You're sure you're okay up there?"

There was no way she was okay up there. He slowed the boat and let it idle. He admired her stubbornness. Hell, he found it sexy. But it wasn't going to be very sexy fishing her out of the ocean. An image of her T-shirt, wet and stuck to her breasts, filled his head.

Okay, maybe it would be sexy.

Ash resisted the urge to turn the boat sharply so she'd fall out. No doubt it wouldn't go over as well as he'd like it to. Although seeing her with her shirt skintight, wet, showing every line and curve on what was no doubt a ten out of ten body, would be worth it. It would be very worth it.

With a sigh of regret, he left the throttle, and took two steps toward the bow, holding out his hand for her. "Come on."

"Honestly, I'm fine up—whoa."

A boat passing by sent out a wave that threatened to make the decision for both of them. Ash stretched out and grabbed her arm moments before it happened. "Gotcha." He took her backpack with one hand and without releasing her arm, helped her to the back of the boat. Heather's eyes were wide, but she didn't look scared. Instead, she looked as if she was fighting back laughter. Sure enough, the moment she plopped down across from him on a bag of rice, she burst into laughter.

He waited a moment, scratched at the scruff on his chin and finally tucked her backpack in beside her before her laughter died down.

"Sorry."

Ash chuckled. "Never apologize for laughing. I'm just glad you didn't go in." That was a lie. The image of a wet T-shirt was still very much in his head. "Besides, it's a beautiful sound."

She blushed at the compliment, the flush trailing down the deep vee of her shirt.

"Are you settled now?"

She looked much more stable situated on the rice in front of him. It would make navigating a little more difficult, but Ash had no complaints staring at the beautiful woman in front of him.

She nodded. "I'm good. Are you sure you can see?"

"I can see everything I need to."

She blushed again, but this time smiled before any conversation was swallowed by the roar of the engine. He navigated the boat past Bocas Town, which literally hovered on the edge of the sea. In places, it looked as if the pieced-together buildings were falling into the water.

Leaving from the main dock, there was a much larger, nicer boat painted bright blue with *Turquoise Cove* painted on the side. It was filled with the resort tourists. Those were the people who'd signed up to spend a week or two at one of the exclusive resorts tucked far enough away from Bocas Town that the guests would be able to forget about the poverty and sense of desperation they'd caught a glimpse of when their plane landed. They had no clue that there was more to the world than their carefully constructed bubbles.

Ash saw Heather watching the bright-blue boat, and could tell she had the same opinion of those people that he did. Not that they were bad, just that they were missing out. He turned the boat away from town and aimed it toward the maze of mangrove forest on the other side of the bay. He used to be one of those people. He'd lived his own carefully constructed life, working twelve hours a day for the promise of a better future. When he did take a vacation, it was exactly what those people were going to: a tropical version of what he had back home. Complete with Internet access and a full office so he didn't have to leave the office behind.

That was a different world. A world he didn't like to think about.

Ash revved the engine, pushing the little boat hard through the waves.

Heather had spun on her perch and was turned away from him, looking out at the water and the thick mangrove forests. No. She wasn't looking at all. Her eyes were closed, her face tilted up into the wind. Some hair had escaped from its tie and whipped around her face and neck but it didn't seem to bother her. Ash felt almost as if he were intruding on a private moment, but he couldn't bring himself to look away.

There was something about her. Beautiful, wild, and sexy as hell.

For the next few minutes, they drove in silence. The boat sliced through the calm waters as they raced toward Casa del Sol. He loved it when the seas were quiet; they often weren't, even sheltered in the mangroves the way they were. But so late in the day the way they were now, it was particularly special to see the shadows dance with their reflections, everything cast in a glow of orange, pink, and yellow as the sun started its slow descent.

He would have happily taken his time to get back to the B&B, and it was easy to see Heather would enjoy the ride. But they were losing daylight quickly and it was never a great idea to drive around in the dark, especially not with a full load. Besides, Sherri would start to worry, and she hadn't seemed like herself the last few days. It was probably better to spare her any type of stress or concern.

Heather turned around and smiled at him in a way that he could tell she hadn't done in a long time. Probably too long.

Screw it.

He turned the boat to the left. Away from Casa del Sol and directly toward a tangle of mangroves.

Chapter Three

HEATHER COULDN'T REMEMBER the last time she'd been so relaxed and completely at peace. It was a feeling that was so completely foreign to her. Even when she'd been on the *Cassiopeia* with Cass and Archer, something still held her back. She tilted her head back a little farther, letting the wind grab the strands of her hair and whip them around her head.

She had no idea where Casa del Sol was, which meant she was totally at the mercy of Ash and wherever he wanted to take her. That probably should have worried her to some degree. Getting into a boat with a total stranger who, besides being extremely sexy, she knew nothing about. As far as she could tell, the man didn't even own a shirt. Not that she was complaining about that detail.

Yes, she should probably be a little more concerned about her safety, but she wasn't. Not even a little bit.

If it was up to her, she would ride in that boat for the rest of her life if it meant feeling the way she did at that moment.

She turned around, wanting to somehow tell him that, or share her happiness with him. All Heather could manage was a smile, but it said more than any of the words she could have come up with.

The skin next to his eyes crinkled when he smiled. It was the look of a man who'd seen things and knew how to appreciate the good. For an instant, he looked as if he was going to say something, but then the boat turned sharply. Heather let out a yelp as she bobbled on her perch and turned around again.

The boat was headed toward the shore and a thick growth of mangroves. They were going full speed. She was no expert on boats, but she didn't have to be to know that if they hit the trees, it would not be good.

She whipped around to tell him to slow down, but he held up one finger to silence her, moments before the boat slowed, and he pointed over her shoulder.

"Look."

She did.

Directly in front of them was a tunnel through the trees. Ash navigated expertly through the opening and the boat fit perfectly. Once inside the tunnel, Heather tipped her head back and gazed up at the branches that rose up to interweave together like arms creating a perfect canopy over their heads.

She couldn't see them, but birds sang all around them as they drifted through the tunnel.

"This is…I just…"

"It's pretty amazing, isn't it?"

"I don't feel like that's enough." Her voice came out on a breath as a brilliant, blue butterfly floated past. "Ash, it's…" She turned, the words evaporating on her tongue.

"I know."

She didn't want to wish away a second of the magical little tunnel, but it wasn't nearly as long as she wanted it to be. The boat emerged from the other side of the tunnel and without saying another word, Ash sped up, whisking them away from the mangrove tunnel and toward Casa del Sol.

It only took them another few minutes of weaving through the mangrove maze before a long dock came into view. Soon, Heather could see the grass-thatched huts on the shore, with a few more peeking through the trees farther up the hill.

"Welcome to Casa del Sol," Ash said behind her.

"Welcome, welcome."

The woman running down the dock to greet them must have been in her sixties, but dressed in a flowing skirt with an impressive variety of shell necklaces draped over her chest and the bikini top that was only a slightly darker shade than her deeply tanned skin, she defied her age.

"I was getting worried, Ash." She scolded him as he pulled alongside the dock and handed her a rope. "It's getting late."

"You worry too much." He hopped out of the boat and gave the woman a big hug. "If you didn't have such a big order this time, it wouldn't have taken nearly as long."

"And I suppose you're going to tell me you weren't enjoying the *entertainment* in town?"

Heather bristled at her choice of words, which was ridiculous considering she'd only just met Ash. She grabbed her backpack and stood as Ash extended a hand down to her.

"You must be Heather." Before she could even fully set foot on the dock, the woman wrapped her in a surprisingly strong hug. She smelled like a mixture of earth and sea, with a faint undertone of sweet jasmine. Heather immediately felt at home in her embrace, like a familiar auntie. "I'm so happy to have you here, love. I'm Sherri." She squeezed one more time.

Heather pulled back to look into warm, brown eyes that she could tell at once were full of a lifetime of experience. "I'm so happy to be here." Surprise tears pricked at the back of her throat. She swallowed hard to keep them away.

"Why don't we leave Ash here to unload and I'll show you around Casa del Sol?" She wrapped a thin arm around Heather's shoulders and guided her down the dock, directly into the first thatched building.

"This is the heart of Casa del Sol. We call it *grande casa*. The big house." She swelled up in pride while she spoke, and with good reason as far as Heather could tell. The place was beautiful. It was rustic, and perfect for the jungle landscape, but at the same time, the decadent finishings made the large room feel cozy and welcoming.

"All our guests gather here for meals, drinks and...well, just for everything." Sherri walked over to a large polished plank of wood that hung from the ceiling. "Our hanging table." She gave it a push so it swung gently. "It truly is the heart of the place. I hope you feel at home here."

There was no way she couldn't. Heather took a minute to walk through the space, letting her fingers trail along the rail that opened out to the ocean directly beneath the building. With the shutters open, it was only a three-sided building, which allowed the trade winds to flow through, keeping it cool. At the back of the room was a large bar that looked well stocked. The other side of the room held a mixture of padded benches, cozy-looking chairs, and hammocks strung up from the open beam ceiling. Paintings and handicrafts hung on the walls, and as the sun set further, small LED lights that looked almost like stars came on to give the space an even more magical feel.

Heather turned and almost stumbled over a black lump on the floor. "Oh, I didn't see you there."

"That's Thor."

"Thor?"

"He's my guard dog."

Heather raised an eyebrow. The dog certainly didn't look like he was guarding anyone from anything. He hardly raised his massive head from his paws when Heather tripped over him.

"I know he doesn't look like much, but you should see him handle a snake."

"Snakes?"

"Hasn't been one inside in years." Sherri pointed to Thor. "Thanks to my boy there."

"Well, I guess that makes me feel a little better." Heather stepped around the dog and went over to the bar, where Sherri was mixing up a pitcher of something that looked delicious.

"Do you like mojitos?" Before Heather could answer, she laughed, a deep throaty sound. "Of course you do." Sherri shook her head. "Everyone likes mojitos. But mine are the best. I make them with mint right out of my garden. There simply isn't anything better. Is there, Ash?"

Heather whirled around. She hadn't heard him come in. His arms were loaded down with supplies. A Panamanian man followed behind with a similar load.

"Nothing better, Sher. I'll be ready for one in about thirty seconds." He winked in her direction before he walked past the bar into the kitchen area.

"Leave all that," Sherri called after him. "Luis will take care of it, won't you, Luis?" The other man nodded. "Of course he will," she added in Heather's direction. "That's what I pay him the big bucks for."

Heather laughed and accepted the drink Sherri held out for her. She'd only been there for a few minutes, hadn't even seen where she'd be staying, and already she knew she wouldn't want to leave. She walked toward the rail and gazed out at the sun setting over the turquoise water.

"It's pretty special, isn't it?" Sherri said beside her.

"It really is."

"And the sunset is pretty nice, too." The older woman laughed. They clinked their glasses together and drank deeply before she put her glass down with a start. "I can't believe I didn't even show you your room. I swear, I don't know where my mind is these days. I can't remember anything unless I write it down. You'd think I'd remember to show you, though." She shook her head, the lines on her forehead deep with concern.

"It's fine, Sherri." She put her glass next to the other and squeezed the woman's hand. "I'm not in any kind of hurry. I think I'd be happy to stay right here all night." She hoped she sounded reassuring. Forgetting small details was never a reason for concern. At least, they weren't for Heather.

"It's not okay, honey. I should have taken you up straight away. A girl like you needs a place to stay, to call home. A place you can rest and recover." Her hands fluttered around her face until Heather took them in her own and squeezed gently.

"Honestly. I'm not in any rush. But if you're ready now, why don't you take me up?"

It took a second, but the woman's face cleared; the panic and worry evaporated as quickly as it had appeared. "Yes," she said, her voice once more soft and serene. "That's a good idea. I don't know why I let myself get worked up about these things."

Heather picked up her backpack and followed Sherri out the back door that led to the garden, passing the kitchen and Ash, who reclined against the doorjamb as he watched them.

"What was that all about?"

Ash reclined in his chair, his feet resting on the swinging table. He'd helped himself to a mojito and was on his second glass but this time, Sherri returned to *grande casa* without Heather.

She retrieved the glasses that had been left on the rail, refreshed her own with ice and joined him at the table. "She's nice," she said, ignoring his question. "I think Heather will be good for Casa del Sol. Maybe as much as it will be good for her."

She drank deeply, draining half her glass. Ash watched her closely. Something was not quite right with Sherri. He knew she'd tell him in her own time. He just wasn't sure he wanted to wait. Particularly after bringing her a boat full of medical supplies. If there was something wrong, he wanted—no, he *needed*—to know. Sherri was the only thing remotely close to a family he had left, and if there was anything wrong, he'd make sure he fixed it.

"Sherri." He looked at her pointedly, and waited.

"I think she has quite a story." She looked straight ahead into the dark night beyond. "I don't know what it is. But I'm sure she has one."

He let out a long sigh and shook his head with a bit of a smile. He wasn't going to get a thing out of Sherri if she wasn't ready to talk. "Why do you think Heather has a story?" he asked instead. Besides, he had a feeling that talking about Heather might be one of his new favorite pastimes. There was no denying that something about the woman captivated him in a way that was unlike anything he'd felt in years. And it wasn't just the sexiness that all but radiated off her. Although that didn't hurt.

Next to him, Sherri clucked her tongue. "Honey, all women have a story. Some are longer than others, most have many twists and turns, and sadly, not enough of them have happy endings. But everyone has one."

"That's a sad thought." Ash thought about it for a moment

before he drained his drink. "Men have stories, too." He sat up and winked at Sherri, making her laugh.

"True enough, honey. True enough. And your story *will* have a happy ending."

He tipped his head, but didn't ask for her to elaborate. He never did. Not because he didn't want a happy ending, but more because he didn't believe her. Instead, he answered the way he always did when she tried to get serious with him. "Fairy tales aren't real, Sherri. But I'm all about a happy ending." He jumped up from his chair and wiggled his eyebrows, narrowly dodging her hand as it shot out to give him a smack.

He took the empty glass she held out instead and headed to the bar to freshen up their drinks. "Where is everyone, anyway? You don't have any guests tonight?"

"One couple. They're very...romantic." She made a kissy face and laughed again. It was one of Ash's favorite sounds. Before coming to Casa del Sol, he'd never met someone who laughed with such authenticity before. It was a true testament of the joy in her heart. She really was a one-of-a-kind woman. "They wanted to be left alone tonight to swim under the stars and revel in their love. I packed them snacks but I'm sure they'll be here first thing in the morning, having worked up quite an appetite."

Ash laughed and ignored the twinge of jealousy in his chest. He'd had that once. A love so on fire they didn't believe the flames would ever be doused.

They had.

"And where's Heather? Don't tell me you left her out in the jungle, all alone?"

He teased, but there was a note of concern, too. Sherri's place had bungalows both set over the water and set back a bit in the trees. It was secluded enough to discourage thieves, but it wasn't humans that were the cause for the concern. It was the jungle and the creatures that could potentially be lurking in the darkness.

"You worry too much." Sherri waved her hand, dismissing his concern. "Casa del Sol is perfectly safe. Besides, I left Thor with her. She's getting settled in. She promised to join us when she was unpacked."

"What cabin did you put her in?"

She narrowed her eyes at him. "*Casa de esperanza*. She's fine, Ash."

There was no doubt that she was fine. There were various snakes and critters back in the jungle, but they hadn't actually had one at Casa del Sol in years. Thor and the handful of other dogs that were usually hanging around took good care of that. But that didn't mean he shouldn't be a gentleman and go see whether she needed a hand finding her way back to *grande casa* in the dark. After all, that would be the considerate thing to do. The fact that she might be grateful enough to show her appreciation in any variety of ways didn't have anything to do with his decision-making process.

Not totally.

"I should go see if she needs any help."

"She's fine, Ash."

"It can be tricky to navigate down the garden path if you don't know what you're doing."

"She's fine, Ash."

"It's pretty dark out there tonight. I wouldn't want her getting lost."

"Take a flashlight."

He dropped a kiss on the top of Sherri's head and grabbed a lantern from behind the bar before he headed out the back door. Sherri's rich laughter followed him out into the darkness.

Chapter Four

IF SHE'D BEEN a little unsure about the job at Casa del Sol, once Heather was shown her room, which was so much more than a room, all doubt vaporized. Sherri called it *casa de esperanza*.

Hope house.

It was perfect.

Built the same as the big house, with bamboo walls and thatched roof, *esperanza* was a much smaller version, only it was better because her house sat directly over the ocean. It was set far enough from the main house that she would have privacy, but it was close enough that she'd be able to take care of things there and easily get back and forth.

The room held only a bed, a dresser, and a chair, but the real living would take place on the wraparound deck. She left her backpack on the bed and walked outside. There was no rail on the deck. Instead, there were hammocks strung in each corner, oversized wooden chairs against the walls, and the best part of all—a large wooden swing suspended just right so she'd be able to swing into the beautiful blue water below.

But that would have to wait.

She had to finish unpacking and then formally accept the job. Sherri had explained it as the manager of the bed-and-breakfast: handling the bookings, client relations, and overseeing the basic staff she had who did cooking and cleaning. It sounded perfect, and if it meant staying in this little corner of paradise, it pretty much didn't matter what the job was—she would take it. From the moment she'd set foot on the dock, she'd felt at home somehow. In only a few minutes, she was calmer, more settled than she'd been in five years in Shelter Bay.

"Knock knock." The voice came from somewhere around the corner of her house. "Anyone home?"

There was no real door, but large sliding shutters that would protect her in the event of heavy rain or a storm, so Heather walked around the porch to greet her visitor, although she already knew who it was. Her body did, too. The heat that flooded her was immediate, intense and unsettling.

Ash leaned against the bamboo wall, looking sexy as hell, totally at home. *And damn, did that man not own a shirt?*

"Come on in." She hoped she sounded relaxed and casual, but she doubted that was the case. "I was just getting settled in."

She turned, knowing he would follow, and questioned the sensibility of being alone with the man. After all, they'd only just met; she knew nothing about him besides he was somehow connected to Sherri and her new job, although Heather still couldn't figure out how. And she did not want to risk losing a job she hadn't even started yet because of a man she didn't even know.

"This was always one of my favorite bungalows at Casa del Sol. Sherri's done such a great job with all of them, though. It's a very special place."

Heather turned to see that Ash had walked right through the room, and was out on the porch in the very spot where she'd just been standing. She left her bag still unpacked and joined him outside in the growing darkness.

"It really is a special place. I'm looking forward to getting to know it."

They stood so close, she could feel the heat of his body and smell the salt on his skin.

"I'm looking forward to getting to know you." He turned to face her, the look in his eyes leaving no question that the attraction she'd felt for him was entirely mutual.

A moment later, when he cupped her face in one hand and used the other to pull her close, any hesitation she had about getting involved with Ash dissolved into the night air. All she could think about was the thrumming in her veins and the need to have his mouth on hers.

It was Heather who closed the distance between them, pressing her lips to his in a kiss. He answered her need by pulling her even tighter to his hard body. His tongue parted her lips, clashing with hers. Heather's hands slid up his bare skin; her fingers dug into the muscles on his back in a misguided effort to control the sensations that flooded her.

Ash's hand left her face and slid down her body to the hem of her shirt. His fingers easily slipped beneath the fabric of the T-shirt. The shock of his touch on her bare skin stopped her.

What was she doing?

From somewhere behind her, Thor, who'd been waiting just outside her room, whined. It was just enough of a distraction to bring her senses crashing down. Heather pulled out of Ash's embrace. Her hand moved to her mouth; her fingers danced uneasily on her lips while she composed herself.

"We shouldn't...I shouldn't... I mean, I'm not saying I don't want to. It's just...well, I just got here."

"Later then." Ash chuckled and when she finally brought herself to look at him, he was grinning. "I understand," he said when their eyes met.

She wasn't sure he did, but he didn't seem all that upset by her sudden change of heart, and that made it less awkward somehow. Although she got the impression that Ash probably didn't get upset about much.

Heather looked at him for another second before she turned out to stare at the darkness. The stars were starting to pop out on the black canvas. It never failed to surprise her how quickly it got dark in Panama compared to Idaho. They stood in silence for a few minutes.

Ash spoke first. "Anyway, that wasn't the real reason I came out here." She could see the lie on his face. "I just came to see if you needed help finding your way back in the dark."

She nodded. "That would be good."

"It can be tricky if you don't know where you're going."

She doubted that.

"Are you ready to go? I think Sherri was going to put out some food."

The mention of food made her stomach grumble. She could eat. "Sounds good." Besides, she probably shouldn't spend too much more time alone with Ash. Not that she didn't want to. She did. She really did. That was the entire problem.

"You were gone awhile."

Ash looked directly at Sherri, who stared at him pointedly when they walked back into the big house.

"Not long enough, Sher," he said just loud enough for her to hear. He didn't want to make Heather feel any more uncomfortable than she clearly already did. That was never his intention. In a different situation, he might think he'd read her wrong, but the way she'd kissed him left no room for doubt.

No, he'd certainly not read that wrong.

"Something smells fantastic." Ash left the women and went

directly to the kitchen and the source of the delicious smells that were coming out of it.

He was greeted by a beautiful smile. "*Gracias*, Ash." Camila, the young woman Sherri had hired to help out with the cooking and cleaning, stood in front of the stove. Her apron was tight across her chest and the heat of the kitchen had left a sexy sheen on her skin. "Would you like a taste?" She tipped her head and parted her lips, making it clear that the only taste Camila was offering would be a taste of her lips.

Any other day, he wouldn't have hesitated, but the familiar attraction he usually felt with Camila wasn't there. The girl was gorgeous and he knew exactly what she had to offer, having been the lucky recipient of her affections on more than one occasion. But today was different.

"I'll wait to eat with the ladies," he said smoothly. He tried not to notice the disappointment on her face. She was a nice girl, but he'd never made her any promises.

He never made anyone any promises.

Not anymore.

He spied a platter of tamales and crossed the room. "Are these ready?" Without waiting for an answer, Ash grabbed the tray and headed back out into the main room and away from Camila's questioning stare.

"Looks like dinner's ready." When he walked in, Sherri and Heather lifted their heads from their discussion. "Am I interrupting anything?"

Sherri shook her head. "Of course not, honey. You're never an interruption."

He knew he wasn't but the wink Heather gave him helped to reassure him.

Sherri stood and gestured to the table. "Set it down, Ash. I'll get wine. We need to celebrate."

"Celebrate?" Heather looked between them. "What are we celebrating?"

"You, silly girl." Sherri put a decanter of wine on the table next to the tamales. "You're here at Casa del Sol and I just know you're going to be perfect."

Ash poured the wine. They raised it in a toast to Heather and drank deeply before they tucked into the homemade tamales and the locally famous salad Sherri liked to make with local ingredients. Ash refilled their glasses at least twice more before they were done eating and he cleared the dishes, ducking them into the kitchen quickly before Camila saw him. On his way back to the table, he stopped at the bar to refill the wine.

Heather had been fairly quiet during the meal, but that was probably to be expected considering Sherri was filling her in on everything there was to know about Casa del Sol and the gardens, including the *crop* of sea grapes that could be accessed across the channel with a quick snorkel and dive. Ash was only half listening to Sherri talk about the food options, it was nothing he hadn't heard before. It was more interesting to watch Heather.

She definitely had a history. Sherri's description of every woman having a *story* replayed in his head. But despite a few well-placed questions about her past, all he could figure was she'd been in Panama for five years but had never been to Bocas. She was single. That much he could tell from her ring finger and the fact that she was there alone. And of course, the kiss.

Damn, that kiss.

To say Ash had kissed his share of women would be a ridiculous understatement. But as many kisses as he'd had, kissing Heather earlier had been different. Very different.

He knew exactly how long it had been since he'd had that kind of reaction from a simple kiss. It was a lifetime ago.

Watching her across the room, listening closely to every-thing Sherri was telling her, it took all the self-control he had to keep from crossing the floor and pulling her back into his arms for a second round.

He hadn't realized he was staring until Sherri looked up and caught his eye. Her mouth was set in a firm line. She shook her head once, but Ash caught it. Sherri was the only one who knew the details of Ash's past. They'd talked about it one time and by unspoken agreement, it had never come up again.

Not once during their friendship had Sherri ever said a word in judgment about his personal life. Except to tell him to stay away from her guests, a fact Ash had always respected. It was no secret that he enjoyed the company of women. In fact, he and Sherri had enjoyed long conversations about the benefits of exploring one's sexuality and embracing a free love style of life. Granted, those conversations had often been after a few bottles of wine but that didn't make them any less valid. It had been a lifestyle that had worked well for him for the last four years.

Mostly.

"Ash." He blinked hard, refocusing on Sherri, whose frown had been replaced by her usual bright smile. "It's not much of a party without music. Find us something fun on my iPod and let's dance."

"iPod?" Heather had to ask. Sherri had just finished explaining to her that they tried to exist as sustainably as possible with solar energy, rainwater, and a garden full of fruits, vegetables, and herbs. Many of which, she'd never heard of. The mention of an iPod seemed at odds to everything she'd just learned.

Sherri laughed at Heather's reaction. "We don't totally live in the dark ages, honey. Music is good for the soul and until I can get my own live-in band, the iPod is the next best thing.

Fire it up, Ash. And bring some more wine over here. I wanna dance."

Ash laughed from behind the bar, where he was digging around for something. "You don't need wine to dance, Sherri." A moment later, music filled the small space. "I don't even think you need music."

Sherri tipped her head back and laughed long and loud. It was refreshing to see someone so carefree and in touch with herself. Sherri was the second woman Heather had met who seemed to live her life only for herself. Just like Josie in San Blas, the two women shared many similarities. Watching Sherri was beyond refreshing. It was downright inspirational.

"Come on." Sherri was on her feet and held a hand out to Heather. "Dance with me. There's no better way to tune into your very essence."

Heather wasn't much of a dancer but that was probably only because of her past. Joe hated dancing with her and told her she had no rhythm. Whenever they had a band brought in to Shelter Bay Marina, she'd sat out or claimed to be not feeling well, or more often than not, she'd make up some excuse to leave early because it was way too hard to sit by and watch everyone else have fun when she only wanted to join them.

She should have.

There were a lot of things Heather should have done over the years.

But one thing was for sure: she was done sitting out.

She took Sherri's hand. A good dancer or not, she didn't care. She just wanted to feel the music. And that's exactly what she did. For the first few songs, which were a mixture of steel drum bands and rock and roll, Heather closed her eyes, put her arms in the air and let her body go.

At first, her movements were a little stiff, but she didn't let that dissuade her. She just kept moving. Feeling the rhythm through her body, all the way down to her toes. It didn't take long before she opened her eyes to look into the serene face of Sherri, lost in the beat herself.

"This is amazing." It seemed like such an inadequate word. Maybe it was the wine, or the long day, or simply the fact that the pounding bass had permeated her brain, but Heather couldn't think of a better word to describe how she felt in the little lodge of the bed-and-breakfast. She turned and her stomach did a ridiculous flutter when she saw Ash, reclining in a chair, his feet on the table, his eyes fixed on her.

Emboldened by the music and wine, Heather crooked a finger and beckoned him to the dance floor. His smile was slow and so sexy it almost hurt, but he shook his head.

Trying not to feel rejected, Heather turned and faced Sherri again. "He doesn't dance?"

"Oh, Ash dances." Sherri spun in a circle.

Heather looked over her shoulder. Ash tapped his foot, but wasn't dancing.

"He's not."

"He will. I can tell by the way he's watching you."

"That doesn't make sense."

"Honey, it makes perfect sense." Sherri laughed and grabbed Heather's hands, taking her along for a spin. "I've seen that look in his eyes before."

"What's the look?" She was pretty sure she knew, but she needed to hear it from her.

Sherri pulled her in to a turn. "Like he wants to devour you." She winked and Heather laughed because that was exactly how Ash was looking at her.

A thought stopped her, and Heather stopped dancing, jerking Sherri to a stop as well. "I just want you to know that I really want this job and I'm excited for…what I'm trying to say is I'm not going to screw anything—"

"Oh, you'll screw something, honey." Sherri winked. "But

whatever your personal choices are, you won't screw up this job with them." With strength Heather didn't expect from her, Sherri grabbed her hand and flung her out into a spin before she pulled her back in. "Just be honest."

"With him?"

Her smile was kind. "With yourself."

She didn't have time to process what that even meant before she was once again spinning across the floor.

Heather closed her eyes and let herself go. It wasn't until two arms—two very strong, masculine arms—circled her waist that she opened them and looked directly into Ash's deep-green eyes. She wished her stomach hadn't done that flip, that her skin didn't spark at his touch, that her center didn't turn to straight-up liquid heat when he touched her.

But it did.

When it came to Ash, she was definitely in over her head. In her whole life, she'd never felt her body light up the way it did when he was near, and dammit, she owed it to herself to pursue that. But Sherri was right. She needed to be honest with herself. Whatever that meant.

But she had a sneaking suspicion it meant figuring herself out before getting involved in any way with anyone else.

There was a lot to process.

Ash had started to move, Heather in his arms. She could have pulled away from him right then and there. Maybe she should have. But at that moment, she needed a dance more than she needed to figure out her thoughts. Besides, a dance was just a dance.

That was all.

At least that's what she'd keep telling herself.

She'd figure out the rest later.

Chapter Five

ASH OPENED one eyelid and waited for Sherri to continue her train of thought. It had been almost a week since he'd brought Heather to Casa del Sol and he knew he was running out of excuses for why he was still hanging around. He'd spent the days picking up guests, shuttling them to nearby beaches and running various errands for Sherri, but mostly he'd been watching Heather, waiting for the perfect opportunity to be alone with her.

There hadn't been one.

"It's not that I don't want you here," Sherri called to Ash, who lounged in one of the hammocks on the side deck. He was in the shade for the moment, but he could feel the hot sun starting to creep over his toes. It wouldn't take long before he'd need to move. Either that or turn a somewhat undesirable and very painful shade of red.

It was unusual for him to spend so long at Casa del Sol but they both knew why he was there. Ash was just surprised it had taken Sherri so long to bring it up.

"Am I in the way?"

"Not currently." He opened his eyes to see her standing over him. "But that's probably because right now you're hanging out here instead of harassing my newest manager."

Ash sat up as best he could in the hammock. "I don't harass Heather."

He didn't. Or at least he didn't think he did. Although he did try to talk to her whenever he had the chance. Not that there were many chances. It was frustrating.

No.

It was a challenge. Because although the attraction between them was still very much there, something had shifted from that first day when she'd rode in his boat, her head tilted back to the sea air, taking it all in. He could have sworn they had a connection. And when they'd kissed...hell. They *absolutely* had a connection. There was no way he'd imagined any of that.

But why then did it seem like she was avoiding him?

"Don't you agree, Ash?"

He blinked hard and in an effort to at least look like he'd been paying attention to whatever Sherri'd been saying, he nodded.

"I'm glad you see it my way."

She slapped her hands together and turned to walk away, leaving Ash with the distinct feeling that he'd just agreed to something he wasn't going to be pleased about.

"Wait." He struggled to push out of the hammock, ending up in an awkward twisted mess as he stumbled to the floor. "Sherri. What did I just agree to?"

He caught up with her across the room. Her smile told him he was in trouble.

"You're going to open up my treehouse today."

"Your treehouse?" Ash was vaguely aware of Sherri's tree-house, which was much less of a treehouse and more of a real house situated about a thousand stairs up into the jungle. He knew the house existed. He'd even been in it once to retrieve some extra pots and pans, but to his knowledge, Sherri hadn't actually used the house in years. She spent her time mostly in *grande casa* so she could be close to her guests. In fact, he couldn't remember the last time he'd heard of Sherri up in her treehouse. "Why?"

"Because it's my house."

"Right…" Ash followed her into the kitchen and let out a sigh of relief when he didn't see Camila.

"Don't worry." Sherri rolled her eyes. "She moved on."

"What are you talking about?"

Sherri put one hand on her slight hip and shot him a look that made it more than clear that she wasn't buying his innocent act. "Luis has been lusting after Camila for months, but for whatever reason, the poor girl thought she had a chance with you. I can't imagine why." She rolled her eyes again and shook her head, but Ash could see the humor in her face. "Anyway, the girl came to her senses finally and it would seem that she's over you."

"That didn't take long." He couldn't help but be a little offended. *Maybe he was easy to get over?* It was ridiculous, but he couldn't help it. *Maybe he should ask Camila what—*

"Get over yourself." Sherri smacked him in the arm. "You didn't want the poor girl anyway. You should have cut her loose ages ago." She shook her head and opened cupboards, pulling various jars off the shelves and placing them in a box.

"I didn't have her on the hook." He didn't need to explain or defend himself, but Ash couldn't help it. It wasn't his fault if Camila had felt something more for him than he was willing to give. *Was it?*

"You did have her on the hook." Sherri paused in her gathering, but only for a moment. "That's the entire problem. You don't even know you're doing it."

"Doing what?"

"Breaking hearts, Ash."

He shook his head and walked to the other end of the kitchen, where he hefted himself up on the counter. "That's not fair, Sherri. I've never made any claim to want a relationship with any of the women I see. I never promise them anything I'm not willing to give. I'm not that guy."

That was true. He was totally not that guy. Before getting involved with anyone, he was always very upfront with his intentions. Always.

"I think you're more of that guy than you care to think." There was no judgment in Sherri's voice. "It's just who you are."

"It's not."

Sherri put the jar of whatever it was she was holding down and turned to him. "Ash. It's not a bad thing but for all the detachment you claim to have, you're just not made that way. You, my dear, are a creature of love. You crave it. You *need* it. At least you *think* you do." He opened his mouth to refute everything she was saying, but she held up one finger to silence him. Obediently, he closed his mouth. "It's not a bad thing, Ash. It's just who you are. And before you object. I know you're honest with every woman you get involved with." She shrugged casually and picked up another jar. "You're just not very honest with yourself."

"That's not true." He jumped off the counter, ready to walk out of the kitchen and away from everything Sherri was saying. She may be the person in the world who knew him the best, and she might very well be the best friend he had, but she had no idea what it had been like for him back in the States. Even if she knew the details, she didn't really *know*. No one did. And Sherri definitely had no idea that no matter what she thought she knew, the one thing Ash didn't want was love. He absolutely did not crave it and he most certainly did not *need* it.

He should have walked out. He should have gotten some distance, because there was no way he was going to even attempt to explain any of that to Sherri. There was no point.

But he didn't walk out, because the next thing that came out of his friend's mouth stopped him.

"And that's exactly why you should be careful with Heather."

"Heather?" Ash moved around the worktable in the middle of the room and took the jar of what looked like Sherri's chutney out of her hand. "What does this have to do with Heather?"

Sherri stood on her tiptoes and kissed him on the cheek. "I see the way you look at her."

"Like she's a beautiful woman?"

"Like you want her to fill a void."

He shook his head, denying her assessment at the same time a blur of motion out the window caught his attention. "Speaking of Heather." He gestured with his head, but Sherri didn't turn around.

"I mean it, Ash. Unless you can finally be real with yourself, you should stay away from her. She can't help you."

He didn't have the faintest idea what Sherri was talking about, but in his experience, that was often the case. She had some very different views on people and love and…basically everything. The thing was, even if Ash didn't agree right away with Sherri's thoughts and opinions, even if he originally thought they were totally out of left field…they were almost always right. Which was probably why he didn't want to hear anything about Heather that didn't support him pursuing her. Because no matter what Sherri said, it wasn't going to change the fact that he wanted her.

Man, did he ever.

Ash handed the jar back to her and turned his attention to

the window, or more specifically, the woman working beyond it in the garden.

In the short time she'd been at Casa del Sol, Heather had visibly relaxed. Not that she'd been like one of the uptight, over-stressed tourists who often showed up looking to unwind. She hadn't been like that at all. But there'd been a tension in the way she carried herself. A tightness in her voice, as if she was afraid to say something she shouldn't. A hesitancy to her actions. It likely wasn't noticeable to anyone unless they paid attention. But Ash paid attention.

He'd also noticed that she'd thrown herself into the running of Casa del Sol at the expense of any quiet time where he could possibly sneak in and have a replay of that kiss. It was almost as if she was avoiding that very situation from happening.

No way. Ash hadn't imagined the heat between them. There was no way she wouldn't want a replay of that.

But the more time that went by without any acknowledgment of their connection, the more he'd started to doubt himself.

Maybe Sherri was right. Maybe Heather couldn't help him. But then again, he never claimed to need any help at all.

"Maybe it's not me who needs help."

It wasn't a question and Sherri didn't answer it. Instead, she shook her head and clucked her tongue like an old grandma who knew enough to know there wasn't a damn thing she could do about him and his *ways.* "Come on." She tugged him away from the window. "Stop peeping on the poor woman and help me out. I have a storeroom full of boxes you brought me that aren't going to move themselves up to the treehouse."

He'd forgotten all about the treehouse. Heather had a distracting effect on him. Ash surveyed the kitchen and for the first time, really looked at what Sherri was doing. She had a box with a selection of jars and cans, another with bottles of water sat on the floor, and a basket full of freshly picked herbs and vegetable from the garden sat next to it.

There were enough provisions for weeks, maybe more. But that didn't make sense. *Why would she go up into the trees by herself for weeks?*

Ash ran a hand through his shaggy hair and for the first time, focused his gaze on her. "Sherri? What's going on?"

Heather knelt in the dirt and took her time picking leaves from the mint bushes. She was going to make a big pitcher of mojitos for the afternoon cocktail hour. Besides the lovebird couple who'd been there when she'd arrived, there were two more arrivals, two girlfriends on a holiday, later that afternoon. She assumed Ash would be going to get them in Bocas Town. But that was a pretty big assumption considering she hadn't asked him.

She'd have to talk to him in order to do that.

Which, of course, would mean she'd need to stop avoiding him long enough to have a conversation. Not that she'd really been avoiding him.

Not entirely. She'd just been giving him some space in an effort to be honest with herself.

It had made sense at the time after Sherri's conversation with her, but as the days went on, she could no longer remember what she was trying to achieve with that plan.

Heather sighed and tried for the hundredth time to ignore the fluttering low in her belly every time she thought about Ash and the kiss they'd shared.

She plucked at the mint bush, filling her little basket with the fragrant green leaves before she scanned the rest of the little garden. There were mostly plants she didn't recognize, which wasn't hard to believe because she'd never been much of a gardener. But in the few days that she'd been there, she was learning a little bit. Mostly, just enough to fetch garnishes for Camila or Sherri, but maybe with a little time, she'd actually be able to identify enough of the plants to possibly even cook a meal. Not that her food would be better than Camila's. It wouldn't even come close to the deliciousness that she could create. But Heather missed a real kitchen. She missed being able to fool around with ingredients and create something.

She'd never been allowed in the kitchen at the marina. Not that she would have wanted to cook anything in there. It was a typical, lifeless commercial kitchen. Food couldn't be created with love when there was no life.

She wasn't in a hurry to get in front of the stove yet, but soon. Just being at Casa del Sol was starting to wake her up. She hadn't fully realized it, but there was part of Heather that had been sleeping, or hiding, for a long time. Even before Joe and his betrayal. Long before. Maybe a little sunshine, sea air, and freedom was what she needed.

She needed something else, too.

That increasingly familiar heat in her belly reminded her that there was definitely more she needed.

But not from Ash.

Maybe from Ash.

Why not Ash?

"Ash!"

Heather jerked backward so fast, her hand caught on the basket and dumped the mint leaves she'd been collecting.

"Shit."

She started to collect the leaves. More like she started to pretend to collect the leaves while she kept her eyes trained on the door of the kitchen, where Ash had appeared, carrying a large crate. At least she was fairly sure it was Ash, as she couldn't see his face through the box he was carrying.

But she didn't need to see. It was Ash.

He took another step out the door and half turned behind him to say something to Sherri, who'd yelled at him from inside. "I got it, Sher."

The older woman appeared in the doorway next. "So help me—if you step on any of my plants…"

Ash laughed and took a few more steps into the garden. Closer to Heather. "I got this. Stop worrying."

"I don't know," Heather said, unable to help herself from joining in. "I'd be a little worried."

Ash jostled the crate and took a step backward, visibly surprised to hear her voice. For a split second, Heather was afraid he was not only going to step on the plants that Sherri was so protective of, but her as well. She jumped up to help him steady the crate as he bent to set it down.

Their eyes met and Heather knew by the twinkle in his green depths that he'd been well aware of her presence all along.

A thrill shot through her. *Cocky bastard.*

"Hi, Heather."

"Hey." She tried for casual, but there was no way she pulled it off. Avoiding Ash was one thing. Trying to pretend that his proximity didn't stir up all kinds of feelings that made her want to throw all her ideals and good intentions out the window was a completely different thing altogether. "Moving out?" Not that he'd even moved in. In fact, it occurred to her that she didn't really know where Ash lived.

"Don't worry." He crossed his arms over his perpetually bare chest. "I'm not going anywhere."

The trip of relief in her gut didn't make any sense.

"The only place you're going, Romeo, is up to the tree-house with that crate. My things aren't going to move themselves."

"Where are *you* going?" Heather looked between them. "What's the treehouse?"

Sherri's smile was broad. "My house, honey."

"I thought you lived…" She trailed off, because, like Ash, Heather had no idea where Sherri lived. She just always seemed to be around.

"I don't live in *grande casa*." Sherri laughed. "Although I'm sure it seems that way. Truthfully, I've been spending my nights there since you came, but it's time for me to go home."

Abandoning her basket of mint, Heather picked her way through the garden toward Sherri. She had to walk past Ash, stepping around the crate he'd set down. She tried hard not to breathe in as she moved past him, but it didn't work. His sexy scent filled her senses and her body shivered involuntarily.

"Cold, Heather?" She ignored him and the laughter in his voice. The man knew exactly what he did to her and she couldn't decide whether that pissed her off or turned her on.

"Sherri." She focused on her friend. "I don't understand. Did I take your room? Where's home? And why…I mean… why are you…"

"Why am I leaving you?"

Heather nodded and Sherri chuckled before she squeezed her arm. "It's not like I'm going far. I'm just going up the hill to my house in the trees."

"But I need—" She stopped herself before she finished the thought. The last thing Heather needed was her new boss thinking that she couldn't handle the job of running the B&B. After all, she'd only just started. She didn't want Sherri to fire her for incompetence. More than anything, she wanted to stay.

"You don't need me, honey. You've got this. Besides, I'll be just up the hill."

"And I'll be here."

Heather squeezed her eyes shut. Ash's presence was both reassuring and unsettling. She couldn't quite make out the expression on Sherri's face. For a moment, she thought the older woman might protest Ash's comment.

Sherri seemed to hesitate before she nodded. "Yes. Ash will be around if you need anything." With a gentle hand, Sherri gripped Heather's chin and looked into her eyes. "You'll be fine. This is exactly where you need to be."

She couldn't find any words that made sense, and afraid she might cry and make a bigger fool out of herself, Heather simply nodded again. She would be fine. And it was ridiculous, because it wasn't as though Sherri was leaving her permanently. She was moving up the hill. She'd be close.

But if that was true, why then, as she watched Ash and Sherri move away from her, down the path and up the hill, did it feel as if she was losing her friend, just as she'd found her?

It took Ash four trips up to the treehouse to get all of Sherri's things in place. Of course, those were four very long trips, as her treehouse was straight up the hill and, as far as Ash could figure, about five thousand stairs away.

And he was pretty sure he wasn't exaggerating.

On the last trip up, Sherri came with him. Even with the heavy crate in his arms, she was much slower than he was. Ash stopped to rest a few times and each time, he turned to see her carefully picking her way up the wooden steps. She was moving slow. Too slow.

Something was wrong. He could feel it. There was more to Sherri's move up the hill than she was letting on.

When he finally reached the top, Ash deposited the crate on the floor next to the others, went to Sherri's small fridge and grabbed one of the beers he'd stashed there earlier. He sat outside on a bamboo chair, cracked his beer and waited.

A few minutes later, Sherri rounded the corner, ascending the last few stairs. "I expected to see you on your way down already."

Ash shook his head. "Nah. I wanted to wait for you." He took a deep slug of his beer, letting the icy liquid slide down his throat. "You know, make sure you got up okay."

She tilted her head and eyed him suspiciously as she stepped up on the porch. Ash handed her his beer, which she took silently, taking a deep drink herself before she sat next to him.

He waited, and a few moments later, she let out a long breath before she spoke. "You want to know what's up."

It wasn't a question but Ash nodded.

"I'm surprised you haven't looked yet."

"It's your stuff." He didn't bother adding that he'd been dying to know what was inside, but then he'd also have to admit that there was part of him that didn't want to know. In his experience, large secret packages weren't always a good thing.

She nodded her head inside, where the crates were stacked and waiting. "Take a look."

Ash didn't immediately get up. Instead, he finished the beer Sherri had handed back, taking his time to savor it before slowly setting it down next to him. "You're sure?"

Sherri nodded.

The crates were typical, nondescript wooden boxes. The only indication Ash had that he wasn't going to like what was inside was the knowledge that he picked them up from the medical center in Bocas Town. He may have put it off as normal medical supplies for the B&B, except for the fact that he'd just spent the last few hours carrying them up the hill where Sherri planned to be on her own.

He picked up a nearby hammer and readied to pry the lid off the first box, but stopped himself. "Are you sure you don't want to tell me something first?"

She looked older and more worn-down than he'd ever seen her when she shook her head.

Ash didn't handle bad news well. He avoided it, choosing to live his life as one ongoing good time, which was the entire reason he'd moved to Panama in the first place. Bad things didn't happen in paradise. But he knew as he pried the first board, and then the second, from the top of the crate, that his perfectly planned good time was about to come to some sort of end. And short of dropping the hammer and heading back down the hill, he wasn't going to be able to avoid it.

He could have done it a whole lot faster, but when he finally had the boards off and stacked neatly on the floor next to him, Ash reached in and pushed the packing material aside to expose long, stainless-steel tubes. He dug further, finding a wheeled base, and a long, stainless-steel hook. He pulled a piece of the contraption out and turned around, a question on his face.

"What is…"

"An IV stand."

He didn't want to know. He didn't want to know. He didn't want to know.

He already knew.

"I'm sick, Ash."

He knew.

He'd known for a long time. She'd slowed down. She looked frail. Smaller somehow. Her eyes were clouded; the life that was usually there had dimmed.

Ash nodded and turned back to the crates. Without speaking, he opened the rest of them before he slowly looked through the contents: saline bags, needles, pills, and boxes containing carefully packaged vials. Judging by the warning labels on the packages, whatever they were, they were some pretty intense drugs.

Sherri didn't say a word while Ash completed his investigation. When he was finished, he got up, went inside and got two more beers before he returned to the porch. He handed one to Sherri and sat next to her.

"Cancer," was all she said. "Second time."

Ash nodded in acknowledgment. There was nothing to say. *Cancer.*

Cancer killed people. It killed people when they were receiving the best possible care in the world, in a state-of-the-art hospital with professional doctors and nurses administering the treatment.

Sherri was alone, in a jungle in the middle of a third world country and from everything he could see, it looked as if she planned on treating herself.

He shook his head, tipped his bottle back and drank deep and long before he wiped his mouth with his arm.

"Why?"

"I've been through it before, Ash. I have leukemia. The doctors told me I'd have to take the medication for the rest of my life and I didn't think I would have to." She shrugged casually. "It's fine, because I'm going to beat it again. It's very treatable and I know what to do."

"You need a doctor." He looked straight ahead, unable to meet her eyes.

"What I need is to be surrounded by life and love."

"You're going to die."

"Maybe. But if I'm going to die, I'm going to do it on my own terms."

Her voice finally shook, and Ash was out of his chair, kneeling in front of the woman who'd become more than a friend to him in the last few years. She was family. She was his only family.

They didn't speak. They didn't cry. They simply sat together. Ash squeezed his eyes shut, willing his energy—his positive, healthy energy—to flow into her. Finally, Sherri squeezed his hand. "It'll be okay."

They both knew there was a good chance that it would be anything but okay.

He nodded and jumped to his feet, determined to help where he could. "Of course it will." He believed what he said. He didn't have a choice. He'd lost too much; he couldn't—no, he *wouldn't*—lose her too.

Heather didn't have time to think about what Sherri was doing up the hill in her treehouse because she still had a job and a B&B to run. While Ash was busy moving crates up and down the stairs, the two new guests had arrived, compliments of a water taxi from Bocas Town.

She had the jug of mojitos ready for the two friends and after getting them settled into the bungalow closest to *grande casa*, they'd returned to partake in the drinks.

One of the best parts of the job, and the part that Heather knew she'd like the most, was the constant change of interesting and creative people. Sandy and Miranda were old friends from California. They'd known each other for twenty years, and made a point every year to go away together for two weeks to escape their lives back home.

From the moment they'd arrived on the dock, they hadn't stopped talking and laughing. They were exactly the type of friends Heather once had back home before she'd moved to Panama with Joe. It brought a smile to her face just listening to them, but it also gave her a little twinge of nostalgia.

She'd given up a lot of things for Joe. Too many things.

But that time was over. She pushed her shoulders back, inhaled a deep breath of ocean air and breathed all the negativity out. There was no room for it at Casa del Sol.

Heck, there was no room for it in her soul. It was time for

her. And she was going to start by joining her guests for a mojito.

She finished mixing the second round of drinks and carried it over, along with a new glass for herself, to the dock where the women were enjoying the late afternoon sun.

"Mind if I join you?" Heather set her glass down before she refilled the other women's cups.

Sandy smiled and waved to the empty wooden chair. "Any woman who makes mojitos as good as these is a friend of mine." She took a long sip with her straw. A satisfied groan escaped her and she laid her head back. "It's paradise."

Heather laughed.

"It really is," Miranda agreed. "You may just be the luckiest woman ever because you actually live here."

She couldn't disagree with that statement, so she didn't. Instead, Heather joined in the easy conversation, learning about their busy lives back home, filled with careers, children, and husbands. No wonder they needed a holiday—it all sounded completely exhausting.

And absolutely wonderful.

It's not that she wanted what Sandy and Miranda had back home.

Not at all.

Heather had never wanted that life for herself. The busy wife and mother route was right for some people, but it had never appealed to her. Even so, listening to the women talking with such love in their voices, despite the stress that obviously carried them through their days, she couldn't help but feel a little envious. She may not have wanted exactly what they had, but she did want the companionship. The love.

She allowed herself a moment of jealousy, but only a moment.

"Who is that?" Miranda sat straight up in her chair, her

mouth all but hanging open. Before she even turned to look, Heather knew exactly who she was talking about.

It could only be Ash.

When Sandy looked over her shoulder to see what her friend was gawking at and had almost an identical reaction, Heather followed their gaze in order to confirm. "That's Ash. He helps out around here."

Just like every other time she saw him, her body lit up with a heat that grew from deep inside.

"And *who* exactly is Ash?"

"If I wasn't married—"

"But you are." Miranda cut off her friend and they both dissolved in giggles.

"True, true." Sandy clucked her tongue. "But if I wasn't… ohh baby."

Heather shook her head. "I should get him to put a shirt on."

"Don't you dare!"

"What?"

The friends yelled at the same time, drawing attention from the object of their conversation. Ash waved, and for a moment Heather was sure the ladies were going to swoon right off the dock and into the water. Although, that might not be a bad thing; they both clearly needed to cool down. Heather made a mental note to make the next batch of drinks virgin.

"Okay, okay." She held up her hands in surrender. "No shirt. I promise. But I should go talk to him and see what's going on." She laughed along with their whoops of approval before she excused herself. "I'll be back, I promise."

"With drinks!"

"Of course." She winked before she made her retreat.

Yes. The next batch was definitely going to be non-alcoholic.

Ash watched her with his signature sexy smile as she walked down the dock toward him.

"Looks like you have quite a party going on down there." He waved a hand toward the women, who burst into a fit of giggles at the attention.

Heather shook her head, but she absolutely loved it. As far as she was concerned, if her guests were having fun, she was doing her job. Especially with Sherri gone, she felt an increased sense of responsibility. Not that she was gone. But for as far up the hill as her treehouse was, she might as well be.

She wanted to ask Ash what was going on and whether Sherri was okay. She wanted to ask him what it meant for her and her job. *What if she had questions? What if she didn't know what to do with a guest? Or had a problem? Or—*

"You look worried." The concern in his eyes was genuine, and there was something else in his gaze. *Sadness, maybe?*

"I am," she admitted. "I mean, is it normal for Sherri to go up to the treehouse? It looked like she was moving up there permanently and I know I haven't been here long, but it just seems to me that she *is* this place. The life-force, you know what I mean?"

"I do." He leaned back against the counter and stared out to the ocean. "And you're right. Sherri built Casa del Sol with her own two hands. Did you know that?"

Heather shook her head. She hadn't.

"She had some help, of course. But everything in this place is her doing. She designed it, hammered nails, supervised it, poured her heart into it. No matter what happens, her spirit is always going to be here."

The hair on her arms stood and ice pricked at the back of her neck. "What do you mean, *no matter what happens*? What's going on?"

Ash immediately realized his mistake. In a flash, the look of concern was replaced by his smile. He ran a hand through his hair. "Nothing's going on. Sherri just needed a little time on her own. Besides, I think she knows that Casa del Sol is in good hands with you. She's not worried about a thing with you around."

He made it sound like more than a professional compliment, but a personal one as well, and Heather felt the blush from the roots of her hair.

"I love it here."

"I love having you here."

Her head snapped up and she stared at him. *Had he really just said that?*

She laughed it off. "I've barely even spoken to you." She moved to the side, needing space from him in order to think clearly.

Yes. Space was good. Space would keep her from jumping into his arms again. Whenever he was near, all she wanted to do was feel his lips pressed on hers again. Whatever space she'd been trying to give herself was becoming less and less important by the minute. "You probably just love having someone else to do some of the work around here." She grabbed a rag and wiped down the bar.

"It's not by choice." He stilled her hand with his own and Heather had to fight to keep her legs from buckling under her, his touch had such a strong effect on her. "You've been avoiding me, Heather."

She started to shake her head but there was no point in denying anything.

"You don't have to avoid me."

She laughed involuntarily. It came out as a bizarre chuckle. "I'm not."

He raised an eyebrow.

"Okay," she admitted. "I was avoiding you. But only because I was busy getting things organized and learning the ropes around here and I really don't have—"

He put his hand on her arm, stopping her words. The touch was gentle but at the same time, Heather couldn't help but feel the heat. She turned to him so they were only inches apart. He looked down at her with an intensity and fire that lit her from deep inside.

She'd done her best to silence her internal voice, but it was currently screaming at her because her body was reacting so incredibly hard to his presence and there was no way that could be a bad thing. She'd given up way too much in the last few years, including her sexuality; maybe it was time to get that back. And if it wasn't, then why was everything inside her telling her to kiss the man in front of her and throw all of her *reasons* and *excuses* into the ocean?

"Heather?" His voice broke the spell she was under and she stepped back out of his grasp. It was a good thing, too, because the ring of laughter from the dock reminded her that her guests weren't far away.

"Are you okay?"

She nodded quickly, took a deep breath and smiled widely. "I'm absolutely fine. I think maybe drinking that mojito out in the sun was a bad idea. It went right to my head."

He nodded, but there was no way he looked convinced. "You should have some water. It probably wouldn't be a bad idea for those two either." He pointed to the friends, who were now tugging their T-shirts over their heads to reveal their bikini-clad bodies. "Getting sunstroke on the first day of a holiday is never a good idea."

"True." Heather moved around the counter to prepare a jug. "And I absolutely don't want to be responsible for that." She forced a lightness into her voice.

"I'll tell you what." Ash was around the counter and so close to her that she didn't trust herself to turn around. "I'll take the water out to them."

She nodded and felt the weight of the jug leave her hands.

Heather closed her eyes and concentrated on breathing to

slow her beating heart. She knew when he moved away, because the air felt thinner, less charged.

She opened her eyes and looked straight into his eyes.

Before he turned away to walk out to the dock, he said, "You can't avoid me forever."

His words felt like a promise. A promise she realized she desperately wanted him to keep.

Chapter Six

ASH KNEW he was playing with fire when it came to Heather, but he couldn't seem to stop himself. Something about her drew him in. He wanted to know her. He wanted to…dammit, he wanted to kiss her again. It was the craziest thing and if he'd stopped to think about it, he might have realized there was more to it than just desire. But he didn't want to think about it.

Not if he could help it.

What he did want was to get her alone again so they could finish their conversation. And soon.

He didn't have to wait long. With the new arrivals into the mojitos early on, they were eager to get some sleep shortly after dinner. The romantic couple staying in the far cabin also begged off early, as they did every night, so they could be alone together. Ash and Heather watched the light of their flashlight disappear down the garden path. It wasn't until the light disappeared into their cabin, and Ash and Heather were finally alone for the first time in a week, that Ash finally spoke.

"Will you let me show you something?"

She burst into a giggle, barely bothering to stifle it with her hand.

"That's not what I meant." He shook his head, but it was no use; Heather was in a full blown fit of laugher. The sound was contagious and soon he laughed along with her until she finally exhausted herself.

"You good now?"

She nodded as solemnly as she could. "I am. That just struck me."

"I can see that." He shook his head, but he didn't mind. Not at all. He loved seeing her laugh. "I *do* want to show you something." He held up a hand before she could break into hysterics again. "And it's nothing like that. I promise. This is totally innocent. But it's pretty amazing. Do you want to see?"

She eyed him, unable to conceal the curiosity from her face. Finally she nodded. "I do."

It was the response he was hoping for. They took the dishes into the kitchen, leaving them for later. Ash grabbed a flashlight from the shelf by the garden door and led the way to the pathway behind *grande casa*.

"Where are we going?"

"Not far."

"Is it safe?"

Thor stood a few steps behind, ready for the adventure that awaited. From the moment she'd arrived, the dog wasn't far away from Heather, as if he'd appointed himself her guardian. He'd been up at the treehouse for a bit with Sherri, but as if he'd sensed that she wanted to be totally alone, the dog had come back down the stairs with Ash when he'd left the final time.

"We have Thor. I'm sure he'll save us from any scary jungle creatures."

Heather shot him a look but he laughed. "I told you, I didn't know Casa del Sol was on an island before I came here."

"I know." He slipped his hand in hers, as if it was the most natural thing in the world. "I'm only teasing." She'd stopped walking at his touch, so he squeezed gently. "Ready?"

Ash could only barely make out her nod in the moonlight, but she walked with him, letting him lead her down the garden path. He hadn't been lying; they didn't have far to go. Ash led them, his hand firmly holding hers, to the little walkway that led over the water to a vacant bungalow. Heather stopped hard when she realized where he was taking her and he had to swallow a laugh because by all appearances, it did look a little suspect.

"I promise it's not what it looks like."

"Really, Ash? I mean, this is a little…"

He couldn't help it; he laughed. "I promise." He released her hand to hold it up in a Boy Scout's promise. "We're not even going inside. I just wanted to use the deck."

She looked at him sideways, but finally agreed. "Okay. But no funny business."

"You have my word."

They walked down the dock and skirted around the bungalow to the deck on the far side. Despite the joke, he hadn't been lying when he said he wasn't going to try anything with her. Not that he wouldn't if she wanted him to. But that wasn't his intention by bringing her to the empty bungalow.

"So, why here?" Heather sat on a bench near the edge of the deck and dangled her feet over the water. She moved over so he could sit, but he had other ideas.

"Don't get comfortable. We're going swimming."

"Swimming?" The moonlight reflected off the smooth surface of the water and provided just enough illumination to see the surprise on Heather's face. "But I don't have a bathing —oh. No." She shook her head. "No way. I am not going skinny-dipping."

Ash was afraid that would be her objection. "Don't think of it like that."

"Like what?"

"Like you are." He moved to unbutton his shorts and she looked away. "You're thinking of it like it's a sexual thing and I promise you it's not." That got her attention. Heather's head turned and she eyed him, so he couldn't help but add, "Unless, of course, you want it to be."

He loved the way her skin looked in the light of the moon, but in that moment, he wished he could see the blush that he was absolutely positive was all over her face.

"Ash, I—"

"Honestly. I *do* want to show you something amazing. And the best way to see it is for yourself, in the water. You can wear your underwear if you want, but I think you're going to be disappointed if you aren't bare in the water."

He had her interest piqued. He had to forcibly stop himself from thinking of all the other things he may have peaked with his words. It was no secret that he wanted her. But he'd behave himself for her sake because he knew just how much she was going to love what he was about to show her.

"And if it makes you feel better," he added. "I won't even look while you get in. But I want you to get in first."

"Why?"

She didn't say no again. That was progress.

"You have to trust me," Ash said. "Can you do that?"

To his surprise, Heather stood and walked toward him. She stared at him for a moment before she finally said, "Turn around."

He did and with a huge smile on his face, he waited until he heard the splash of her dive.

———

She could not believe she was doing it, but something about the way he asked her to take her clothes off and get in the ocean actually made it seem like a totally reasonable request. But the craziest part was that she was going along with it.

Before she could talk herself out of it, Heather stripped the T-shirt off her head and shimmied out of her pants. She stood for a moment in her underwear before she shed them as well. With one last glance at Ash, who'd kept his back turned as promised, she pointed her arms over her head and dove gracefully into the ocean.

The water was warm and instantly she was happy she'd made the decision to remove her underwear. There was nothing quite like feeling the water on your bare skin. She let herself glide under the surface as long as she could before she surfaced. With her eyes still closed, she kicked gently to keep herself afloat and slicked her hair back off her face before she turned around and opened her eyes.

Ash was watching her, but that's not what captured her attention.

In the water she'd just swam through, there was a bright-blue streak that led right to her. It looked like the sea was lit up with neon lights under the surface. She dropped her hands into the water and instantly saw the splash of bright blue.

"What...how..."

"Isn't it magical?"

Heather looked up to Ash. In the moonlight, she could see the smile on his face. She had no words for what she was experiencing. Instead, she nodded and kicked onto her back, watching the water around her light up.

A moment later, there was a splash, a streak of blue, and Ash appeared in front of her. He ran his hands through his hair, smoothing it back from his face. Heather swallowed hard, her attention momentarily diverted from the beauty of the water, focused instead on the beauty in front of her.

"It's pretty impressive, isn't it?"

"You—I mean, yes. It is."

Ash laughed. She splashed him; the water lit up with neon refocused her attention. "What is it?" She watched her hands as they traced back and forth under the surface. "It's so incredible."

"It's bioluminescent phytoplankton."

"What? Really?"

"It's totally safe," Ash said. "I promise. It's pretty cool, isn't it?"

She relaxed and nodded. "It's amazing. I've never seen anything like it."

He swam close to her, so he was only inches from her face. "I'm glad you like it." His voice was soft and when he reached out a finger to trail down her cheek, she didn't push it away. "Your face is glowing now." Ash's smile was tender, and for the life of her, Heather could no longer remember why she'd been avoiding him.

Maybe she did owe it to herself to give herself space and time to come to grips with her new life. But maybe, more than that, she owed it to herself to stop thinking altogether and actually start to experience life. Things exactly like what she was experiencing at that moment. Thanks to Ash.

"I love it. Thank you." Her lips were so close to his, she was sure he could feel the puffs of air from her words.

His hand cupped her cheek and he closed the gap, touching his lips to hers in a soft, slow kiss.

It was over before it started, and in a flash of blue, he kicked away from her. "Do you see now why I wanted to bring you out here, instead of off the main dock?"

It took Heather a minute to decide whether he was talking about the bioluminescence or the kiss. She'd half expected that he had a hidden agenda by bringing her out by the empty bungalow, but with the taste of him still on her lips, she was positive she didn't care anymore.

"It makes sense," she said. "It's darker out here."

"And we can swim out to the platform from here if you want."

She rolled to her back, floating for a moment before she remembered she was naked. In a splash of blue neon, Heather ducked under the water.

"Don't cover yourself on my account, Heather." With an easy stroke, Ash swam up next to her. "You're beautiful and I honestly don't think I can remember ever seeing a sight as magnificent as your breasts all lit up like that."

She should have been embarrassed, but there was nothing but honesty in his voice. So with an easy flip, she returned to her back and looked up at the stars. A moment later, with a slight splash, Ash was stretched out on his back as well.

They floated in the quiet for a few minutes, the stars lighting up the sky above, the phosphoresce lighting them from below.

"This truly is the most incredible place. I can't believe how lucky I am to be…" Heather couldn't finish her thought. Emotions she'd done her best to shove down threatened to spill over and the last thing she wanted to do was cry. Especially when she wasn't even truly upset. In fact, she'd never been happier.

"Are you okay?"

She nodded, even though Ash couldn't see her.

"I am." For the first time in a long time, she meant it. "I think from the moment I got here, I've been okay. I know it's only been a week, but it feels like a lifetime. Like I was meant to find Casa del Sol and Sherri, and…even you." Heather knew how that sounded, but she didn't care because she knew Ash wouldn't be offended. "Do you think maybe that sometimes the universe sends you exactly what you need, exactly when you need it?" It sounded ridiculous when she heard herself say it, just like it had when she'd heard the same words of advice from Josie, the older, and clearly much wiser, woman in the San Blas Islands. But for the first time, Heather actually believed it.

Ash didn't say anything but she knew without looking that he was listening because a moment later, his hand found hers in the water. He twined his fingers through hers and squeezed, so she kept talking.

"It wasn't that long ago that I was totally at a loss with my life. I had nowhere to go, no one to…well, no one who cared about me." Saying it out loud for the first time hurt less than she thought it would. Probably because it wasn't true. Joe may have stopped loving her, but there were others who did.

"Heather, that can't be—"

"It isn't true." She cut him off. "But it felt like it. At least for a little while. The point is, now it feels different. Like, I have a place where I belong." She let the words float on the air in the darkness as a shooting star zipped across the sky.

"Did you see that?"

"I did," she answered. "Did you make a wish?"

Ash laughed and tugged her closer. "I can't tell you that. It won't come true."

"You kind of just admitted it." Heather laughed. But the laughter died on her lips when he pulled her close, righting her in the water, so they were face-to-face. Ash's skin was speckled with neon blue and she was sure hers was the same. "You might as well tell me your wish." It was bold, especially given the tension between them, but something about the water and the darkness and the man she was with emboldened her.

"I think you already know what I wished for." His lips curled into a small smile so sexy a simple kiss wouldn't do it justice.

In an even bolder move, Heather reached out, trailing her fingers, and a streak of blue, down the side of his face. She left her fingers resting on his jaw, ready to take the kiss she was craving, but he beat her to it.

With a slight splash, Ash wrapped his arm around her and pressed her hard against him before his lips crashed to hers. There was nothing tentative about the kiss, and there was definitely nothing tentative about the way her body responded to it.

He'd half expected her to swim away and when she didn't, it took Ash a second to realize it. But only a second before he pulled her closer, her wet skin hot against his, her lips moving against his.

"I don't believe in wishes," she said when she came up for air.

"Is that right?" Ash slid a hand down her back until it rested on the curve of her buttocks. "Because it would seem to me—"

She silenced him with another kiss. Her boldness sent desire ripping through him, focused between his legs.

Damn, he'd never expected her to be so forward with him. But then again, from the moment he'd met her, he hadn't known what to expect from her. But if the surprises kept coming and they were even half as good as the kiss, he was perfectly okay with it.

"That's right," she said, answering him. "Wishes are nothing but empty promises to yourself."

Something about her choice of words stopped him, but he didn't have time to respond before she bit his bottom lip and sucked it into her mouth, kissing him hard. She wrapped her legs around his waist.

The water wasn't deep, but he wouldn't be able to hold them up in the water indefinitely. He pulled away from her kiss, gently sucking on her bottom lip as he did so. "Hold on."

"Are we going for a ride?"

"Something like that." He kicked his legs hard beneath him, and used his arms to pull them a few feet into the shallower waters. As soon as he put his feet down and they touched the sandy bottom below, his hands wrapped around Heather once more, this time pressing her closer to him and his growing hardness between them.

A low moan escaped her lips when he moved his kisses to her neck. A shudder ran through her, encouraging his attentions on her neck. He sucked, nibbled, and left a bite or two as he worked his way down her body. Her groans intensified the lower he went, so he lifted her easily, exposing more of her gorgeous body from the water.

Her breasts glistened with the blue luminescence in the moonlight. He hadn't been blowing smoke when he'd told her earlier she was the most beautiful thing he'd seen. She truly was. Her body with curves in all the right places was just right for holding and squeezing and kissing. And that's exactly what he wanted to do.

Needing to taste her again, Ash slid her wet body down his chest until they were once again face-to-face. Her breath was coming in short pants, but he didn't give her a chance to recover before once more taking her mouth in his. He slipped his tongue between her lips while at the same time his fingers found their target between her legs.

He swallowed her gasp with his kiss, his own excitement building with her reaction. She was so incredibly responsive to his touch; it was only moments before he felt her body clench around his fingers, followed by a shudder and a low moan that built low in her chest before it escaped her throat.

He waited while she recovered from her orgasm. He'd thought she was beautiful before, but watching her come completely undone in his arms was very likely the sexiest thing he'd ever experienced. There was just something about her. He couldn't get enough. More than that, he didn't want to.

"Ash. We…I…"

"Don't." He kissed her words away.

She lifted herself in his arms so she looked directly at him. "Don't what?"

"Don't tell me we shouldn't have done that."

Her laugh was rich and loud and took him completely off guard. "I was not going to say that."

"You weren't?" He eyed her suspiciously. Every indication she'd given him from the moment they'd begun their cat-and-mouse game told him she'd be running now. Every time he thought he made a step in the right direction with Heather, that's what she did. And if this wasn't a huge step, he didn't know what was.

"No." She shook her head with another laugh and grabbed his face between her hands. She kissed him deep and any lingering thoughts of her running disappeared. Especially when she said, "I was going to say that we needed to get out of the water so we could take care of you properly."

A rush of heat flooded his groin at her words. He pulled her tight to his now throbbing erection. "God, you're amazing." He pushed one hand through her wet hair and kissed her again. "But I don't want to go anywhere." His voice was rough with need. "I need you now."

She wiggled against him and for a moment he thought he might come completely undone right then and there. Ash moved a hand to her hips to still her.

"What? You just said—"

"I know what I said, but I also know we need to be safe." The thought of stopping made him want to scream, but he wasn't completely unreasonable. There were precautions, and he was a grown man. He could wait.

"I'm safe," she said. "I'm protected and…well, I know I'm clean."

Ash's mind spun. He never had unprotected sex. *Ever.*

Which was how he knew he was clean.

With her legs still wrapped tightly around him, he stilled her, staring into her eyes. "You're sure?"

She nodded and despite all the reasons he had to stop, he kissed her. Hard.

His hands found her hips again and then he couldn't have stopped for anything. He lifted her slightly before bringing her down again, slowly so his hard length buried inside her.

For a moment, he held her still, unmoving and allowing her a chance to adjust to him. When her eyes once again focused on his, he started moving, slowly at first. And then faster.

"Ash. You…." Her words were lost as he increased his movements.

Every thrust inside her sent electrical pulses racing through him, spurring him on. He wanted to make it last, but he also knew there'd be time for that later.

Heather nuzzled her face into his neck and bit down as another orgasm crested inside her. She was his undoing, and his own climax built rapidly.

With one hand holding her to him, his other hand found her chin, tilting it up so he could look directly into her eyes as they went over the edge together.

She clung to him and a shudder traveled through them both.

Ash didn't know how much time passed as they recovered from their coupling, but as soon as his heartbeat returned to normal, he kissed her again. Softer this time; the need for her was still there, but without the edge of urgency there'd been earlier.

"I thought you promised me no funny business." She winked at him playfully and unwound her legs from him before she kicked away from him in a splash. She turned and said, "I think you owe me."

"Oh yeah?"

"Come on," she called. "I'll race you to the platform."

She took off before he could object. Not that he would. His body was still vibrating from the memory of her and he could barely form a thought. Without a doubt, he knew one thing with certainty: now that he'd had a taste of her, Ash wasn't sure he'd ever be able to get enough of her.

Chapter Seven

IT HAD BEEN a week since she'd had her late-night *swim* with Ash, and although every morning Heather had woken to the sounds of the waves outside her window and the birds in the trees behind her bungalow, in the last week, her morning routine had changed a little bit. Now, as well as listening to the peace of Casa del Sol, she woke up with a fire deep inside her that only Ash had been able to quench. Or maybe he just fueled the flames? Either way, she liked it.

She stretched her arms up over her head and let those sounds of peace and tranquility wash over her before she slipped out of bed to sit on the swing over the deck. It was the perfect way to start her day, and she didn't think she was ever going to tire of it.

Although, she could think of a few other perfect ways to start her day. All of which included waking up to Ash, his hands on her body—touching her, stroking her...

"Mmmm." Heather squeezed her eyes shut and let her mind drift for a few minutes.

The night of the swim, and every night after that they'd spent together, Heather almost invited Ash to spend the night in her bungalow. But every time, at the last minute had changed her mind. Not that she didn't want to sleep next to him, his arms holding her close, her head on his chest. Oh yes, she wanted all those things, but it was too soon. And they'd been having such fun together, she didn't want to ruin it by moving too fast.

She stretched her body, reaching her arms over her head and squeezed her eyes shut again. Her body came alive with the simple memory of his fingers touching her, coaxing things out of her that she didn't even know she was capable of feeling. It was hard to believe that she'd allowed herself to let go so completely.

Was it?

Maybe not. After all, she'd been surprising herself a lot lately. And maybe Ash was able to stir things in her she'd never felt because she was finally allowing herself to be open to those things.

Maybe. Whatever it was, she liked it.

A lot.

With one more stretch, Heather left the comfort of her bed and moved outside to her swing. She'd come to love the morning ritual, if it could be a ritual in only a few weeks. Either way, it was her time to sit and reflect before things got busy. And after her romantic nights with Ash, she certainly had a lot to think about.

She felt almost like a teenager using the word romantic, even in her thoughts, but there was no other word for it. Everything with Ash *had* been romantic, in a way she'd never experienced before. Heck, she thought she was beyond romance.

She didn't need it. She never had. Joe certainly hadn't been romantic. Once upon a time, she'd liked his *realism*. At least that's how she used to think about it. Excuse it.

The truth was there was no romance with Joe because there'd never been any love. Not like there should have been.

But that was over.

She should be sad or heartbroken or…something. But all Heather could feel as she swung gently over the ocean was relief. Her body was still deliciously sore from Ash the night before, but she knew their coupling had nothing to do with how she was feeling about her marriage dissolving. Although, one certainly wouldn't have happened without the other.

Things had a funny way of working out.

Not that anything with Ash was *worked out*. Heather laughed at herself. She'd never been the crazy type who assumed there was a relationship just because there'd been sex. Besides that, she didn't want or need a relationship of any kind.

She laughed again and tossed her head back, letting the feeling fill her.

"I love that sound."

Ash's voice startled her and she sat up as she twisted around in the swing.

"Good morning, beautiful." Ash leaned up against the side of the bungalow, a single orchid in his hand. "I didn't mean to scare you."

She smiled. "You didn't. Come sit."

He crossed the deck and caught her by the waist in mid swing. She tipped her head back and he kissed her thoroughly before he tucked the orchid behind her ear. "You're beautiful." She thought he'd kiss her again. Instead, he released her with a gentle push so she could resume her swing. "Although I'm a little disappointed by your sleeping attire."

Heather blushed and looked down at her old Mickey Mouse T-shirt.

"That mouse wouldn't stand a chance if I was lying next to you."

She turned and gave him a wicked smile. "But you weren't."

"I wasn't invited."

Heather shrugged casually. "Maybe one day."

If he kept looking at her with those sexy eyes full of even sexier promises, that day would come sooner rather than later.

"If I play my cards right?"

She hopped off her swing and stood across from him. "I'm pretty sure it won't have anything to do with cards."

Just as she hoped he would, Ash grabbed her waist and pulled her close. "You drive me crazy," he whispered roughly before he kissed her with a need that backed up his words.

The feeling was completely mutual, and her body thrummed with electricity. She was breathless when he finally pulled away. But as much as she'd like to put out the fire in her veins, she had work to do and her presence was needed at *grande casa*. Preferably before her guests woke up.

Ash would have to wait.

Heather put a finger to his lips and stepped back. "We'll have to finish this later."

He didn't release his grip on her.

"I have work to do," she insisted, but he only raised an eyebrow. "I do not want to get fired."

He moved one hand down to her bare thigh, gently moving his fingers along her skin. "You aren't going to get fired."

"Oh, I don't know." She tried—without much luck—not to get distracted by his attentions. "I can't imagine that Sherri would like it if I was too busy making out to do my job."

"Sherri won't mind." He kissed her again. "She doesn't even have to know."

Of course, she probably didn't know what was happening between Ash and Heather at all since she moved up to her treehouse. It wasn't the first time Heather had wondered and worried about the older woman. She'd asked Ash a few times, but he always managed to change the subject whenever it was brought up.

"Hey." His thumb stroked her cheek. "Where did your smile go?"

Heather shook her head, but he wouldn't have it. Ash held her head and looked into her eyes. "Seriously. What's up?"

"I was just thinking about Sherri," she admitted. "I can't help but worry about her and wonder how she's doing." She wiggled free from his arms. "Aren't you concerned at all?" She turned and looked out to the water. "No. Of course you're not. You know what she's doing. I don't know anything." Heather crossed her arms over her thin T-shirt. "I shouldn't even be worried. I mean, it's not like it's my business."

"Of course it is." His hand rested on her shoulder, and he gently turned her. "Sherri is as much your business as she is mine."

"Is that right?" She knew she was pushing things, but Heather had never been one to back down when something was important. She wasn't about to start now. "Then tell me the truth."

Of course she wanted answers. She deserved them. Heck, he was surprised it had taken as long as it had for her to push the issue. She didn't seem like the type of woman who would let things go easily.

But he couldn't tell her.

Not without Sherri's permission.

"We should probably get to *grande casa*," he said instead. It was a terrible attempt at avoiding the matter, but he didn't know what else to do. Not without talking to Sherri first. "Your guests will be up soon and I have a feeling they're going to want some help figuring out how to spend their day."

She shook her head, opened her mouth as if she were going to object, and finally closed it again, her lips pressed into a thin line. Ash didn't know what was worse: Heather pushing him to tell her something he couldn't, or her being upset with him when only the night before, she'd been so happy.

The memory of her body pressed against his, the way she felt when he moved inside her, the sound she made when she lost control—*damn*. He didn't think he'd ever get enough of that.

She turned to walk back into her bungalow, but he grabbed her hand, spinning her around, and held her tight in his arms. "Don't be mad." Ash kissed her neck. "I know you're worried." He kissed her again. "And I think it's really sweet of you to be concerned, but Sherri's fine." He nuzzled into her neck, unable to look her in the face while he lied to her. "She just needs a little alone time for a while."

"She's fine?"

Ash nodded and kissed her again. Distracting Heather was quickly becoming his favorite thing to do.

"Would you tell me if something was wrong?"

He couldn't lie to her again, so instead, he took her face in both hands and kissed her thoroughly. When he was finally satisfied, not that he thought he'd ever be satisfied kissing her, he released her. "I'll tell you what," he said. "I'll start the coffee. You take your time getting ready for the day."

Before she could object, or challenge him on the fact that he didn't quite answer her question, he gave her another quick kiss and left her to get ready.

He wasn't going to be able to avoid her questioning forever and he hated to lie to her. Particularly at the beginning of their relationship, whatever that was. It didn't matter what it was between them; he wasn't going to keep lying to her. He may be a lot of things, but a liar was certainly not one of them. Which was why as soon as breakfast was finished, and Heather was busy with her guests, organizing a day of activities to keep them busy in the sun, Ash packed a basket of supplies and headed up the hill to Sherri's treehouse.

He took his time going up the stairs, partly because he wasn't in a hurry to see what was waiting for him at the top, and partly because he loved the journey. The rainforest was full of the most beautiful flowers and creatures. When he'd first moved to Panama, he'd barely noticed his surroundings, losing himself in booze and women and pretty much anything else that would dull the ache inside him. It had worked for a little while, but then he'd met Mick at the Bitter End and shortly after, he'd introduced him to Sherri. It was only after that meeting, when he first came to Casa del Sol, that Ash finally started noticing his surroundings. *Really* noticing them.

And they were incredible. The colors, the scents, everything. He almost couldn't believe that he hadn't noticed the beauty of Panama before.

Almost.

He'd been way too closed off to notice anything besides his own misery. Almost as if he'd been in a long sleep. But that was a long time ago. He hadn't been that guy for a while. The guy who moved through the days in a fog, unable or unwilling to open his eyes to the life that was happening to him.

But he was no longer that guy.

His eyes were wide open now.

And he planned to keep it that way.

Before he took the final flight of steps to Sherri's house, Ash turned and looked out at the bay below. The water always looked especially peaceful from up here. A ring of laughter rang out and soon, the forms of two women on a paddleboard came into view. Heather hadn't wasted any time getting the guests situated with the water toys. He watched for a moment, wondering why both the friends were on one board. Sherri had two paddleboards for the guests to use. His answer came in form of the new guests. A couple who were backpacking through Central America. They were only spending a few days with them, but it looked as if they didn't want to waste a minute of it. They paddled into Ash's view, looking much more graceful than the two women who'd come before them. They were still laughing and clearly having balancing issues while the other couple paddled peacefully around the bay.

Their peace only lasted a moment before one of the ladies jumped from their board, swam over and knocked the couple into the water. Ash shook his head and laughed. It looked like fun. No doubt Heather was on the dock, laughing at them all.

Just like Sherri would have.

Remembering why he was headed up the hill in the first place, Ash took the last few steps two at a time until he was outside Sherri's little house. He knocked once and entered.

"Sherri?"

He kept his voice low at first, but called out again when she didn't answer. "Sherri, I hope I didn't wake you." He kept his voice calm, trying to infuse some of that same calmness into himself. He had no idea what to expect, and the unknown was never a good thing. "Sherri? You okay?"

The house wasn't very large, consisting mostly of one big open room with a few comfy chairs and pillows scattered around, and a cooking area tucked into one corner. There was a bathroom with a compostable toilet out the back, and just like the buildings down by the ocean, the water was supplied from a large cistern full of rainwater. The main room was empty, although it definitely showed signs of life from the last time he'd been there, dropping off crates. The large windows were open, letting the crosswinds blow through the space, and there were little pots with different plants scattered around the room.

Signs of life. But no Sherri.

Ash crossed the space to the ladder on the far wall that led to the sleeping loft. If Sherri was sleeping, he didn't want to wake her. But if she wasn't sleeping…he didn't want to think about it.

"Sherri?"

Still no answer. There was no other choice. He shook his head and took a deep breath. "You shouldn't be up here on your own, Sherri. Not with all the medicine and no one to help you. And this loft is even stupider." She could be up there, unable to move, stuck in her bed. With his hands on the ladder, he climbed up slowly, muttering the entire way. "So help me, if I have to carry you down this ladder, I'm going to—"

"Ash?"

He started, and only nearly caught himself before sliding backward off the ladder. Ash took a moment to compose himself before he turned around to see Sherri, looking quite healthy and in no way incapacitated in her bed, standing behind him. "Sherri."

"As I live and breathe."

"Funny." He shook his head and climbed off the ladder. "How are you?" He wrapped her in a hug and tried not to notice that she looked a little bit smaller than the last time he'd seen her. Or at least he thought she did. Maybe it was just his imagination. He hoped it was. "Seriously. How are you?"

She didn't look sick. Her house didn't look like the house of a sick person. It was sunny and airy and everything it should be. But then he took a closer look. There were pill bottles lined up on the counter, the IV pole shoved in a corner, a bandage on the inside of Sherri's arm. "Are you taking care of yourself?"

She smiled and patted his arm. "Ash, I'm fine." She moved slower than he remembered as she crossed the floor to the fridge. But then again, maybe it was all in his head. "Now tell me, to what do I owe the honor of your visit?"

He followed her across the room and took the bottle of

juice from her hands so he could pour it for her. "Sit," he ordered. "I'll get us a drink."

To his surprise, she didn't protest, but did as she was told, sitting in a large wicker chair that looked out into the jungle. "But only juice for me," she said. "You better have a beer."

"It's not even noon."

She laughed. "Suit yourself then, but it's special juice." She held her hands up in air quotes and shook her head.

He was pretty sure the type of special Sherri was referring to had more to do with the bottles of medicine and a lot less to do with any type of special anything he might care to entertain. "Beer it is."

As soon as the drinks were ready, he sat down next to his friend and waited for her to talk. It didn't take long.

"So, you didn't say, what brings you up here?"

"You do."

"And?"

"I brought you supplies." He pointed to the basket he'd left by the door.

"I don't need anything." She chugged half her drink and grimaced. "This stuff is awful." She drank the rest and put the empty glass on the table next to her. "Besides, I've been growing a few things and getting my garden going again. Do you know that when I first moved here, I spent most of my days up here? I preferred it to the water. It was more peaceful. I'd forgotten that." Her eyes took on a faraway look for a moment. "It's nice up here."

"You're not lonely?"

"Should I be?"

Ash wasn't sure how to answer that. He would have been lonely all on his own, but he wasn't Sherri. And it wouldn't surprise him if she was perfectly content on her own. "No," he said after a moment. "You shouldn't be. But how are you feeling? Your medicine…" He nodded to the empty glass. "It's okay?"

Her smile was warm and reassuring, just as he was sure she meant it to be. "I feel good. The drugs aren't so bad if you pair them with some herbs to help with the side effects. So far everything is fine."

He examined her closely for any indication that she was lying to him, but her face gave nothing away. "You promise that you'll tell me if you need anything, right?"

"I'll call you right away." She laughed again and despite the fact that he knew she was teasing him, he didn't mind as long as it kept her laughing.

"Maybe not." He raised an eyebrow and took a deep slug of his beer. "But I'm serious about it, Sherri. I need you to let me know right away if you need anything." He looked her straight in the eye. "Anything at all. I'm going to come up here as much as I can, okay?"

She started to shake her head, but he stopped her. "That's the only way I'm going to agree to leave you alone, Sher. Like every two days. I'll be here." He waited until she nodded. "I won't stay long if you don't want me to," he continued. "But I need to know you're okay."

"Okay."

He blinked. He'd expected her to put up a much bigger fight. "Really?"

"Really." She nodded. "If that's what makes you feel better."

"It does." It made him feel unexplainably happier. He'd been more worried about Sherri than he even knew. Although he'd still be worried, maybe that could be lessened somewhat if he was able to come up to visit and check on her with his own two eyes. Not that he couldn't have done that before but now he had her blessing, which would ultimately make things easier. "One more thing."

She narrowed her eyes, no doubt ready for a fight. Sherri may be the most relaxed, easy-going person he knew, but she was also the most stubborn when she put her mind to it. She was fierce and under normal circumstances, he wouldn't be willing to go up against her.

These were not normal circumstances.

When she didn't speak, he continued. "I need to tell Heather about what's going on with you. She's worried and I think—"

"No."

"Sherri. I think if you—"

"No." She pushed up and out of her chair as if the subject was closed.

It wasn't.

It couldn't be.

Ash followed her out to the deck that was all but right in the canopy of trees. There was a bit of space between the trees where you could look down on Casa del Sol. Even though they were far up the hill, you could still see the buildings, the people playing in the water and hear the laughter floating on the air. Ash stood next to Sherri and watched the activities in silence for a moment before he pressed the issue.

"If Heather knew what was happening, it would really put her mind at ease."

"No, it wouldn't," Sherri said simply. "It would only worry her."

"She's already worried because she doesn't know what's going on."

"It's a different type of worry." She shook her head. "She doesn't need that right now."

Frustration built inside him. Sherri was being ridiculous. *Cancer was not something you could fight on your own.* He hadn't said anything about the ludicrous notion she had about treating herself. He'd stayed quiet when she told him she'd be administering her own treatments; he'd respected those wishes. But this was different. She needed support. She needed friends and positive energy and love. And how could she presume to know what Heather needed? Especially when she'd been hiding away. *If anyone knew what Heather needed, it was—*

"Get out of your head, Ash." She interrupted his thoughts. "Say what you need to say, but don't stew on it. It's not healthy."

Her words calmed him, the way they always did because even though it drove him crazy, she knew. Sherri always just *knew*.

His hands gripped the railing. He took a breath. "Heather's doing fine."

Sherri's smile told him that she'd already guessed just how fine Heather was doing. "I'm sure she is. But this is my story to tell, Ash. And I'm not ready to tell it yet, okay?"

Her words shut down any further argument because he couldn't argue with that. She'd always respected his story. The least he could do was return the favor. He swallowed back the objections that were still on the tip of his tongue. Finally he nodded. "Okay. But I'll be here every two days."

"I know you will."

It was almost time for lunch by the time Ash reappeared. He hadn't told Heather he was going anywhere, and despite the fact that she was hyper aware of his presence, she'd been so busy with her guests, she hadn't even noticed he was gone until about thirty minutes before he walked into *grande casa*, holding a bouquet of exotic flowers.

"For you, beautiful."

"They're gorgeous." She took the bouquet from him and inhaled their blossoms. "And they smell amazing."

Ash wrapped an arm around her waist, pulled her close and kissed her quickly. "They are not nearly as gorgeous as you and trust me when I tell you that you smell a whole lot more amazing than they do."

Heather shook her head at his cheesy line, but she couldn't help but feel a warmth at his words. She'd never been spoken to like that before. With tenderness and...it was *way* too early to even think about the *L* word. But there was no other way to describe the way she felt when he spoke to her like that. She cleared her throat and wiggled away from his grip, needing space before she let her mind get carried away with a fairy tale.

"Well, they're really pretty." She dug out a jar from behind the bar and filled it with water. "Thank you for thinking of me. Where were you, anyway?"

"I went to visit Sherri."

She froze and turned slowly. *Was he finally going to tell her what was going on with the other woman?* "And?"

"And she's doing great." He joined her behind the bar. "Please tell me you have bottles of water in the fridge. I'm parched."

Heather grabbed a bottle, but held it close to her chest instead of handing it to him.

Ash grinned and crossed his arms. "You're not going to give me the water?"

"Are you going to tell me?"

"Tell you what?"

"Sherri."

He tilted his head as if he had no idea what she was talking about. She was smarter than that. "Seriously," she said. "Tell me what's going on with Sherri. You just said you were there visiting her, so tell me what's going on with her."

Ash dropped his chin to his chest for a moment before he looked up. "Honestly, there's nothing going on with her. She's just taking a little vacation in the trees."

"A vacation?"

"Is that hard to believe?"

It was. Heather looked around her. She was in the middle of paradise. *How could anyone want a vacation from that?* She nodded and Ash laughed.

"Remember, you just got here. This is Sherri's home."

"Sherri's incredibly lucky."

"She is. And so are you. Because you're here now…with me." He wiggled his eyebrows and she laughed. "Seriously, though. She just wanted a break for a bit from the running of things and besides, I think she just wanted to give you space to do things your way. It's no big deal."

He didn't make it sound like a big deal. Maybe it wasn't and she was just worrying about nothing. It certainly felt like something, though.

"I swear," Ash added when she didn't respond. "It's nothing. Don't worry about it. Sherri's just like that. What's been going on around here? I heard lots of laughter."

For a minute, Heather contemplated pressing the issue, but there didn't seem to be much point. Besides, Ash said she was just on a vacation. Although, why she didn't tell Heather that herself was kind of a mystery. Still, it didn't seem like something she needed to worry about. At least not until there was something to worry about.

"It's been a busy morning around here." She pointed at the dock, where all the guests were lounging while they took their turns on the paddleboards, having given up on trying to go two at a time. If all her days were like this, Heather would have no problem getting used to life at Casa del Sol. *Who was she kidding —she'd already gotten used to it.*

"We should go join them," Ash said. "It does look like a lot of fun." He turned to head out to the dock but she hesitated. "You coming?"

She nodded. She wanted to let it go. But the thing with

Sherri still niggled at her brain. Something just didn't feel right.

"Are you okay?"

She nodded again, but Ash crossed the space and took her hands in his. "Ash?" He nodded. "You'd tell me if something was really wrong, right? I just need to know that you'll be honest with me if it's needed. Then I won't need to worry."

A flash of something crossed his face so quickly she couldn't be sure she'd even seen a change, and then just like that, his smile was back. He squeezed her hands. "Of course."

Chapter Eight

THE DAY, like most days at Casa del Sol, passed in a blur of activity and fun. The romantic couple retreated to their room shortly after lunch. Heather didn't begrudge them the time alone. If anything, she was a little jealous of it. She'd never had such a connection with a man before. The idea of abandoning fun in the sun to sneak off for sex was a completely foreign idea.

She snuck a glance at Ash, who was organizing snorkel gear at the end of the dock.

Maybe it wasn't a completely foreign idea.

Maybe she could entertain the idea of spending some time cloistered in a hut over the ocean with Ash.

Oh yes. That could be a possibility.

He looked up from adjusting a mask to see her watching him. "Hey. Like what you see?"

Heather shook her head, but she couldn't help but laugh. Ash could get away with the cockiness. "I do." She blew him a kiss and quickly turned away.

She closed her eyes and let the heat of the sun wash over

her face. She'd never been so forward before. Never flirted so openly. It was unlike her. She liked it.

Besides that, it was fun and there was nothing wrong with fun.

"Seriously. He's so hot." Sandy, who sat in the chair next to her, nudged Heather with her elbow. "You're a lucky woman to have such a hot boyfriend."

"Oh, he's not my—" Heather stopped herself. There was no point getting into details with her guests. "But I am very lucky. Ash is a good guy."

"If you know what I mean?" Sandy laughed, clearly looking for details Heather wasn't prepared to give. But she also wasn't going to shatter the illusion for the woman, so she settled for wiggling her eyebrows before she excused herself.

"I should go see what Camila's planned for dinner. If you ladies want to go for another snorkel before it gets too late, I'm sure Ash could hook you up."

She felt kind of bad about pushing the women on Ash that way, but she knew he could handle it. Besides, she probably should take a look in the kitchen. Not so much to check up on Camila, who was most likely preparing something absolutely delicious for dinner, but it was past time to take a look at the inventory on the shelves and see what they were getting low on. It might be time to organize a trip into town soon.

It didn't take her long to go through the kitchen, and the list wasn't as long as Heather thought it might be. Camila was amazing at using a lot of the ingredients that grew locally and managing the supplies that were harder to get.

Still, they could always do with a few things next time a trip into town needed to be made. With any luck, it could be organized around the guests coming and going to reduce the trips that needed to be made.

Casa del Sol ran on solar power, and Heather had found it to be remarkably well wired. It was an interesting combination between primitive and modern. Heather liked to call it rustic luxury but it still made her shake her head in wonder every time she fired up the laptop that handled all of the bookings and connected her to the Internet.

Sherri had shown her the passwords and log-ins for the website. Heather tried to look at it every two days at the latest, in case someone sent an email inquiring about a booking. There were usually a few, but not as many as she thought there should be. And not nearly as many bookings as they could handle.

She made a mental note to check with Sherri about the idea of listing Casa del Sol on a site like Airbnb, where she was positive they would get more hits, and therefore more reservations. The property had enough rooms to handle up to ten people comfortably. Heather would love to have a full house. It would be a lot of work, but it would also be a lot of fun. Not to mention the whole business side of things. Heather had always liked a challenge. Not that Casa del Sol was a *challenge*—but if she could increase the guests and therefore the revenue…well, that would be something.

It took her a few minutes to go through the emails and send a few to upcoming guests. She jotted down their arrival times, which coincided conveniently with everyone else's departure. There'd be two more couples coming in and judging by their correspondence with Sherri, it looked as though they were up for a little fun and adventure. It could be an interesting week.

Heather was just about to power things down when she decided to do something she'd been avoiding since she'd arrived.

She clicked over to the Internet, opened a new window and typed in the address for her online email account. Right before she'd left for Bocas, Heather sent her mother an email, telling her about the divorce and Heather's relocation. She knew how her mother would react, and she wouldn't have told her at all except, well…she was her mother.

Just as she knew it would be, Heather's inbox was full. There were at least ten messages from her mother. With a sigh, she scrolled up and clicked on the first one.

Heather!! Her mother always did have a flair for the dramatic. Why use one exclamation mark when you could use two?

What the hell is going on? I told you Joe was no good for you. You must be crushed. There it was. Just about as much motherly sympathy as she'd get.

He always was a deadbeat. In actuality, he wasn't; he just wasn't a good match for Heather. That was one thing her mother had gotten right. Which was why Heather had steadfastly ignored her every time her mom had told her that.

At least now you can get out of that godforsaken country and come home where you belong. Her mom had never understood why they'd gone to Panama; she'd refused to visit them—not like it was a big loss—and she was always trying to encourage Heather to come home by sending her articles on yellow fever, hurricanes, and crime rates in Central America.

It wasn't helpful.

Call me when you can. I'll send you a ticket home. Yeah. That wasn't happening. The phone call or the ticket home.

Panama *was* home.

Heather clicked off the email and scanned the others. They were more of the same.

There was no help for it; she'd keep writing her until she responded. They hadn't always seen eye to eye when she was growing up, but she knew her mother cared about her. She'd always wanted the best for her, and even though she didn't have a great way of showing it, her mom loved her. It had only been the two of them after her father died when Heather was only five and her mother, who'd seemed fairly normal up until then, became both very detached and completely overbearing all at the same time.

Joe and Panama had been Heather's escape. Looking back, it hadn't been the most mature response to dealing with her mom, but it got her out from under her influence and ultimately, it had probably been the best thing for their relationship. After all, Heather didn't totally cringe now when she spoke to her. That was progress.

Heather opened a new email and wrote quickly.

Mom,

Thank you for your concern. I'm doing fine and I have a great new job managing a beautiful bed-and-breakfast on the other side of Panama. I won't be coming home, so please don't send a ticket.

I hope you're well and keeping yourself busy.

It really is paradise here in every sense of the word. You have to see it to believe it.

Love, Heather.

She sent the email before reading it over, clicked through a few other messages, including one telling her that the divorce was final and everything had been settled easily. No doubt, Joe and his baby mama would be tying the knot soon, if they hadn't already, now that he was free. She almost felt like emailing Joe to congratulate him but it didn't seem appropriate. She didn't really know what was appropriate when it came to Joe. It was a very odd thing to be hurt and relieved about a divorce all at the same time. But the overwhelming feeling was one of relief and freedom.

She looked around at the beautiful waters, the palm trees, the hibiscus and orchids blooming, the birds singing in the trees behind her. She took it all in and let out a long breath.

Yes.

Definitely freedom.

"Good night."

Ash kept a smile on his face until the last guests left out the garden door to their own bungalows for the night. The second they were gone, he turned to Heather, and his smile became very different. He'd been waiting all night. No. He'd been waiting all day to get her alone again.

He'd never thought of himself as an impatient man, but Heather was changing a lot of the things he'd once thought about himself. Including the fact that he might not be a one-night stand type of guy after all.

At least not the way he thought.

The fact that after his night with Heather in the ocean, he not only wanted to see her the next morning, but for the rest of the day, was telling. Never mind the fact that he hadn't been able to stop thinking about her.

He never let a woman get to him like that. *Not since—*

"What's that smile for?"

Heather interrupted his train of thought. From the way she walked across the room, a sultry swing in her hips and a sexy smile of her own on her face, he was pretty sure he was going to like the interruption.

"I'm just happy to have a little alone time is all," Ash said.

"With me?"

He hooked a finger in the hem of her shirt and tugged her close before pressing his lips to her neck.

"You'll do." He nipped the skin under her ear. "Oh, you'll do all right." He kissed her again, sucking her earlobe between his lips. "You'll *definitely* do."

"Oh, I'll more than *do*." Her voice was little more than a breath on the air.

"Damn right." He walked her back to the bench of cushions that served as a couch in the corner of the room until her legs pressed against it and she sat down. Gently, Ash pushed her back until she was on her back, looking up at him straddled over her body. The look on her face was full of want, and he was more than ready to answer her need.

Ash pulled a thin blanket over their bodies and cuddled Heather closer. They'd worked up a sweat, and the breeze coming off the ocean could be cool, especially after the heat they'd created faded. Not that he thought it would. Not really.

She nuzzled into his chest, a perfect fit, and Ash felt something in his chest hitch. He'd never spent so much time with a woman. Not like this. *Not since Carlie.*

It was the first time he'd allowed himself to even think her name in months. Maybe years. The fact that he did so while holding another woman stopped him. His fingers, which had been tracing circles on Heather's back, froze. It wasn't until Heather pulled away and propped herself up on one elbow that he realized he'd been holding his breath.

"You okay?"

He nodded but it took him a moment to recover from the sudden wash of emotion. "I'm good." He pulled her closer and kissed the top of her head before he slipped off the couch. "I was just thinking there might be a storm coming in." He grabbed his pants and tugged them on. "It feels a bit cooler than usual. We should check the weather. If there's something coming in, I might need to take the guests back early."

Ash was aware that he was being an ass, but he couldn't seem to stop himself. It was too much to be next to her at that moment. He just needed a little space so he could think and clear his head. It was far worse to lie next to Heather and be thinking of another woman. Even if it was Carlie, even if—*no. He needed to stop.*

"Do you want a drink or something?" He went to the bar and rooted around for something strong. "Scotch?" He selected a bottle from the shelf and grabbed a glass.

Heather watched him from the couch, the blanket pulled up under her arms, covering her body. She shook her head, so he poured himself a dram and swallowed it fast.

"You're sure you're okay?"

Ash nodded. "Fine. Just thinking about the weather."

"Right." She nodded slowly. "Well, if you're this worked up by it, maybe you should fire up the computer and check. If you're right, we'll have to make arrangements for everyone to go early." She slipped off the couch and, keeping her body covered, fetched her clothes from where he'd thrown them. Ash's guilt grew as he watched the way she worked to get dressed without the blanket slipping. He'd done that. He'd created an awkwardness between them. And after the closeness they'd just shared.

He was an ass.

He poured another measure of the amber liquid and tossed it back quickly before he reached for the laptop and powered it up.

There were a million places he could have looked while the old laptop took its time powering up, but like the coward he was being, he stared at the black screen until it came to life. Heather came to stand beside him, and his reflex was to put his arm around her, but he stopped himself.

He knew she was feeling the sudden strangeness between them; she had to be. But instead of pulling away the way he expected her to, she slid her hands over his shoulders and squeezed. "Well?"

Ash turned and took her hand. "Heather, I—"

"The weather, Ash. How is it?"

It took him a moment to process the fact that she wasn't going to call him out for being a jerk, and it was just the thing he needed to snap out of whatever it was that was going on in his head. Ash grabbed her face with both hands and kissed her hard.

"What was that for?" Heather laughed when he finally let her up for air.

"For acting like an idiot." He hated lying to her, especially more than once. It just wasn't the right time to tell her about Carlie, and it certainly wasn't the right time to tell her what kind of man he really was. "I was just thinking about the weather and then I got worried that the guests would be stranded and miss their flight, and—"

"It's okay." She kissed him softly and smiled. "You don't owe me anything, Ash."

He opened his mouth to disagree, although he didn't know what he'd say, but the incoming ding of an email interrupted.

In fact, there were multiple dings and the email program that had been left open lit up with the incoming messages that filled the screen. "Looks like someone is pretty popular."

Heather's arm shot across him and slammed the lid shut. "It's nothing."

It was most certainly something and he said so. "You don't like email?"

She reached around him and slid the laptop away from him. "We need to check the weather." With the screen turned away from him, she flipped it up and started to click buttons.

Whoever it was sending her emails, she certainly didn't want him to see. A spark of jealousy flared in his gut. "A boyfriend?"

He couldn't believe the question came out of his mouth. He had no right to ask her that. Especially after the way he'd just been acting. Besides, whatever it was they were doing together, it wasn't serious. He didn't do serious and he likewise, he couldn't reasonably expect any kind of exclusivity from her. "I mean, it's fine if—"

"No boyfriend." She cut him off. "And before you ask, no husband either. I'm not that kind of girl."

"I didn't mean to imply that you were. I just… well…sorry."

"Don't be." She laughed. "I had a husband up until very recently. It wasn't right and it ended." A wave of relief washed over him, which was ridiculous because, like he kept telling himself, they weren't serious. "And that's why my mother keeps emailing me. She wants me to go home to *recover*."

"Ah, a mother." He took her hand and threaded his fingers through hers. "And I take it you don't need to go home and recover?"

She looked straight into his eyes. "I think I'm recovering just fine right here. Not that I need to recover," she added quickly. "Like I said, it wasn't right. And sure, there are some hard feelings for sure, especially since he decided to end it like a coward by finding someone else." He could see the hurt in her eyes when she told him that, but as they talked, and Heather told him the details, he could also see the sense of relief in her face as she let it all out. While she was talking, Ash realized she was sharing her *story*. The story Sherri told him all women had. Everything in the past had helped shape her and define who she was. He wasn't sure what it was, but it was clear to see that Heather's story had made her stronger.

"So, then I came here," she finished her story. "And I think all things considered, I'm doing okay."

Better than okay, Ash thought. And he couldn't help but think he was at least a small part of that. "I'm happy to hear that." He squeezed her hand and then tugged her close for a kiss.

"I told you about my past," she said when his lips left hers. "Tell me about yours. How is it a guy like you isn't married?"

"A guy like me?" Ash hoped his chuckle hid his discomfort. He didn't talk about his past with anyone and he didn't want to start now. But it didn't look as though that was going to be an option for much longer.

———

Heather knew she was risking the easiness between them by asking about his past but she had to do it. It's not that she was looking for anything between them, but whether she'd been looking or not, there was something. And if it was going to continue, she needed to know.

She waited.

"I was married once."

She hadn't expected that. "It didn't work out?"

"I wasn't there for her the way I should have been."

It wasn't quite the response she'd expected. Not that she really knew what she expected, but maybe something more along the lines of infidelity or money issues. Not that she thought he had either of those problems…it was just…she had no idea.

"What do you mean?"

"I worked a lot," he said. "No. That's an understatement. I was a total workaholic."

"What did you do?" It was a question that the old Heather would have asked right away. The fact that they'd known each other for as long as they had and she didn't know such a basic fact about him should have been strange. But that was the old Heather.

Ash shrugged. "Without getting into too many details, I invented a computer chip technology. It was pretty cutting-edge and in high demand. I should have brought on a manager to run the business side of things but I couldn't let go. It was a power trip for me and as a result, I worked too much. It's not that I didn't know it was a problem—I did. We had more conversations about it than I can even remember. I knew everything could be on the line, but I still couldn't seem to make myself slow down. It was always 'after this project' or 'as soon as I get this proposal done' or…well, it doesn't matter." His eyes got a faraway look, as if he were remembering saying those exact things to his ex-wife. "It doesn't matter because I never did seem to find the time to slow down and put her first." He shook his head and managed a wry smile. "I can't even tell you how many holidays I canceled because something 'more important' came up."

"Holidays? No?"

He nodded solemnly. "One time we were supposed to go to Mexico for her cousin's wedding but at the last minute I had this huge project come up. I couldn't say no. As a start-up, you have to take every opportunity that comes your way. No matter what. No matter the cost."

"Oh no." Heather's hand flew to her mouth. Joe had made a lot of mistakes, but he'd never made her miss her cousin's wedding. "And you guys had to miss it?"

Ash shook his head. "No. She was a bridesmaid—she couldn't miss it."

"She went without you."

Ash nodded.

"Wow."

"Wow indeed. I was a total dick."

She couldn't disagree with that, but it wouldn't have helped to say anything, so she didn't. "I bet she was mad?" It occurred to her that he hadn't told her his ex-wife's name. "Was *she*?" Heather emphasized the word, hoping he'd get the hint.

"That's the thing. She wasn't mad." His eyes clouded as he got lost in a memory and Heather couldn't help but feel a twinge of jealousy. "She was never mad. She always under- stood. I could see it hurt her when I canceled or left her at parties alone, or didn't come home because it was easier to sleep at the office. But she never once said anything."

If she'd never complained or gotten upset, then how did they get a divorce? Heather couldn't wrap her head around what he was telling her, but he didn't look as if he was ready to explain. "So, what happened?"

He looked startled, as if he was lost in a memory and she'd interrupted him. In fact, that's exactly what had happened. Heather felt like an intruder watching the emotions play on Ash's face. He was clearly lost in his thoughts. She asked again. "If she never got mad, then what happened?"

"We just didn't get our happily ever after is all. It happens sometimes."

"It shouldn't happen," she said simply. "I still believe in happy endings."

He wiggled his eyebrows. "Do you now?"

She couldn't help it; Heather laughed and smacked him on the arm. "You're ridiculous."

"You're crazy." He winked and grabbed a pillow from a nearby chair and tossed it at her before taking off, running across the room.

It may have been a diversionary tactic, but it worked because she wasn't thinking about failed marriages or past relationships anymore. Her only focus was on catching Ash and making him pay for his crazy comment.

If making him pay meant pinning him down and having her way with him, then all the better.

He let her catch him. Mostly because only good things could come from Heather straddling him on the floor. And all those things most certainly happened. And then some.

After they pulled themselves together for the second time and scrounged up some semblance of breakfast, it was long past time for opening up the rest of Casa del Sol and checking for storm damage. Screwing around was fun and all, but it didn't help them get their work done. And he really should head up the hill and check on Sherri. It had been too long as it was, and he should make sure there was no damage on her place, and do any repairs if they were needed. But first, there was something he needed to take care of.

He waited until the dishes from their pieced-together meal were in the sink and he'd helped her open most of the shutters. "I know you feel like you're failing at things."

"Gee, thanks." She rolled her eyes and shook her head.

"That came out wrong." He reached for her hand and pulled her close. "That's not what I meant. All I was saying is I know you've had a run of bad luck the last few days. So what if I showed you something that I think would help?"

She tilted her head, waiting for him to continue. "What did you have in mind?"

"I want to show you how to run the boat."

"The boat?"

He nodded. It had seemed like such a good idea in his head. The wooden panga could be a little tricky and if she knew how to handle the boat, it might make her feel more in charge of things and secure if she ever needed to go somewhere and he wasn't around. Although he couldn't think about where he'd be or why he wouldn't be around. He didn't plan to go anywhere anytime soon.

"I've driven a boat before."

That's right; she had said she'd been at a marina with her ex-husband. But something told Ash he hadn't been the type of guy to let her participate in a whole lot. "So you know how to drive a boat then?"

"I've done it." She put one hand on her hip.

"You didn't answer my question."

"I did."

"Okay then." Ash clapped his hands together. "Let's do it."

He started to walk out to the dock and the tied-up panga. "Show me your skills, girl."

He knew she'd follow and sure enough, by the time he got out to the boat, she was right behind him. "I don't think we have time to do this today," Heather protested. "There's still so much clean-up and I should check the guest rooms to make sure they're—"

"Chicken?"

That had the desired effect, just the way he'd been hoping it would. But instead of answering his question, she crossed her arms over her chest, planted her feet and stared at him. "Who are you calling a chicken?"

"You."

"Me?" She jabbed a thumb at her chest.

"Yes, you."

"You're calling *me* a chicken?"

He nodded. "That's right."

She nodded slowly, and a smile crept over her face. "Okay. Let's do it."

Before he could offer her a hand into the boat, she jumped in and went straight for the bow rope.

"Whoa." He was right behind her, stilling her hand. "One thing at a time, sweetheart. Never untie the boat before you get the engine started. And this particular engine can be a bit finicky."

"Right." She squeezed past him and stood in front of the old two-stroke engine. Ash watched as she pulled the starter cord. Once. Twice. Three times.

Nothing happened.

Heather straightened up, hands on her hips, and stared at the engine before she turned to him with a question on her face.

"Try the choke—make sure it's on idle."

"Right."

He waited while she made the adjustment and pulled the starter cord again. Once. Twice. Three times.

Nothing.

Ash fought back his chuckle. "I thought you said you've done this before."

He couldn't help it; when he saw the fire in her eyes when she turned around the second time, Ash couldn't hold back his laughter any more. He quickly swallowed it back though when he saw she might hit him. "Okay, okay. I'm not being fair. This boat is a little tricky. Can I show you the trick?"

Heather nodded and stepped aside. "By all means."

It wasn't a lie; the engine was tricky, but it wasn't impossible. "Look here. Sometimes the fuel hose gets a little loose. You just need to make sure it's snug and secure. Be careful when you're driving, too, because sometimes the line can be jostled and if you're not connected, then you know what that means."

Heather tilted her head. "I do."

"It sounds simple, but make sure you check it. Every time."

She nodded. "That's it?"

"That should be it." He moved to the side and let her try again.

Ash watched while she checked the fuel line, making sure it was tight, adjusted the choke and pulled.

Once.

Twice.

The old engine fired up with a sputter and a roar. Heather turned, a huge smile on her face. She jumped up and kissed him on the cheek. "I did it."

"You did." He untied the bow line and sat back while Heather navigated the boat away from the dock and out into the water. He reclined in the sun and let her have her fun until finally the boat slowed and she navigated it back to the dock.

"That was awesome."

"You did great." Ash tied the bow line and helped her out. "See? It's not all bad. You've got this."

She held his face between her hands and kissed him long and slow. "Thank you."

"It's all you, babe. All you."

Chapter Nine

THE NEXT MORNING, the clouds were quickly gathering to the west as Heather did her best to load her guests and all their things into the boat as quickly as possible. It was a lot harder to say good-bye to Sandy and Miranda than she thought it would be. Probably because they'd been with her for two weeks, they were her first real guests, and their departure was more rushed than she'd like it to be. That was why it was so hard. It wouldn't always be so hard.

At least that's what she kept telling herself.

"I'm so sorry you have to go like this." Heather hugged Miranda tight. "If I would have known yesterday was going to be your last day, we would have done something special."

"It's okay." Miranda smiled and her whole face lit up. "This absolutely was the best vacation."

"It was," Sandy agreed. "I have never felt so totally relaxed and at peace with life. This place is pure magic."

"Agreed."

Heather hugged Sandy next. "I am going to miss you both, so much. Thank you for being my first guests and letting me break myself in on you."

Miranda waved her away. "You don't need any practice at all. You're a natural."

"Isn't she?" Ash walked by the dock and dropped a quick kiss on her cheek as he moved on, loaded down with more bags.

As soon as he was out of earshot, or maybe not, Sandy leaned in and whisper-yelled, "If I wasn't married, I'd definitely give you a run for your money."

"You wouldn't stand a chance." Miranda gave her friend a playful shove. "Haven't you seen the way he looks at her?"

"True." Sandy clutched her hands together and pretended to swoon. "Maybe one day…"

"I'll be sure to tell your husband that you're keeping your options open." They both laughed and gave Heather one more hug before they climbed into the boat.

"We should get going," Ash called across the dock to her, where he was adjusting a rope. The wind was starting to pick up and she knew he was right. If they didn't get going soon, the weather might get too wild for a safe trip. As it was, it was probably going to be a wet ride into town.

"Just give me one second." She held up a finger and ignored Ash when he tried to disagree. She turned and almost ran into the new couple who'd only just arrived and now had to leave so quickly. "I'm so sorry your trip was cut short," she said to the woman. "It's really too bad."

The woman waved her hand in dismissal. "It's just the weather and Lord knows we can't control that."

"Besides," her husband said. "It's all part of the experience. We're at the mercy of this beautiful world."

Heather nodded. It was kind of a hippie way to look at things, but they were right. "Well, I'm sure glad you got at least one day out here."

"Us too."

Heather left them to load up into the boat and ran down

the dock into the kitchen to find an old tarp or even some garbage bags to provide some type of shelter from the open boat. After a quick dig around, she grabbed some old plastic tablecloths and turned to run back out to the boat where everyone was waiting. With her hands full, she didn't even look up until she ran straight into a very solid and very familiar chest.

"Slow down." Ash laughed and tightened his arms around her shoulders.

Her body reacted immediately to his touch. It was insane to her that she could feel both completely safe and very much in danger by his proximity. She looked up into his eyes. "I wanted to make sure I got this to you, and I know you were getting ready to leave."

He kissed her forehead gently. "I wouldn't leave without saying good-bye."

She knew that. Well, she thought she knew that. She also knew that she was about to prepare for the first storm she'd ever had to deal with at Casa del Sol and she had no idea what to expect.

"I do have to get going, though. The wind is getting serious and it's going to be a rough trip."

She opened her mouth to interject, but he silenced her with a quick kiss before he continued. "It'll be safe. Don't worry. Just rough. And rainy."

Heather held up the tablecloths in a lame gesture. "It's not much. But maybe they'll help keep you a little dry."

Ash smiled. "They'll be great. At the very least, they might be able to keep some water off the bags."

He took Heather's hand and they walked outside again. The wind whipped her hair against her face. They were running out of time. Ash took the tablecloths from her and handed them down to the passengers, who tucked them around their bags as much as possible. He turned to her, held her face in her hands and kissed her hard. "You need to close up the shutters and secure the swim ladders, okay? And then all you need to do is stay warm and dry and ride it out. I'll be back tomorrow."

"Tomorrow?" Of course he couldn't get back in one day. Logically, she knew that. It was upsetting to hear him say it out loud and even more disconcerting that she was upset by it. It was only because there was a storm, she told herself. It didn't have anything to do with the fact that she might actually miss him.

Not at all.

Before he could object, or tell her she was being ridiculous, which she already knew, Heather gave him a quick kiss. "Go," she said. "Be safe." She turned and said one more good-bye to her guests as Ash hopped down into the boat before untying the bow line and tossing it into the boat.

Ash didn't waste any time before whipping the boat off. Amid a handful of waves and hoots, they were gone, zipping across the water toward Bocas.

Heather stood on the dock until she could no longer see them. Thor, whining at her heels, reminded her that there was still a lot to do.

They'd be fine. Her guests. Ash.

He'd stay the night in Bocas and be back in the morning. It was the safe thing to do. Besides, it's not as if they were married or anything. He certainly didn't need to risk his life in a tropical storm just to return to her when they were only…*what? What were they?*

It didn't matter and she didn't have time to think about it. Refocusing on the mounting to-do list at hand, Heather forced thoughts of Ash out of her head and got to work. She managed to get the shutters secured and tied down on *grande casa* without much trouble, but the rain started by the time Heather headed out to the bungalows to make sure they were secured. Camila had retired to her own little house in the trees earlier, so she was on her own to get the guest rooms protected before it was too late.

By the time she had the majority of the bungalows secured, Heather's clothes were drenched and stuck to her skin. Her hair was pasted in wet streaks across her face and she was chilled to the bone. Despite the fact that it was a tropical rain, it was really freakin' cold when you were stuck in the middle of it and the wind whipped all around you. Damn cold.

She tucked her chin to her chest and went out into the storm one more time to check the far bungalow. The same bungalow she and Ash had gone swimming off of. There hadn't been anyone staying in it, but she hadn't checked it and if there was a shutter loose, it could cause massive amounts of water damage inside.

Heather tugged on the door and walked around to check each shutter. They were secure but something out in the water caught her eye. The swim platform. Or more specifically, the ladder on the swim platform.

The water level was rising with the increase in rain. It was something Heather didn't expect, but then again she'd never experienced a tropical storm in the jungles of Panama before. The rainwater, combined with the fresh water coming off the streams in the hills, was causing a rise in the level, which meant the ladder on her swim platform was no longer resting on the ocean bottom, but was lifting and getting dangerously close to floating away.

"Dammit."

If she lost the ladder, it probably wouldn't be the end of the world, but at the same time, it would be a pain and they did have more guests coming soon. Besides, that would be the first really big screw-up she'd made since being in charge.

She didn't want that. Not at all.

The canoe.

It was tied to the main dock and it wouldn't take much to paddle it over and secure the ladder. Then everything would be taken care of and she could get inside and ride out the storm.

Her decision made before she'd thought it through, Heather rushed back to *grande casa* and out to the dock. The canoe had already been tied tightly and with her cold fingers, it took a little bit longer to work the knots, but she managed and jumped in with the paddle.

The waves were bigger than she'd expected and despite the short distance she had to travel, the paddling was hard. She finally reached the swim platform, grabbed the rope in the bow and hopped out. It would be easier to tie up the ladder from on top of the platform.

The rain came harder now, and Heather's teeth chattered together painfully from the cold. But she was almost done. It would only be a few more minutes and she could go warm up.

It took her a few fumbling tries to tie the canoe to the cleat on the side of the platform and then she quickly turned her attention to the ladder. After a quick assessment, she decided it would be best to pull the ladder up instead of leaving it in the water. It was a job that would have been easier to handle with another set of hands. But she was on her own. She could do it. She'd prove to Ash and to Sherri that she was a good manager and Casa del Sol was in good hands with her. Trying to get some leverage, Heather stood and tugged on the ladder. But the wood was slick beneath her feet and they slid right out from under her, sending her crashing to her ass.

The pain from her tailbone radiated up her spine, but she didn't have time to think about it. The waves were getting bigger and started to wash over the platform. Some of the larger waves crashed over the top and filled the boat.

"Come on, Heather." She gritted her teeth and pushed to her feet. "You got this."

The truth—if she was honest with herself—was that she

most certainly did not have it. She reached down one more time and tried to get a grasp on the slippery ladder, but once again she crashed to the dock. This time the pain from her tail-bone was sharper. Heather knew if she hadn't cracked it, she'd most certainly done some major damage. But she couldn't give up. She was invested now. One more time, Heather picked herself up and reached down for the ladder. This time, she squatted deep and heaved with her legs. The ladder moved. She gritted her teeth and heaved again. It moved more. And then it was coming up onto the dock. And on top of her.

Right before the ladder came all the way up, she was able to wiggle out of the way and avoid being completely crushed by it. But she didn't have time to celebrate, because the wind had picked up and with it, the waves. Now, almost every second one washed up and over the dock. And into the canoe.

"Shit."

She scrambled on her stomach to the cleat and lashed the ladder down so it was secure before she turned her attention to the canoe, which was now half filled with water.

She needed to bail. And fast.

"Where's the…"

Her words were swallowed by the wind. Not that it mattered, because there was no bailing bucket. There was nothing. And if she didn't do something, soon there would be no canoe. It was filling quickly.

Too quickly.

Heather looked around in vain. There was nothing she could use. Worse than that, there was no one to come and help her. Just because there was nothing else she could do, she scooped her hands and tried to push some water out of the boat. But it was no use. The waves came faster than she could deal with them.

At least it was tied to the raft. In a last-ditch effort to save the boat from total loss, Heather loosened the rope as much as she could so it wouldn't bash against the platform before she sat in the middle, wrapped her arms around her knees and tried her best not to cry.

At that very moment, Ash should have been sitting at the bar at the Bitter End with a beer in his hand, or tucked into a warm bed with an even warmer body tucked up next to him.

He wasn't. Not only was he not at the bar or in bed with one of his lady friends, the surprising part was that he didn't want either of those things. Sure, the idea of a beer wasn't bad. But the idea of being in bed with anyone except Heather was even less appealing than sitting in the driving rain that assaulted him from all sides as he powered through the waves in his little boat.

He wiped the spray from his face, but it was in vain since the rain was coming down in stinging blasts, soaking through his clothes.

He should have stayed in Bocas Town. At that very moment, he could be warm and dry and safe and *alone*. Because he would most definitely not be in the arms of anyone who wasn't Heather.

Not that he felt that it was cheating. It couldn't be cheating if they hadn't defined their relationship.

It wasn't a *relationship*.

He didn't use that word.

But it was *something*.

Something he was enjoying. And despite how much he'd been dreading it, telling her about Carlie the night before had been a relief. And whatever it was between them, he wasn't going to screw it up with someone in Bocas Town.

The wind howled, and he aimed the boat directly into it, taking the waves head on, letting them smash against the hull of the little boat. It was foolhardy to be out on the water. He should have stayed.

But he hadn't. Because the only thing he could think of was Heather.

Heather alone at Casa del Sol. Heather trying to batten down the shutters as best as she could with the wind snapping them out of her hands. He'd done it before. It wasn't easy to secure the bed-and-breakfast with two people; it would be incredibly difficult to do it all by herself. And what if she forgot something? She was still so new to Bocas and Casa del Sol. She'd beat herself up if she missed something.

No.

Maybe the smart thing to do would have been to stay put until the storm cleared. But when it came to women—some women—Ash had never made the smart choice.

He twisted his hand on the accelerator and urged his boat to move even faster through the wind and the waves. The sooner he got there, the better.

As soon as he got the boat behind a stand of mangroves that broke the wind a little bit, it was easier going and he was able to give himself a moment to think. Chances were good that by the time he got there, everything would have been done and she would be inside *grande casa*, wrapped in a blanket and with a cup of tea in her hand. He was being ridiculous. He almost laughed at himself, but then he navigated around a corner. The very corner that would put him within sight of...

Heather?

"What the—"

It had to be her.

He didn't have time to think. He pushed his little boat even faster toward Casa del Sol, and more specifically, the swim platform tied up outside of *their* bungalow.

It was difficult to make it out in the rain, but it looked as if there was a very distinct human form huddled on top of the dock. A human form that looked a whole lot like Heather.

What the hell was she doing out there? Had she swum? What was she thinking?

She must have heard the roar of the boat's engine, because her head lifted from her knees. A little bit at first, and then more.

He called out, yelling her name.

She jumped to her feet and was almost immediately knocked down by a wave.

"Stay still," he yelled. "I'm coming."

There was no way to know whether his words reached her over the howling winds. But just calling to her made him feel better. As soon as he got close enough, he slowed the boat so as not to crash into the platform and he could see the rope stretched from the platform cleat.

He didn't have to ask to know it was the canoe. He'd have to cut it free. It might wash up on shore; it might be lost. But at least it would have a chance.

"Get in," he told her as soon as he was close enough. "I'll get as close as I can, but you'll have to jump."

She nodded in understanding. Ash could see her teeth clattering, the white tips of her fingers and the fear in her eyes.

Heather did as she was told and all but fell into the boat the second she could. Ash pulled his knife out of his pocket and sliced through the rope, before quickly tucking it away.

"The canoe."

He nodded. "It'll be fine." It was most likely a lie and they both knew it, but he had to say something. Everything else would have to wait. As quickly as he could, he pulled the boat up alongside the dock and quickly tied it. She was clearly frozen, and likely incapable of making any fast moves, so as soon as the boat was secured and the engine cut, Ash jumped up to the dock and reached down for her. He scooped her up into his arms and carried her into Casa del Sol.

The door was open. Likely from when she'd ventured out with the canoe. As soon as he got her settled onto the couch with the heaviest blanket he could find pulled over her knees, he went to work securing the door and mopping up the floor where the water had snuck in.

A quick look around showed that all the other shutters had been closed. Casa del Sol was secure. Heather had done good. And now she was safe.

He climbed up onto the couch behind her and pulled her back against his chest. He was cold to the bone himself, but compared to her, he was smoking hot. She couldn't talk for a few minutes and he didn't push it. She needed to warm up. That was the most important thing. There'd be plenty of time for her to explain what on earth she'd been thinking by being out on that platform in the middle of a tropical rainstorm. *She could have been killed, for God's sake.*

Her body was so cold. Her clothes were soaked and not helping, so he eased her forward just enough to pull her clothes from her body, and then his own before settling back into the cushions with her between his legs. His body reacted at once to the closeness of her naked skin, but he ignored it.

Slowly, he could feel the warmth returning to Heather's limbs. He slowly rubbed her arms, and then her thighs. Her murmur of pleasure let him know she was warming up. "Feeling a little better?"

Heather nodded and rested her head against his chest. "I was so cold."

"You were."

"I didn't even think it was possible to get that cold in the tropics." She twisted her head around a little to look at him. "I think the last time I was that cold was back home in Idaho when I was a kid and stayed out too long sledding."

"What were you doing out there, Heather? You could have been killed." Just speaking the words aloud made it even more real to him. The idea that he could have lost her slammed into him.

"You told me to secure the ladders."

Did he? He probably had. But he certainly hadn't meant for her to go out onto the water to secure anything. That was crazy. "I told you to secure the shutters and get inside." He ignored the fact that he may have in fact told her something he hadn't meant. "You're just lucky I came back. What was your plan? Were you just going to stay out there and freeze to death?"

She shook her head, but didn't speak for a moment. Her pretty eyes glistened with tears. "I was...well...I was going to..." A tear slipped down her cheek. "I was going to wait until the wind died down and then swim back."

Ash shook his head. She was crazy. But at the same time, he could see that she didn't have many choices. He reached out a finger and wiped her cheek.

"I didn't think you were coming back."

"I wasn't going to." He nuzzled into the crook of her neck. "But I couldn't stay away." It was true. He absolutely couldn't have stayed away and even though he couldn't explain that feeling, he didn't care because thank God he'd come back. "I'm so glad I came back."

"Me too." Heather wiped at the tears that streamed down her face in earnest and turned away. "I don't know what I was thinking. What would have happened if you hadn't come back? I was all alone out there." She sniffed and wiped at her face with the blanket. "I was totally alone and—"

"It's okay."

She shook her head. "No. It's not. I was just trying to show you that I could do it."

Ahh. There it was. He knew there had to be a reason she'd risked her life for a ladder.

"I wanted to show you that I was capable of running Casa del Sol and taking care of everything all by myself. And Sherri, too." Heather whipped around, her eyes wide. "Oh my God. Sherri!"

Panic rushed through Heather. Any and all thoughts about how her own life had been in danger vanished at the thought of the older woman up in her treehouse all alone. "I can't believe I didn't even think to go check on her."

She tried to wiggle free of Ash's arms, but he held her tight.

"You're not going anywhere."

"I need to go check on her, Ash. She's all alone up there and this storm—"

"Is still raging." It was true. The wind was still whipping against the shutters and through the trees behind them. "There is absolutely no point in risking our lives again to go up there. She's fine."

"How do you know that? And it's not like we're going back out on the water. We're going up—"

"Through the trees with falling branches and who knows what else. It's almost more dangerous, Heather. You're staying put. So am I. Because she's fine."

Frustration built up inside her until she was sure she was going to burst. *How could he be so sure Sherri was okay? How did he think it was okay that she was all alone up there with no one to help her if something went wrong?*

"Settle down." He kissed her forehead. "Although I do love your concern."

That's it. She was going to hit him. In a burst, Heather

wrestled herself free from his grip. The blanket fell from her body and she jumped up in front of him. She would have taken a swing at him if the look on his face hadn't stopped her. "What?"

Ash wiggled his eyebrows. "You're sexy as hell when you're all worked up. I need to remember that."

"That's not funny."

"I'm not trying to be funny." The grin slid off his face into sincerity. "I think it's incredible that you're concerned about Sherri."

"But then, what about—"

"Come here." He extended a hand and that she still kind of wanted to hit him, she took it and let him pull her back into his embrace and the warmth of the blanket. "Sherri's fine. I'll go check on her after the storm has died down, but I spoke with her before I left Bocas and she's all settled. She managed to get the shutters secured and was holed up with Thor."

Thor! She hadn't even thought about the dog.

"It's not your job to worry about the dog," Ash said, reading her thoughts. "You had enough to worry about and the dogs around here can more than take care of themselves. They probably know better than we do about taking cover and staying safe." He shot her a look. Which she pointedly ignored.

"Wait." What he'd just said finally registered in her head. "What do you mean, you spoke with Sherri before you left Bocas? How?"

Ash had the sense to back up on the couch slightly. Not that she'd hit him. But she might.

"I called her," he said tentatively.

"You called her?"

"On the phone." He slipped his battered cell phone from his back pocket and held it out.

"You have a cell phone?" She immediately felt stupid for asking the question. Everyone had a cell phone. But everyone in the middle of the Panamanian jungle? Maybe it wasn't such a stupid question. Besides, no one had mentioned a phone before. She hadn't taken her own cell phone out of her bag since she'd arrived. "You have a phone?" she asked again.

Ash shrugged in response. "It's not like I use it. Not really. It's mostly for Sherri to get a hold of me when she has guests to pick up or something for me to grab from town. And of course situations like this."

She could have been angry, but there was no point. Besides, what business was it of hers whether he had a phone or not? Never mind the fact that he hadn't offered to give her the number. But then again, maybe their relationship wasn't at that point yet.

Whatever that point was.

Or even if they had a relationship.

She shook her head. It was all too confusing to think about. All she wanted to focus on was the fact that she was sitting there, inside, out of the storm and in the arms of the very sexy, very naked man who'd saved her.

She snuggled back against him, feeling his hardness against her back.

Yes.

That was definitely what she was going to focus on.

Ash wrapped his arms around her and pulled her tighter to him. One hand secured around her waist held her in place and the other found her breast, gently cupping and massaging it. He nuzzled into her neck and whispered in her ear, "Is that okay with you?" When she didn't answer right away, he tweaked her nipple and elicited the exact response he was looking for.

She moaned and pressed back into him. It was more than okay with her. Although, if she'd been asked at that exact moment what exactly they were talking about, Heather wasn't sure she'd be able to give an answer. At least not a coherent one, but one that started with a moan and more than likely would end with her turning in her seat, wrapping her arms around his neck and kissing him until neither of them could remember what they'd been talking about.

"I thought so," Ash murmured and bit the sensitive skin directly below her ear. "Are you all warmed up now?"

She shook her head and twisted around so she faced him. "Not entirely." She kissed him, sucking his bottom lip between her teeth. "But I think I know how you can help fix that."

Chapter Ten

WAKING up in Heather's arms was just about the nicest thing Ash had experienced in...well, longer than he wanted to remember. Sure, the couch in *grande casa* wouldn't have been his first choice for a bed, but given the circumstances, he'd take what he could get. And at that moment, what he could get was the warmth of a woman who felt good in his arms.

No. She felt *right*.

It had been a long time since a woman had felt *right*. A really long time. Normally, Ash would fight it. Push it away. Run from it. But with Heather, things were different.

They were easy, comfortable, sexy as hell and...*right*.

Dammit.

She was sleeping soundly and after the day she'd had before—not to mention the night—she needed her rest. But Ash needed to get up and stretch. And think. He slid his arm out from under her and slipped from the couch. His shorts, which he'd shed in an effort to warm her the night before, were still lying in a crumpled damp ball on the floor, as were her clothes. Ash scooped everything up and left out the garden door.

The sun was shining, the heat of the day already building although it couldn't be more than seven in the morning. To say it got hot in Panama was a huge understatement. Even after four years, the heat took some getting used to. Living in California most of his adult life, it's not that he was any stranger to the heat, but it was different. And of course, unlike Panama, there had been a bit of a reprieve from the stifling heat. He'd once enjoyed the cool mornings when the world was still waking up. When everyone, including Carlie, was still in bed and it was only him and the other workaholics on the roads into the office. He'd roll down his window, and let the cool air hit his face on the thirty-minute commute before he spent his entire day inside an air-conditioned building, breathing recycled air, just to turn around and drive home in the dark, long after the sun went down, with the same cooler air hitting him in the face to keep him awake before he got home to his beautiful wife, who more often than not would already be in bed.

Ash hung up the damp clothes on the line and tilted his head to the sun, allowing the heat of the day to warm him while he breathed in fresh, tropical air.

Thinking about Carlie hurt less and less. Maybe his friends —no, he never had friends back home, not really—his coworkers had been on to something. Time did ease the hurt. But it wasn't just time that had helped him heal from his loss. It was this place. Panama. The jungle. The wildness. The easiness.

It was so different than his old life. It was the exact opposite, really. The change had saved him from total destruction. When he'd lost Carlie, Ash hadn't thought he'd ever recover. A part of him would never fully heal, and although it had taken awhile, even after he'd landed in Panama City and then found Bocas Town, he'd been able to take a breath without the pain in his chest threatening to destroy him. And then soon, he could take two breaths. And one day, he woke up and it didn't hurt to live.

It had taken longer to think of Carlie without the hurt dropping him to his knees. A lot longer. It was only recently that he hadn't needed to lose himself in the arms of another woman just to forget her touch. Things with Heather were different. It wasn't about forgetting with her. It was about remembering.

Remembering that once upon a time, he'd felt something more than an empty, dull ache.

Holy shit.

The revelation stopped him in his tracks in the middle of the garden. *Did being with Heather really do all that for him? Was it more than just a fun fling?* He almost laughed at himself. He *knew* it was more. He'd known since their first kiss. Whether he'd wanted to open his eyes to it or not.

He wouldn't be able to ignore it forever. More than that, he wasn't so sure anymore that he wanted to. Ash picked his way through the garden, clearing palm fronds the storm had brought down. He piled them next to the path as he worked in the quiet morning. The storm hadn't been as destructive as he'd thought it might be. At least, not in the garden. There were a few crushed plants, and an undeniable mess to clear, but it wasn't as bad as it could have been and it wouldn't take long to fix up. When Ash was done in the garden, he moved down the path toward the far bungalow. Heather's bungalow.

From the outside, it looked like it, too, had weathered the storm. There might have been some water that leaked through, but he couldn't tell from the outside and he didn't want to intrude on her privacy. He walked around the deck, untangled one of the hammocks from its support pole and straightened the swing that hung over the water's edge. Using his bare feet, he swept the debris into the murky water below.

The seas had been churned up by the storm, but he knew from experience they'd settle out in a day or two and be back to their usual crystal-clear, bright blue.

He spent the next few minutes checking out the rest of the guest bungalows and opening the shutters to let the rooms air out, and when he was finished, he made his way back through the garden, stopping at the clothesline to pull his now dry shorts off. He tugged them on and gathered Heather's clothes before going back inside *grande casa*. He expected to find her still sleeping, but she was up and in the kitchen. With no clothes to wear, she'd tied a thin batik blanket around her body, sarong style. Her hair was piled on top of her head and she looked absolutely ravishing standing in front of the stove, a spatula in one hand and a pan in the other.

"Good morning."

"It is now." He knew he sounded cheesy and cliché, but didn't care one little bit. "You look…fantastic."

She laughed and the hand with the spatula in it went to her head, leaving a drop of batter in her hair. "I don't know about that. I woke up and found you'd stolen my clothes. But I was starving and couldn't wait."

Ash held her now dry shorts and tank top out. "I'm not sure I want to give them back. I like this look on you. It's very bohemian. And sexy as hell."

Her smile was wicked. Ash almost ripped the thin sheet off her right then and there, and he would have, too, if whatever it was she was cooking hadn't smelled so good. His stomach growled, reminding him he hadn't eaten since before leaving for Bocas Town the day before. "What's for breakfast?"

Her smile was immediate and radiant. "I've been dying to get in here and make something. But I'm starting slow. Banana pancakes."

"That sounds delicious." He crossed the room and kissed

her. "Almost as delicious as you." It was cheesy but it made her blush, and that's all he was trying to achieve. He traced a finger down her neck and over the curve of her naked shoulder, smiling when she shivered in response. He kissed the sensitive spot on the nape of her neck before he retreated to let her continue cooking. He would absolutely love to have her for breakfast, but he wasn't so sure that it would do much to quench either of his appetites.

Ash gave himself distance by hopping up on the far counter to watch Heather work.

"Where did you run off to this morning?"

"You looked so peaceful, I thought I'd let you sleep and see if there was any damage from the storm. Besides, I don't sleep much."

She shot him a curious look over her shoulder. "And was there? Any damage, I mean?"

"Only superficial from what I could tell." He filled her in on what he'd seen outside and how he'd opened up all the guest bungalows except for hers. "After we eat, I can go with you to see if your place sustained any damage," he added. "But I don't think it did."

Heather flipped a pancake from the pan and poured more batter in. "Do you want the first taste? Or can you wait?"

Ash's stomach growled in response. "I'd rather eat with you."

She winked at him and turned back to the stove. "Why can't you sleep?"

The question took him off guard. "What do you mean?"

"You said you don't sleep much. Why not?"

"The heat." The lie immediately felt sour on his tongue and he shook his head. "No, that's not true."

Heather tilted her head and waited.

Ash hesitated in telling her the truth, but for the life of him, he couldn't come up with a good reason why he wouldn't just tell her. "I haven't had a full night's sleep in years." He glanced out the window and watched a parrot in the trees for a moment. "Memories become dreams when you sleep and sometimes those dreams become nightmares. I like to wake up." It was the most he'd said about his *story* since he'd told Heather the little bit about Carlie a few days ago. But maybe it was time for the full truth.

"Not all dreams have to be nightmares."

"Mine are." He didn't mean to sound as sad as he did, but there was nothing happy about his truth. "You can't rewrite your memories, Heather. They just are."

She turned away from the stove, her face lined with worry. "But why? I mean, why do you have such unhappy memories?" She crossed the kitchen and put her hands on his bare knees. Something about her touch encouraged him to talk.

"Once upon a time, I lived a very different life," he said simply. "And I lost it. Those are the memories I can't forget. Don't you have memories you'd rather forget?"

"We're not talking about me."

His lip crooked up in a wry smile. She had him there. "Touché. But we will. One day." He took a deep breath. He liked Heather; it wasn't fair that he continue doing whatever it was they were doing without the truth. He might as well get it over with. He took a breath. "Remember when I told you I was married?"

She tried to hide it, but Ash saw her cringe a little, before she nodded. "I remember. Is there more to it?"

This was always the part he struggled with. Over the years, it had gotten easier to think about Carlie. Heck, he could even talk about Carlie sometimes. But he couldn't talk about what happened with them. He still could barely bring himself to think about it.

It was a time he wasn't proud of. Although it should have

been. No, it *could* have been. If he hadn't have screwed everything up. *Things had been going so well before—*

"Ash?"

He focused on the woman in front of him.

"Talk to me."

He didn't answer her right away. Instead, he stepped closer, bridging the gap between them, and took a strand of her hair between his fingers. "This is crazy."

"My hair?" She laughed, but it was controlled. Something was certainly going on with him, and she wasn't sure she was going to like it. "What's crazy about that?"

"No." He dropped a kiss on her nose. "This. You. Me."

She stilled in his arms. *What was he talking about? And what did it have to do with his dreams that were more like nightmares?*

Finally, she spoke up. "What's so crazy about this? You were talking about your marriage."

"Was I?"

"You know you were." She wasn't going to let him out of it so easy. Clearly he had something to tell her. "Talk to me, Ash."

Ash shook his head. "I don't do this."

"Do…"

"This."

Heather pulled away, putting a little distance between them. "Looks to me like you're doing it." She struggled to keep her voice even, at the same time hating herself for letting him affect her so much. *It wasn't supposed to be serious.* She shouldn't care what he had to tell her, or why he was being so strange while he was doing it.

"I really enjoy spending time with you."

She looked at him warily. "As do I."

"But I need you to know that it can never be more than that. Us spending time together."

"What do you mean?"

Ash took a deep breath. "I think there's something I should tell you."

She sighed, the last of the easiness between them slipping away completely. "Right, about your ex?"

"My *wife*," he corrected her. "I vowed to never put myself in that position again," he said simply, as if it explained everything.

"What position is that?" She tried to keep her tone light. "Marriage? No one mentioned anything about that." She giggled a little, but it fell flat.

"No—love. I vowed never to love again. And I'm not saying that..." He held up his hand and shook his head, clearly backing himself into a tight spot.

She didn't know what to say about the *L* word; instead, Heather ignored it and tried to refocus him. "What? She screwed you up so badly that you think you can never feel something again, so you vowed to never again let yourself get hurt? That's a pretty common story, Ash. Hell, I could say the same thing. Don't worry about it."

He took a breath. "That's the thing. We didn't get divorced. She died."

The words fell on the air, landing heavy between them.

Died?

"Ash, I'm sorry." She put her hand on his, needing to connect with him, but he shook off her touch.

"Don't be. It was my fault. Remember when I told you I worked all the time? That I missed holidays? Parties? Anniversaries?" She did. "Carlie was always so understanding about my need to build the business and work hard. She never complained. Not like you'd expect. But there was one time when she asked me to please not cancel our date." He closed his eyes. "I left too early that morning for her to ask me, so she texted me. It was our third wedding anniversary and we had dinner reservations at her favorite restaurant. She told me she had something special to talk to me about and to please not cancel."

"You didn't."

He nodded sadly. "I didn't mean to. I had no intentions of canceling, but at the last minute, an important investor came into town and…it doesn't matter. I let her down. Badly."

"What happened?"

This was the part that was so hard. The part he'd replayed in his mind repeatedly for months. He swallowed hard. "When I didn't show up, she was upset. Like, really upset." Heather nodded. "She called me. From the car."

Heather shook her head and squeezed her eyes shut. "No."

He nodded when she finally looked at him again.

"She was crying. Yelling. Calling me names. She'd never done that before and I tried to calm her down. I tried to tell her to pull over and call me back when she wasn't driving."

Heather put a hand to her mouth but didn't say anything. There was nothing to say. She must know what was coming next.

"I heard the squeal of the tires, the scream and the crunch of the metal. Then nothing. I didn't even know where she was to go to her. I didn't know where to send help. I just screamed her name over and over again."

"Oh, Ash. I can't even imagine how terrible that would have been for you."

He shook off her touch again. He refused to let her feel sorry for him. No one should ever feel badly for him. It was his fault. It was all his fault.

"The man in the other car died on scene." He couldn't even look at her as he spoke; he knew what he'd see in her face. "They airlifted Carlie to the hospital but the internal damage was too much. By the time I got there, she was gone." He heard Heather gasp, but still didn't look because he wasn't done. "At the hospital, they gave me this plastic bag with all her things in it. There was her purse and her cell phone, of course. But there was something else. The reason she was so adamant that I didn't cancel on our date. The special thing she wanted to talk to me about." He didn't even have to close his eyes to relive the moment. It would be forever burned in his mind. "The sonogram picture of our baby. She was four months along. She'd written Happy Anniversary on the top. It was her gift to me, to tell me I was going to be a dad. And I destroyed it all. I destroyed my family. And all because I was too stupid to know what my priorities were."

"It's not your fault, Ash."

"But it is."

"No." She put her hands on his face and forced him to look at her. "It wasn't your fault. It was an accident."

He shook his head. She wasn't the first person who'd tried to tell him that. Not by a long shot. "I didn't tell you this so you'd feel sorry for me." He reached up and took her hands in his.

"Then why did you tell me?"

The look on her face told him that she already knew what he was going to say.

"Because you need to understand that I really enjoy spending time with you, Heather." She nodded. "But I vowed a long time ago that I'd never do that again."

"Do what? Love? That's ridiculous, Ash. It wasn't your fault. What happened with your wife was a tragic accident. That's all. You think that by keeping your heart closed off, you'll never have to hurt again? That's bullshit."

"No." He shook his head. She didn't understand. She didn't understand at all. "It's not about me, Heather. Carlie died because of me. Because she loved me. I won't let that happen again."

"You won't let someone love you again?" Heather chuckled, but she wasn't smiling. She stood, taking the blanket with her. "You might sit there and think you're protecting someone else by closing your heart to love. In fact, it's possible that you've told yourself that story so many times that you even believe it now. But it's bullshit, Ash. And this is why."

He reached for his shorts and tugged them on before sitting again. Heather clearly had something she needed to say and he had a feeling that he wasn't going anywhere until she got it all out.

"Are you so self-centered that you think you get to decide who gets close to you?"

He didn't answer.

"Do you really think that just because *you've* decided not to love again, that no one will fall in love with *you?*"

"That's not what I'm saying."

"That's exactly what you're saying. And I have news for you." She crossed the floor and stood in front of him. "What happened to your wife was tragic. It was terrible and devastating, but it was not your fault. Sure, you might have been a different guy back then with a fucked-up set of priorities. But that didn't make the accident your fault. It made you an asshole."

He grinned at her boldness. And because she was right.

"She didn't die because she loved you." Her voice was softer. Ash stood so he was directly in front of her. "You can't stop people from falling in love with you. And if you try, you're only hurting yourself because no matter what terribleness life has thrown at you, no matter what type of heartbreak you've been through in the past, there will always be the potential for love. The real tragedy is allowing yourself to believe otherwise."

There was so much passion in her words, her voice, her body. Ash reached out and cupped her face with his hand. "What are you saying, Heather?"

"Exactly what I just said. The potential for love always exists. I believe that."

They stared at each other for a moment, neither of them speaking. He couldn't help but think she might be right. Not that he loved *her*, necessarily. After all, it was too soon for that even if he was open to it, which he'd just finished explaining to her could never happen. *But maybe...* He shook his head and pulled away before he could allow himself to finish the thought.

"Okay, so now you know where I'm coming from." He heard her sigh, felt the puff of air on his face.

"I do," she said slowly. "Thank you for sharing that story with me. It couldn't have been easy."

He shook his head.

"And I get it."

"You do?"

He expected a number of reactions from her, but that wasn't one of them. "I don't expect anything from you, Ash. But thank you for telling me the truth. Trust is so important, no matter what the relationship is. Or what's going on between two people."

It might have been the choice of her words, or the truth of the situation—which was that she shouldn't trust him at all—but a tight knot formed in his gut. When she kissed him again, her lips were soft and sweet. It pulled even tighter because he knew that despite the fun they were having, no matter what she said, he couldn't be the man she thought he was. The man she needed him to be.

She needed to know more, a lot more. His confession had just given her more questions than answers. Including some big ones: *Why would he choose that moment to tell her the truth about his wife? Why would he stand there and confess that he'd vowed never to love again?*

Did he think she was falling in love with him? He had mentioned the *L* word.

Did he think she was getting too close?

Before she could ask any of the questions on the tip of her tongue, they both caught the scent of burning pancakes at the same time. Heather whipped around to see smoke coming up from the pan that she'd stupidly left on the burner. "Oh, shit." In two steps, she was across the room but she couldn't find a potholder to grab the pan with. Tears of frustration pricked at her eyes and she was about to reach out with her bare hands when Ash reached around her, a towel in his hands, and grabbed the pan.

"Watch out." He deftly moved around her and dumped the whole smoking mess into the sink before he turned on the faucet. "Got it. It's okay."

"It's not." The pesky tears were still threatening to spill. She bit down on her bottom lip to keep it from happening.

"Hey." Ash stood in front of her. So close she could feel his heat. Or maybe it was the heat from the burnt pancakes. *How could she have forgotten about the pancakes?* She could have burned the whole place down.

She didn't stand a chance at keeping her tears at bay. Everything was just too much. She just wanted to do something right. It was bad enough getting stranded on the dock like an idiot. But now she couldn't even manage to cook breakfast. *What kind of bed-and-breakfast manager was she anyway?* The tears slipped from her eyes and she didn't even bother trying to stop them.

"It's okay." Ash pulled her into his arms, but she wasn't ready to be hugged and she pushed away. "It's okay, Heather."

"It's not." She snorted loudly. "I just want to be able to do something right. I can't believe I'm messing this up so bad."

Ash froze and looked at her with a raised eyebrow.

"I'm not talking about you." She threw a nearby towel at him. "God. You really are a self-centered bastard."

The minute the words came out of her mouth, she felt bad. He'd just told her a tragic story about his past. She had no right calling him names. If he was offended, he certainly didn't show it. Instead, Ash did the exact opposite of what she expected. He laughed.

He bent over, his body racked with the laughter. When he finally looked up at her, Heather couldn't help but join in. "You're crazy."

The laughter stopped, and Ash looked at her with false seriousness. "Remember what happened when I called you crazy?"

She certainly did. It had ended up with her chasing him around the room until she caught him and straddled him on the floor, followed by... "Oh."

"Oh yes."

It didn't take her long to get what he was saying. A moment later, she took off running, but he was too quick. Ash caught the edge of her sarong and with one firm tug, it fell to the floor.

"That's more like it."

She let him pull her close and kiss her hard. When his hands slipped down her bare skin, she groaned with the need he brought out in her so easily. And when he reached down between them to unfasten the button on his shorts, she pushed his hands aside and did it for him. Because whatever it was that they were doing together—whether or not either of them wanted a relationship, or believed in happy endings, or love, or getting too emotionally invested—the one thing they had in common was their intense desire for each other. And for the moment, that would have to be enough.

Chapter Eleven

IT TOOK him longer than usual to get up the steps to Sherri's place, with all the fallen debris and broken tree branches littering the way. Ash took his time to clear it and by the time he got to the top, he was more than ready to enjoy one of the cold beers he'd brought up with him in a cooler full of supplies for Sherri.

But the beer would have to wait, because something was wrong. Very wrong.

When Ash spoke to Sherri before the storm, she'd told him she'd been able to secure the shutters. She'd told him not to worry.

He should have worried.

The shutters had not been secured. Or at least, not all of them. Some were hanging off their hinges; others were still wide open. And only a few that had been secured were still that way and unopened.

"Sherri?"

She should have opened them by now.

Ash dropped the cooler at the front door and tried the

handle. "Sure. It's locked." He shook his head and yelled again. "Sherri!"

He threw his shoulder into the door and the wood gave way with a crack big enough that he could reach inside and unlock the door. Ash pushed through the splintered wood and looked around. "Sherri? Where are you?"

The house was a mess; water and branches and leaves littered the floor. Glasses were broken and dishes had been scattered across the counter. Medicine bottles laid among the mess. Fortunately, from what he could tell, the lids were all on, and the medicine inside was intact.

He moved straight for the loft, silently cursing the stupidity of having the bed up a ladder and away from any help. If she was hurt or too sick to move, it would be very difficult to get her down. Keeping her condition from Heather, a fact he liked less and less, would no longer be an option.

"Sherri. Are you up here?"

A noise that sounded like a whimper came from across the main room. Not in the loft. He took the last few steps up the ladder just to be sure. The loft was empty. Completely empty. No mattress, no blankets. No Sherri.

Ash all but jumped down the ladder to the floor and spun around to see the large pile of blankets that had been heaped in the corner moving.

"Sherri?"

A blanket moved, revealing his friend's face. Her very pale, very tired face.

He crossed the distance in two steps and was down on his knees in front of her. "What's going on? Are you hurt? The storm—it was worse than we thought. I shouldn't have left you up here. What do you need? What's—"

"I'm fine."

She wasn't. Her voice was thin and thready. The hand she

reached out to him, weak and frail. Whatever was going on, Sherri was much sicker than she'd been letting on.

"You're not." Ash dug through the blankets and saw she was resting on her mattress. Confused, he looked up toward her sleeping loft and back to Sherri, who shrugged and attempted a small smile.

"You were right. Maybe sleeping up there was a bad idea." It was a bad idea and more than anything at that moment, he wanted to reaffirm his opinion on that, but it clearly wasn't necessary and there were bigger problems. "After you left last time, I pushed the mattress off the ledge and made myself a nest. It works better."

"I would have helped you." He *should* have helped her. "Your stubbornness is going to be the death of you." He spoke before thinking and immediately wished he hadn't. "I mean…I shouldn't have…"

"No." She laughed, but it lacked her usual gusto. "It likely will be the death of me. But if I'm going to go, I'd rather go on my own terms, don't you think?"

He didn't and he told her as much before helping her sit up, fixing her a drink and a snack of applesauce. Which he all but force-fed her in order to be sure she got it all into her body. She looked so frail and thin. *How had she gotten so thin in only a few days? It had only been days since he'd been up to see her, right?*

No.

It had been longer. A lot longer. *Shit.*

He'd said he'd come every two days, but then life got busy. That wasn't true. Heather had happened. Guilt flooded through him as he held a straw to Sherri's lips and she took a few small sips of water before she shook her head away. She was behaving like a palliative care patient. She wasn't palliative.

Not yet.

And if Ash had anything to say about it, she'd never be.

"I shouldn't have left you up here, Sher. I'm sorry."

"I told you to."

He shook his head. "It doesn't matter. I shouldn't have listened."

Sherri laughed, and for a moment, she sounded like herself. "And what makes you think you stand any kind of chance against what I want?"

He joined in and chuckled right along with her. It was true. He didn't stand a chance fighting against what Sherri wanted. But that was healthy Sherri and it was more than clear that he was no longer dealing with healthy Sherri.

"How about the storm, Sher? You lied. You weren't okay." He gestured around with his arm. "This does not look okay."

She paused for a minute, obviously weighing what she was going to say. "It's fine. I think it looks worse than it is. Besides, what was I going to say? That I needed help?"

"Yes. That's exactly what you should have said."

"And then what, Ash?" Her eyes flared. Two spots of life in her gray face. "You would have left Heather? You know you wouldn't. You wouldn't have taken the guests to Bocas. They would have missed their flights."

He racked his brain for a rebuttal. *What would he have done? What choices did he have?*

He didn't.

She was right; it would have been an impossible choice. His loyalty would have been to Sherri. Had he known she was as bad as she was, he would have gone to her.

The guests would have waited. Missed flights or not. Heather was a smart, capable woman—whether she thought she was or not—and she would have been fine. Sherri would have been the clear choice.

And she would have hated it.

"You still should have told me."

She shook her head softly. "I'm telling you now."

"It's not the same," he chastised and then added, "But I know it's the best I'm going to get."

"Smart boy." Sheri patted his hand and he got the oddest sense that she was consoling *him*. Shouldn't it have been the other way around?

Despite the storm and the whole incident on the swim platform, Heather felt great. It could have been the warm sunshine drying the pools of standing water and heating up the last traces of chill in her bones. It could have been the fact that she'd had a successful run learning how to drive the boat. And she'd loved it. Feeling the wind in her hair and the independence of being able to move around had been amazing.

It could have been either of those things contributing to Heather's good mood, but she knew it wasn't. It was more than that. It was Ash.

It was *definitely* Ash.

How could she be feeling anything for anybody after what she'd been through with Joe? She could keep denying it, but there was no point. She was developing feelings for Ash. There was no way to know what they meant or what on earth she was going to do about them. But they were there and they were making her feel fantastic.

For the moment, that's all she needed to know.

Even after what he'd told her. Maybe it was *because* of what he'd confessed. He'd been through a lot. They both had, in their own ways. Ash's story was tragic, that was for sure. And he'd said there'd never be anything more between them because of his past. That should have bothered her.

But instead of letting it get under her skin, it actually made her feel,...well, she wasn't sure. But the one thing she did know for sure was that the storm had been cleansing.

It was a new day and she was ready to face it.

It didn't even bother her that Ash had gone up the hill to visit Sherri. Not that it should bother her. But she knew something was wrong with the older woman and it was killing her that Ash wouldn't tell her what was going on. Maybe she could help. Even if she couldn't, she'd be able to lend an ear. A loving hug. Whatever was going on, it could only be better if she knew what was going on.

There was no point dwelling on that, though. She'd asked. Multiple times, but she was no closer to knowing what was going on. He'd tell her whatever she needed to know when she needed to know. Of that she was sure. Until then, she wasn't going to worry about it.

With all the major clean-up done, and the sun drying up the last bits of water that had snuck through the shutters, and no guests to entertain, Heather found herself with too much time on her hands. She glanced over at the bar, where the laptop was. She should be checking reservations and emailing potential guests, but Heather knew what would happen the second she turned on the computer. And there was no way she wanted her mother, or even her mother's words, invading her space on this day, when she was finally feeling good. No way.

But after puttering around *grande casa* for another twenty minutes, there was no more avoiding it. She had new guests arriving in a few days.

"I should probably check to make sure they weren't delayed by the storm." Heather spoke to the dog, in the habit she'd gotten into over the last few weeks whenever she found herself alone. Thor always seemed to be at her feet, and she didn't mind. She'd never had a dog of her own before and she found his constant companionship comforting.

Thor whined in agreement or defeat—she couldn't be sure, but it didn't matter. There was no putting it off any longer. Ash could be back any minute and she'd certainly rather spend her time with him, especially when they were alone, in a million different ways.

As it always did, the computer took a few minutes to fire up, but as soon as it did, the email program lit up with unread messages. She filed those away and focused on the notes from guests, and potential new guests. Finally, when she was finished organizing a few more reservations, she went to open the emails from her mother, only there weren't any.

"That can't be right."

Heather scrolled through the inbox again and clicked on her web-based email program and checked it as well. Still nothing. "Maybe she finally gave up on me," she said to Thor, who lifted his head from his paws and yawned before laying it back down. "That's kind of how I feel about it right now."

There were probably a million explanations for why there were no messages, half of them might even be reasonable reasons, but there was no point in worrying about it.

Not when there were more fun things to do.

Heather closed the computer and walked out to the dock, Thor at her heels. The water was calm and just as gorgeous as it usually was. It was hard to believe that not even twenty-four hours ago, there'd been a tropical storm whipping up those very same waters. She gazed out across to the mangroves on the opposite shore from Casa del Sol.

"What do you think, buddy?" She squatted next to the dog and scratched his head. "Do you think I can get those sea grapes over there that Sherri was talking about?" Thor whined and licked her face, making her laugh. "It shouldn't be too hard, right? I can take the canoe."

The canoe.

She'd forgotten all about the boat she'd inadvertently sunk the day before. Looking toward the swim platform, where she'd last seen it, turned up nothing but the frayed rope hanging from the cleat where Ash had cut it in an effort to save it. "But if he'd cut it…" She scanned the shoreline. "Where would it have gone?" Her question was answered when she finally spotted what looked like could be the canoe, or at least the tip of it, sticking out in the water by the mangroves at the far end of the property.

At least it wasn't totally lost. *Maybe with Ash's help, they could dig it out enough to bail and save it?* Hopefully. In the meantime, she definitely wouldn't be taking the canoe to find the sea grapes, but now that the idea was in her head, she really wanted to get some. Besides, if she could make a delicious salad with some of the herbs and lettuces from the garden, the sea grapes would be a crunchy addition. And then maybe she could redeem herself from the burnt breakfast fiasco.

Once the idea was in her head, Heather couldn't shake it. She glanced up toward the treehouse, but there was still no sign of Ash. She'd have time.

Besides, she'd just successfully completed instruction in the panga, so there was no reason not to take the boat out on her own. "You wait here, Thor."

She ran over to the boat and started up the engine on the first try, just like Ash showed her, before untying the bow line. Thor ran along the dock, barking as she backed the boat away from the dock and the bungalow. As soon as she was a safe distance away, she pressed down on the throttle and urged the boat to go faster. The trip across the channel to the grove of mangroves wasn't far, but since she was out there, there was no harm in going for a little spin to enjoy herself.

The wind whipped through her hair, tangling it around her face, but Heather loved it. She always enjoyed a boat ride, especially in the little wooden panga, but as she was discovering, she absolutely loved it when she was alone and in total control of the boat. It was empowering knowing that she was in total control of the boat.

And her life.

She pushed the boat to go even faster out through the channel and around the corner of the mangroves into another bay. She tipped her head back and let out a shriek of joy. And another. And another until she was laughing with the thrill of it all.

It felt strange and wonderful. Inappropriate and entirely perfect all at the same time. In the middle of the ocean, surrounded by mangroves. The sun high in the sky, butterflies dancing over the bow. Heather let herself laugh. Tears of mirth streamed down her face and when finally the last chuckle faded away, she wiped at her face, looked around to get her bearings and put her hand back on the throttle.

She gave the boat a little gas. It leapt forward and then....

Nothing.

Heather flicked her wrist, trying to rev the boat, but nothing. She tried again. And a third time, but the boat wasn't going anywhere.

"Dammit."

The fact that the boat had stopped wasn't terribly concerning. Or at least it wouldn't have been, if Heather had any idea of where she was. She looked around again. All the mangroves looked the same, and she couldn't find a landmark that gave her any indication of where Casa del Sol might be. Not that it would help much considering she'd barely gone out in the boat since she'd arrived at the B&B.

Worse—Ash had no idea where she was. And there was no way to tell him.

He spent the next few hours moving around the house, cleaning the floors, gathering the debris, and opening the shutters to let some light shine in.

As Ash worked, Sherri stayed in her little nest of pillows

and blankets in the corner of the room. From time to time, he glanced over to see how she was. Most of the time, she was sleeping, but a few times he caught her watching him.

When he was finally finished with the major clean-up, he moved to the kitchen area and examined the bottles of pills that were scattered about. Some of them were prescription, not that they were specific to her, but that wasn't unusual for Panama where medicine was readily available, but most of them looked to be vitamins or some types of supplements. And of course, there was a healthy amount of weed in a baggie.

"For the pain," Sherri said when he lifted the bag for closer inspection.

"You're awake." It wasn't a question. "Are you in pain?"

"At the moment?" She shook her head. "No more than usual. It also helps with the nausea." She paused and finally admitted, "It just helps."

"Fair enough." He shrugged and put the bag back where he found it and continued to tidy. No longer because the house was in shambles, but more now because he wanted to see what she was taking. He took a minute, finished up with the bottles before finally grabbing himself a beer.

Ash settled down next to Sherri on her bed, took a slug of his beer and finally asked the question that had been on the tip of his tongue all day. "Tell me how you're doing."

She opened her mouth to say something. But before she said anything, she closed it and pressed her lips together.

"Tell me how you're *really* doing. I'll know if you're lying. Tell me, Sher. Please." The last word came out as the plea he meant it to be because he needed to know. Yes, after seeing what he'd just seen, he *needed* to know.

"It's fine. I'm taking my pills and following the protocol and—"

"Stop." Ash shook his head and looked down at his lap. "Do not tell me any bullshit about pills and supplements and for the love of God, do *not* tell me a goddamn thing about protocol. Not one. Just tell me what's going on, Sher. Tell me you're going to be okay. Tell me you're taking care of yourself and you're just about to turn a corner or please, please tell me you're going to let me take you in to the hospital."

Sherri didn't say anything right away. When the silence stretched out to the point where it was almost unbearable, Ash turned to see whether she'd fallen asleep again. Her dark eyes stared back at him, unblinking. "Sherri." His voice was barely a whisper. "This is crazy. Please."

She shook her head slowly. So slowly it barely moved, but he saw it. More than that, he saw the small tear that formed in the corner of her eye but didn't fall. "No," was all she said.

"Sherri." He stopped himself just short of begging. He didn't want to beg, but he would. Without a doubt, he'd get down on his knees and beg the woman he loved more than his own mother to let him take her to the hospital in any kind of last-minute effort to save her life because clearly she was dying right in front of him and he couldn't let that happen. He *wouldn't* let that happen.

Her hand reached out from the pile of blankets. The touch on his arm was so light, it tickled the skin. "I have to do this my way." He opened his mouth to protest, but the look in her eyes stopped him. "No, Ash. I know you don't understand. I know it's hard and you just want to fix this but some things can't be fixed with medicine and doctors."

"That's bullshit." He curled his fingers around the bottle of beer. "This *can* be fixed with medicine and doctors. Or at the very least, it will give you a fighting chance, Sherri. And that's better than what you're doing right now. You're up here in the tree, hiding and waiting to die."

"Is that what you think? Really?"

He nodded. "I do."

She took a minute, as if the very effort of formulating an

argument was costing her precious energy she didn't have and Ash felt a pang of guilt at the idea that he was costing her that energy. "Ash. You know I love you."

He did.

"You know I think of you as my own."

He knew that too.

"And you know that I have no problem telling you when I think you're being an asshole."

He smiled, because he already knew that.

"This is mine, Ash." She took a deep breath and he could have sworn he heard the air filling her thin, fragile lungs. "This disease is mine. It's my battle to fight or to win. On my own." She held up a finger to silence him before he spoke. "And when I go into battle, it's up to me to choose my arsenal."

"But what if you're purposely turning down the best possible army in favor of—"

"Of what?" With effort, she pushed herself up so she looked directly into his eyes. "Of nature and energy and faith? Yes. I am. I'm choosing that over an army of medicine with pockets lined with big business, corruption, and greed whose number-one purpose isn't to cure me—it's to pad bank accounts. But don't forget, I haven't totally given up on the drugs. I'm taking them, too. Remember? But just the minimum. I don't need to give them any more of my money if I can help it. So if that's what you think I'm doing, then you're correct."

She was exaggerating. She was overblowing what was probably a small issue, but Ash couldn't totally disagree with her. Especially the part about it being her war to fight. She was right about that. He had no business telling her what to do. No matter how badly he wanted to scoop her up and carry her into a hospital. It might be killing her. But it wasn't his battle to fight.

But he could help.

"Okay."

"Okay?"

"Okay," he said again. "If this is what you want to do. Let's do it."

She looked at him with narrowed eyes and tilted her head sideways. "Do what?"

"Let's fight." The idea flooded through him with so much intensity he wanted to jump up and sort it out right away. "We can fight it your way. But I'm in."

"You?"

"Yes. Me."

"You're in."

"I'm in."

Sherri was quiet for a minute but finally she asked, "What does that mean?"

"You have some herbs and vitamins up here." He waved his arm in the vicinity of the counter and the bottles he'd just finished organizing. "You even have some modern medicine."

She nodded because he wasn't telling her anything she didn't know.

"But we can do better."

"We can what?"

"Do better."

Ash swallowed hard. He'd done his best to protect his personal life and more importantly, details of his past from anyone in Panama. Including Sherri. She knew about Carlie. She knew what he'd been through. But she didn't know everything. "I can help."

"You already do, Ash." Her hand squeezed his.

"No." Ash stared into her eyes. "I can *really* help, Sherri. I have…resources." It was an understatement of the largest degree, but he didn't know what else to say. How else was he supposed to explain that he had more money than he'd ever be able to spend in ten lifetimes? He couldn't. So he didn't try. "Whatever you need. I can make it happen."

"I have everything."

"You don't. We can do better. So let's do it."

"Ash, I—"

"No, Sher. Let me do this. You can do this your way. It's your battle to fight. But let me be your army. Let me fight for you the best way I know how."

A tear of his own slid down his cheek but he didn't move his hand to wipe it away. They sat in silence, his hand in hers. Finally, after what seemed like forever, Sherri spoke. "Okay."

She was definitely not having much luck when it came to boats. *First the canoe, and now the panga.* When she got back to land, she was totally not going to be in a hurry to get back in a boat anytime soon, that was for sure.

If she got back.

Heather looked around for what had to be the dozenth time but still there was nothing she recognized. All she could see was mangroves. Lots and lots of mangroves. And that was it. There was a current Heather didn't expect dragging her through the trees. Was she going farther into the maze or out to sea? She had no idea but what she did know for sure was that if she didn't get the boat started soon, she was only going to get more and more lost.

She should have put an anchor down and she would have too, if there'd been one. Just like she would have started paddling if she'd had a paddle. Heather was going to have to have a talk with Ash about outfitting the boat properly when she got back.

If she got back.

She tried the boat again, pushing the negative thoughts out

of her mind. She couldn't dwell on what *could* happen. It wouldn't get her anywhere and she'd never been one for looking at the negative side of things. But it was certainly very, very hard not to at that moment. All she wanted to do was sit in the floor of the boat and cry.

A tear slid down her cheek at the same time that a swell of panic started to rise inside her gut. *No.* She couldn't let bad thoughts take over. She couldn't give them space to fester and grow. What she needed to do was figure out the boat.

"Okay, Heather." She spoke to herself calmly, forcing the words to come out strong and assured. Even though that was the exact opposite of what she was feeling inside. "Pull it together. You've got this."

She smoothed her hair back and took a deep breath before she turned to face the engine.

"Let's start from the beginning." Heather sat down, adjusted the throttle to choke and pulled the cord. Nothing. "Okay," she said to herself. "Try it again. Take it slow and start from the top." She took her own advice and this time went over every detail, pretending Ash was there talking to her. Still, nothing.

"Stupid boat!"

The anger and frustration welled up and this time, she didn't even try to stop it. Heather dropped to the bottom of the boat and let the emotion wash over her. Tears fell hard, hot and fast down her face, over her hands and onto her bare legs. And she let them. She let herself cry hot tears that she'd been holding in for months. Maybe even years.

It was a messy cry. A hard, hot cry.

It was exactly what she needed.

She cried for herself. The years lost, the missed opportunities, the love she'd never had. She cried for Ash and everything he'd confessed to her. She cried for his wife and unborn child and his heart that might not ever heal again. She cried for them and the chance they might not ever have.

Heather didn't move from the bottom of the boat until she'd exhausted every last hot, salty tear. And not even then did she move. She sat and she waited. For what, she didn't know. But she let it all out and when she was finally completely wrung out, she sat a little longer.

The boat had probably floated halfway to Costa Rica by now but if she just didn't open her eyes to see, she'd never know. And sometimes, ignorance was bliss.

Just like it had been with her ex-husband's affair. Everyone at Shelter Bay thought she'd been caught off guard—the jilted wife. Not true. Not at all. She'd known about Joe and Maria from the start. Heck, she'd known before they did. She wasn't stupid. She saw the way they'd looked at each other that first day when Maria had walked in, asking for a job. If Heather hadn't already been so jaded on love and the idea of it all, she might have likened that first meeting to something in one of those cheesy romantic comedy movies she used to like to watch. The ones where the heroine was always just a little bit unsuspecting and the hero was in need of a life shake-up and together they found who they were and what love was all about.

That was exactly what Joe and Maria had been like. Just like they might have if their lives had actually been in a movie, they probably tried to fight their attraction at first. After all, Joe was married and even if it was already a dead marriage, it was still a marriage. But if they had tried to fight it, it hadn't lasted long before they finally gave in to their attraction.

And then came the baby.

She hadn't seen *that* coming. Not in a million years. But when Heather had first noticed Maria's stomach start to swell and her uniform started to get a little tight, she could have laughed with the ridiculousness of it all. But still, Joe didn't come to her and confess. It was as if they were all living in some kind of delusional dream world where, if they just ignored what was playing out in front of them, it wasn't really happening. And Heather was just as bad. She could have said something. Confronted them. Yelled and screamed and forced Joe to make a choice. She could have done all of that.

But she didn't.

Because then there'd be no turning back. And when you didn't know where you were going or what you wanted, it was sometimes easier to keep doing what you were doing and pretend that there was nothing wrong.

But there was.

And when finally Maria went into labor in the middle of the marina restaurant, Joe made his choice right there on the spot, choosing his girlfriend and the child they were about to bring into the world.

Heather should have been mad or humiliated. But all she felt was relief at being given an out.

The only problem with her relationship falling apart was she could no longer keep her head in the sand about what *she* wanted and what she wanted to do with the rest of her life.

Ignoring it wouldn't make it go away.

Just like sitting in the bottom of the boat and crying about it.

Heather sat up, wiped her eyes and smoothed her hair back, fixing her ponytail. "Okay, Heather. You're better than this." She wasn't one for talking to herself, but sometimes a girl just needed a pep talk and if there wasn't anyone else to do it, she'd just have to do it for herself. "Pull yourself together. It's not like you haven't been in tough spots before."

She got up and moved to the back of the boat. With her hands on her hips, she stared down the engine. "I can do this." She walked herself through all the steps again, this time letting Ash's voice guide her.

The fuel hose gets loose sometimes, he'd said.

There was no way it could be that simple, but it was the one thing she hadn't checked. Heather followed the gas line to where it disappeared under the plywood bench where the gas tank was kept. She lifted the seat board to gain access and there, lying in a small puddle of what she assumed to be gasoline, was the end of the fuel line.

"Oh my God." The words came out as a half laugh, half cry and she shoved the line back on to the fitting, making sure it was secure. "You have to be kidding me. If this works..." She refused to jinx herself by saying anymore. Heather quickly put the seat board back in place and went back to the engine. She stared it down one more time and followed all the instructions to start it.

This time, with a choke followed by a roar, the engine sputtered to life.

If she hadn't already spent all her tears, Heather might have collapsed onto the floor one more time. But she'd wasted enough time. And one thing she knew now: she was done wasting time on things she couldn't change.

It was time to look forward and go after what she wanted. And no matter what Ash said about not letting anyone get too close again, one thing was for sure...he didn't have a choice in it.

She was in love with Ash. And she didn't know entirely what that was going to look like yet, but she did know one thing —she was going to tell him. Because no matter what happened, Heather was tired of sitting back and letting life happen to her. She was taking control.

Chapter Twelve

ASH HAD SPENT way longer in the treehouse with Sherri than he'd intended, but it was okay. They'd come to an understanding and at least he could feel good about her being up the hill all alone. Well, maybe not *good*. But he felt better knowing that she would let him help her. And dammit, that's exactly what he was going to do. He didn't know exactly how yet, but he had the resources to find the best natural medicine doctors money could buy. Naturopaths, dieticians, chefs, massage therapists: whatever it took to help Sherri, that's what he'd do.

He'd spent some time fixing a few easy meals for Sherri to grab if she didn't feel like preparing anything and while he worked, she sat, bundled in the corner, watching him and peppering him with questions about the B&B.

"Everything is fine down there," Ash said for the dozenth time. "Heather's doing a great job."

"I'm sure she is."

"Then why do you keep asking?" He scraped the rice out of the pot and into a glass container.

Sherri chuckled. "That's not what I'm asking, Ash."

She was silent for a moment, so finally he took her bait. "Then what are you really asking?" *As if he didn't know.*

"How are things between the two of you?"

And there it was. Ash knew she'd been dying to ask for details about the two of them. Frankly, he was surprised it had taken her so long to get around to it. "What makes you think there's anything between us at all?"

Sherri's smile was a weaker version of the one Ash was so familiar with, but it was still hers and something about seeing it made him both happy and a little sad. "When you get to be my age, Ash, you learn a few things. And when you've spent enough time around people as I have, witnessing all aspects of love, from the blossoming, to sometimes the unfortunate break-down or destruction of it, to the comfortable peace of a secure love, well…you get to see a few things. And I've seen it all."

"Is that right?" He put the pot in the sink and ran a bit of water into it. "And what do you see?"

"I see two people fighting what could be their greatest love."

Greatest love? No way. He shook his head. He had his greatest love already. There could only be one. And he'd destroyed it. He liked Heather. Hell, he *really* liked Heather. More than any other woman he'd met in the last four years. But love?

No way.

Although he *had* told her the story about Carlie. *Why?* So she'd keep her distance? To scare her? Because what if he was falling for her?

"Don't shake your head—it's true."

"It's not, Sher. Sorry. You're not right on this one."

She took a moment to think before she shook her head. "No," she said. "I'm right. You like her."

"Of course I do. But that's not love."

Ash couldn't look at her when he said that because he was afraid she'd see something on his face. Even when he spoke the words, they didn't sound quite right. But he refused to let himself think of the alternative.

As if she read his mind, Sherri spoke up. "It's okay to let yourself love again, Ash."

But it wasn't. And Sherri should agree with him too. *After everything he'd told her, how could she possibly think it'd be okay to love again?*

He turned his focus to the dishes in the sink. He'd been there too long; he should get back down before it got dark and see whether there was anything else that needed to be fixed thanks to the storm.

Ash cleaned in silence for a few minutes and he thought maybe Sherri had fallen asleep again, but then he heard the soft padding of her feet approach. "Sher, you should be in bed. I've got these dishes and you—"

"I'm fine." She put her hand on his arm. "What do you think I do when you're not here?" She shook her head, because neither of them really wanted him to answer that question. "You should go, Ash."

"I'm going to," he said. "Just as soon as I finish these dishes for you."

"No. That's not what I mean." Something in her voice made him turn around again.

"And what do you mean, Sherri? Where should I go?" He wasn't sure he wanted the answer to that question but he needed to ask. "You want me to leave?"

She squeezed his arm. "I love you, Ash. You're like a son to me. You know that. And I'd be happy to have you around for the rest of my days, no matter how many of those there may be." He shot her a look and she smiled. "But I also want you to go live your life."

"I am—"

She held up a hand to stop him. "You've been hanging around Bocas and Casa del Sol for how long now? Five years?"

"Four," he corrected her and immediately felt stupid when she tilted her head.

"Okay, four. But that doesn't make it any better. What are you doing?"

He didn't know how to answer that question. He was living his life. He was doing what he wanted because he could. He was living his dream. Everyone's dream, really. Didn't everyone dream of making their fortune and retiring before they were thirty to live life as a beach bum? That's what he was doing. And it was everything he wanted.

Wasn't it?

"What makes you think I need to leave?" he challenged her. "Why can't I live my life right here? What makes you think I'm not already living my life exactly how I want to?"

She didn't answer that. She didn't need to.

Ash continued with the dishes, stacking them in a drying rack next to the sink. When he was finished, he turned to Sherri, who still stood close. He opened his mouth to object to her argument again, but she stopped him.

"I don't mean you need to leave Bocas, Ash. I didn't even mean that you had to leave Casa del Sol."

He was confused and told her as much.

"I'm sorry if I'm not making much sense these days. The medicine muddles me." She took a moment to compose herself and tried again. "I just want you to live, Ash. I want you to go into your future. I want you to leave your past in the past and stop letting it keep you from living your future. You owe it to yourself. You owe it to—"

"Don't." He held up one hand and looked down at the ground. "I get your point."

"Do you?"

He nodded. "I think so."

"Good." There was a lightness to her voice he hadn't heard all day. "So get down there and tell Heather exactly what you feel. Even if you don't fully understand it yet. Tell her. Can you do that?"

He wasn't sure he could, but Sherri made it sound so easy, so he nodded.

"You make it sound so easy."

"Silly boy. It *is* easy. You only get one shot to live life, so do it on your terms. Put the past where it belongs, behind you. Focus on the here and now. And I think we can both agree, Heather is the here and now. And possibly...even the future." She winked and in that moment, she seemed so much like the old Sherri, Ash couldn't help but pull her into a hug.

"But..."

"But what?"

He swallowed hard, not wanting to voice his deepest worry. "What if I lose her?"

"That's what you're worried about?" She reached out and stroked his cheek. "Oh, Ash. What happened to Carlie was tragic, but that's not going to happen to Heather. The only way you're going to lose her is by not letting yourself love her."

He let the words sink in and it didn't take long. "You're right."

"I know I am." She smiled and smacked his cheek gently. "Now go."

"Okay. You win. I'll go."

"Good. And when you're done, send that girl up to me. I think I'd like a few words with her myself."

He was practically running down the stairs to *grande casa*, over-flowing with ideas and eager to get on the computer to start his research for ways to help Sherri and of course, to see Heather and tell her how he felt.

Maybe.

He wanted to. He really did. But he couldn't help but be cautious, too.

He'd made a vow four years ago to never let anyone get too close again. To never again let anyone love him or depend on him. He would never again put himself or anyone else in the position he and Carlie had been in. He'd loved her more than life itself and she'd loved him. It was that love that had destroyed her because he couldn't live up to it. In the end, he couldn't be the man she needed or deserved and her love for him had been the end of everything.

Never again.

That wasn't your fault.

The stupid voice in his head, the very same voice Ash thought he'd silenced years ago, piped up. It took him off guard and he stopped halfway down the steps back to the bungalows, needing to sit down.

Years ago, right after everything with Carlie happened, the voice in his head would tell him that things would be okay and that it wasn't his fault and all sorts of other lies. He'd worked very hard to silence that voice. Mostly with whiskey and women. Lots of whiskey and women. It took a solid six months, but he'd managed to do it. He'd also managed to alienate what few friends he had left and his own parents barely spoke to him. If he hadn't have had that five minutes of sobriety where he managed to sell his company, he would have lost that too.

But it would have been worth it. Because one day Ash woke up and the voice was gone. As were all the others.

No one, especially his own conscience, was telling him how none of what happened was his fault, and how things would be okay and he'd go on to love again.

It was quiet.

Two weeks later, he sold his condo, his sports car, and everything else he owned and moved to Bocas Town.

But now the voice was back.

Dammit.

Ash dropped his head into his hands and squeezed. When he looked up, the voice was gone, but instead there was a roaring.

A roaring?

It took him a minute to realize the roaring he heard was the sound of the panga and from the sound of it, it was coming from quite a distance. He jumped to his feet and looked through the trees out to the ocean. He scanned for a moment, until finally he saw it. *Would Heather have taken the boat out? And what the hell was she doing way out there?*

From his vantage point, he couldn't see the dock where the boat should have been tied up, and it was too far out to tell whether it was in fact the panga that belonged to Casa del Sol, but either way, it was headed directly toward them. And he intended to be there when it arrived. Sherri was right: even if he didn't fully understand it himself, it was time that he let himself go. He might not know what that meant, but without a doubt, despite all the voices in his head—or maybe because of them—he knew that somehow, in some way, letting himself go involved Heather. And he couldn't wait to tell her so.

It took her awhile to figure out where she was. Especially considering she'd barely been out in the mangroves and they all looked the same to Heather. Or at least that's what she'd thought before. After a few minutes of puttering around in the mangrove coves, she started to notice familiarities and even a few landmarks. She didn't let herself get frustrated, or panic about her situation either. Instead, she stayed calm, used her head, and methodically worked her way through until she got to a larger opening and finally the ocean.

Once she was able to leave the shelter of the trees, it was easier to spot familiar places, like the cantina one island over from Casa del Sol. From there, she worked her way around until in the distance she could make out the familiar thatched roofs of the place she'd already learned to call home. She pushed the engine harder, anxious to get back to the dock.

To Ash.

She'd been told once that crying was therapeutic: your body needed the opportunity to cleanse you from all the emotions that were bound up inside, and crying was the best way to do that. At the time, she was sure she called bullshit or something equally enlightened. But now, after having just sat on the bottom of her boat, lost in the middle of the mangroves, crying like a baby, for the first time, she believed that there might be something to that *bullshit* because she felt like a completely new woman.

She could have laughed at how cliché she probably sounded or even looked, standing in the back of her boat, wind blowing through her hair, a smile on her face. But she didn't care.

Not. One. Bit.

Heather felt great and it had been way too long since she could say that. More than that, she knew what she wanted and what she wanted was Ash. A laugh grew deep in her gut and she threw her head back and let it out as she whipped toward the dock and the figure she knew to be Ash ran down the dock to greet her.

It was him. He caught the bow of the boat as she slowed and brought it alongside the dock.

"Where've you been?" Ash tied the rope to the cleat and turned, right as she stepped onto the dock and into his arms. He caught her with a chuckle that she cut short with the press of her lips to his mouth. "Mmm, I still don't know where you've been," he said when he pulled back. "But I'm sure happy you're back."

"Me too."

His hands slid down her body and pressed her close to his need for her. More than anything, she wanted to answer that need.

"I didn't know you took the boat out." He bent and nibbled on her neck. "Were you gone long?"

The laugh burst from her throat before she could stop it.

"What's so funny?" Ash pulled back and looked at her as if she'd totally lost her mind, which she may have.

"Was I gone long?"

"Were you?"

"You could say that." She took Ash's hand and led him up the dock into *grande casa*. She was suddenly overcome by thirst. *How long was she out there, anyway?* "I need a drink."

"I'll get some beers."

"No." She stopped him. "Water for me. I…" She paused long enough to guzzle half the bottle from the fridge. "I didn't realize how thirsty I was."

"You're acting crazy." He shook his head, but there was a smile on his face. "What's going on? Where did you go?"

"I don't know."

Ash tilted his head and waited. Heather laughed at his confusion.

"I took the boat out to get sea grapes from across the channel," she started to explain.

"Why didn't you take the canoe?"

Heather raised her eyebrows and Ash laughed. "Oh yeah. I guess we should rescue the boat later, too."

"I guess we should." She chugged the last half of her water bottle before she continued. "Anyway. I took the boat out and I was enjoying it so much, I decided to go a little bit farther."

"How far?" Concern started to show on Ash's face.

"That's the thing." She laughed. "I have no idea. I was driving along somewhere in the mangroves and the engine quit."

"It quit?"

She nodded, eager to get the story out and tell him exactly what she was feeling. It was almost bursting inside her. "As it turns out, there is no anchor and no paddle in the boat." She tried to look stern, but she couldn't stop the smile. "So I floated. And floated and floated."

"What the hell, Heather?" He put his hands on her shoulders and shook her a little. "Are you okay? You got it started again? Well, obviously."

"I did." She nodded and moved to the fridge to get the beers. Now that she was hydrated, a beer was in order. After all, she was celebrating. What exactly, she couldn't quite articulate. But she felt good. Damn good. And that's all that mattered. "Cheers." They clinked bottles and she took a long pull before she answered him. "I have no idea how long I was out there. Long enough that you didn't notice." She pointed the bottle at him accusingly.

"I was up at Sherri's for a long time." He waved his hand, dismissing it. "We can talk about that later. But seriously. Were you out there the whole time I was gone?"

"Maybe not the whole time," she said. "But long enough that I was able to have a good cry." She couldn't even believe she was admitting that to Ash, but somehow it felt right. It felt as if she needed to somehow try to explain how she'd just come to an epiphany about her life. And him. Definitely him. So much...him.

Before he could ask her again whether she was okay, she kept talking. "It was just me out there and I got mad. And then I got sad. And then...I was okay." She smiled so wide, it almost hurt her face, but she couldn't help it. There was no other way to explain what was going on.

"I needed it," she continued. "I needed to come to grips with everything and I think the boat breaking down was just the tipping point. Almost a representation of my entire life. Does that make sense?"

Ash shook his head slowly. "Not even a little bit."

She wasn't discouraged. "I'm tired of coasting. I'm ready to drive my own boat. Set my own course. And decide where it is that I want to go."

"Okay." He nodded slowly. "And where is that?"

She took the step that closed the distance between them and stood directly in front of him. She'd never felt more sure of anything in her entire life. It almost didn't matter how he'd react, because Heather knew with complete certainty that what she was about to do was exactly what she needed to do. "It's not so much that I want to go somewhere." She paused. This was it. The moment where she could choose her path. Go after what *she* wanted. It was about her now. "I wanted to tell you that I—"

The blare of a horn cut her off, jarring them both from the moment. The horn sounded again, and she turned toward the noise, to see a wooden panga, a water taxi from Bocas Town, heading toward the dock with a passenger.

"Are you expecting a guest today?"

Heather shook her head. "I just checked things. No one for…" There was something familiar about the passenger in the boat. Even from a distance, she could see the person held themselves very straight. Very proper. Very much like…*her mother*.

Chapter Thirteen

HEATHER RELEASED his hand and stared at the incoming boat. She said they weren't expecting anyone, but the way she shook her head and stared toward the boat told him different.

"What is it?"

She didn't answer.

"Heather?"

"It can't be." Heather's hand went to her mouth. She turned then to look at him and gone was the laughter in her face and the excitement he'd seen only moments before when he'd been so sure she was about to tell him exactly what he didn't even realize he wanted to hear. But he *did* want to hear it and he wanted to tell her the same thing, too. But now…something was wrong.

"What?" He took her by the shoulders and forced her to look at him. "Who is it? What's wrong, Heather? Talk to me."

She shook her head again slowly but this time she answered him before she pulled out of his grip. "It's my mother."

"Your *mother*?"

Heather didn't answer him because she was already walking, zombie-like, toward the dock.

Ash shook his head and followed Heather down the dock. Whatever was about to go down, he knew without a doubt he should be there.

Heather stood frozen on the dock as the boat pulled up alongside. He vaguely recognized the driver as a local from Bocas Town. "*Hola, amigo.*" Ash grabbed the line the driver handed him and tied up the boat before he had a chance to take a good look at the passenger.

She was an older version of Heather, with the same glossy dark hair and cute little nose. He couldn't tell whether mother and daughter shared the same gorgeous eye color, because the woman wore oversized sunglasses. Despite that, it was easy to see there was a family resemblance. But that's where the similarities ended. The older woman held herself bone straight in the front of the boat, as if she'd been positioned on a stick. It must have been incredibly hard to maintain that position for the long ride, but Ash had no doubt she had. Her mouth was set in a firm, straight line, with no indication of the smile Heather always wore, even when she'd first arrived to Casa del Sol.

"Mom. What are you doing here?"

"I came to see you," she snapped. "What do you think I'm doing here?"

Heather made no move to help her mother out of the boat and it was clear to Ash that the woman very much would like to get out. With a quick glance at Heather, he extended the woman a hand. "Welcome to Casa del Sol, Mrs. …"

"Weaver." She looked at Ash's hand with some level of disgust and, obviously deciding it was the lesser of two evils, took it and let him assist her from the boat and up to the dock, where she promptly dropped Ash's hand.

Heather still didn't say anything. The two of them didn't embrace the way Ash would have expected a mother and daughter reunited to do. Instead, they stared at each other somewhat awkwardly. At least for him.

"Let me get your bags, Mrs. Weaver." She dismissed him with a wave, so Ash took the large, totally inappropriate suitcases from the driver and when it was clear that he was going to be expected to also pay the man, he dug into the pocket of his shorts and handed over a few bills.

Even after the boat drove away, Heather still hadn't said anything to her mother. By the looks of it, they were in some sort of stare down, a contest of wills. Regardless, the sun was hot, and Mrs. Weaver looked as though she might melt at any given moment. The last thing Ash needed to deal with on top of the drama that was already unfolding was a wilted woman with heat stroke.

"Why don't we go inside and get a cold drink?" He ushered both the women in the direction of *grande casa*, and dragged the suitcases behind him, bringing up the rear. Once they were inside and out of the sun, Heather seemed to have snapped out of whatever trance she'd been in and was at least communicating and acting somewhat like a hostess.

"I just don't understand why you're here," She handed her mother a glass of water with a sprig of fresh mint in it. It was a little touch she'd started adding to greet the B&B guests.

"You told me, and I quote, '*It really is paradise here in every sense of the word. You have to see it to believe it.*'"

Heather almost choked on her own glass of water. "I didn't mean you should come."

"But that's what you said." Mrs. Weaver picked the sprig of mint from her glass, looked at it with disgust and tossed it to the side. "Why is there a weed in my drink?"

Heather rolled her eyes and Ash decided it wasn't worth saying anything. He sat back to watch the familial exchange with interest.

"I also said I was fine, Mom. And I am. You shouldn't have come here."

"Then why would you tell me to?"

"I didn't." Heather dropped her head to the table and Ash jumped in.

"Well, now you are here, Mrs. Weaver, and we're certainly very glad to have you."

The woman turned to him for the first time with a look of interest. "And who are you?"

"My name is Ash." He extended his hand again, but she still didn't take it, so he dropped it. But he wasn't deterred. "I help out around here."

"You mean you work here?"

"No. Let's just say that I like to help out wherever I can." It would be impossible to try to explain his presence and there would likely be little to no benefit, so he didn't bother. "And right now, I'd like to help you out, Mrs. Weaver. Where did you travel from today? It's never easy to get to Bocas. I'm sure it was a long day, and you could do with something to eat." He gave her his most charming smile, and sure enough, it worked.

She pressed her lips together as if she might protest, but then said, "Thank you, Ash. You're right. It has been a long day to get here. Something I don't think my daughter appreciates. I would love a snack and maybe a chance to freshen up."

"Of course, Mrs. Weaver."

"Oh, and don't be silly. Call me Val."

He was positive if he could see her face, Heather would be rolling her eyes when he winked and said, "As you wish, *Val.* Why don't I show you to a room?"

"Oh, she's not staying." Heather jumped up from her chair and put her hands on her hips. "She needs to get on the next boat back to town and—"

"Heather!"

"You're being ridiculous." Ash smoothly stepped between

mother and daughter. "It's already late in the day. And we don't have any guests right now anyway. Why don't I get her set up in *de la paz* bungalow and then we can talk?"

She set her jaw, but she nodded. It was as good as he was going to get to consent, so before they could get into it again, Ash took Val's bags and led her out the back door through the garden and into the nicest bungalow they had. Not that Val seemed suitably impressed. At least not on the outside. But Ash got the distinct impression that her primness was mostly an act, and likely the woman was just overwhelmed with the situation she found herself in. And who wouldn't be? Bocas Town was a lot for a well-seasoned traveler to handle, let alone a woman who, Ash could tell by the age and condition of her luggage, probably hadn't done much traveling at all, and definitely not anywhere out of the continental United States.

He took his time showing her how to use the facilities and made sure she'd sat in the rocking chair so she could fully experience the stunning beauty she was surrounded by before he took his leave. By the time he'd left Val, she was smiling and she seemed much more at ease. *Clearly neither mother nor daughter were immune to his charms.*

Just thinking about Heather made Ash want to rush back to her. They had a lot to talk about, not the least of which was the conversation they'd started before they'd been interrupted. He *really* wanted to get back to that because he had a feeling it was going in exactly the direction he wanted it to. But he also knew it was probably going to have to wait. And when he walked into *grande casa* and saw Heather sitting at the swinging table, a glass of what looked almost like whiskey in front of her, he knew for sure it would have to wait. She obviously had bigger things on her mind.

He'd waited long enough to tell her how he was feeling. Hell, he'd waited long enough to *figure* out how he was feeling. He could wait a bit longer.

"I can't talk about it."

Heather heard him come in and she knew exactly what he was going to say. Ash would want to know why she was acting so crazy with her mother. He'd want to talk about it and the very last thing she wanted to do was that. *Why was she there? What could she have possibly said that would have made her mother get on a plane and leave the country for the first time in twenty years to travel to Panama, of all places?*

"You don't have to talk." Ash slid into the seat across the table from her and took the glass of whiskey away. "But you also don't have to drink this. It's not going to help anything."

"I know."

"Do you even drink whiskey?"

She shrugged. "Seemed like a good time to start."

He chuckled. "Trust me, it's not." He took a sip.

She raised an eyebrow but didn't say anything. He was probably right. Getting drunk wasn't going to make the situation any better. Her mother would still be there. In her paradise. Only she'd be drunk. No, it definitely wouldn't help the situation.

"Why would your mother drive you to drink anyway?" he questioned. "She seems like a nice enough lady. A little straight, but nice."

"I told you I don't want to talk about it."

"No." He raised his glass again. "You said you *can't* talk about it. But I don't believe that. I think you can. And more than that, I think you *want* to."

Heather shook her head and looked down at the tabletop. She couldn't talk about it because her relationship with her mother was complicated. It wasn't always that way, but that was before. Before Heather had decided to marry Joe and leave. Everything had been fine between them until then.

Only because you did what she wanted.

"If you're not going to let me drink whiskey, I at least need a glass of wine."

Ash smiled. "Deal." He got up to pour her a glass.

Heather took the moment to collect her thoughts and figure out the best way to try to explain the situation to him in a way that didn't sound ridiculous.

She couldn't come up with anything.

"Here you go." He put the glass in front of her. "Better?"

She took a sip before she answered. "Much." She took another sip and licked her lips. "It's not that I don't love my mother."

"Of course." Ash returned to his seat across from her.

"It's just that she doesn't get me." She shook her head because it sounded so adolescent. "And I don't mean that the way it just came out. I mean, ever since my dad died when I was a kid, she's been crazy protective. She wouldn't let me do anything. And I mean *anything.* She would have put me in a bubble if she could have gotten away with it. I know she was just trying to protect me. She was so terrified that something bad would happen to me if I left."

"Left the country?"

"Left the country. The state. Hell, even if I left home." Heather shook her head, remembering the stifling environment she'd grown up in. "It made me crazy. The older I got, the more I felt trapped. I did everything I could to try to get away. I mean, I loved her and everything, but I needed to get out and live, right?"

"Of course."

"I applied at schools out of state after high school; I even got accepted to a few. But when the time came to send in tuition, she claimed the money was gone. The house needed a new roof. The car died. Whatever. I couldn't go."

"That's terrible."

That was an understatement. It was the first time that Heather had really understood how deeply disturbed her mother was. It was also the first time that she realized that if she didn't do something drastic, she'd get sucked down right along with her.

And then she met Joe.

"So I got married."

"Married?" Ash almost spat out his whiskey. "That seems drastic."

"It was. But I needed to get out. I was drowning in my mother's worry for me. I couldn't live like that anymore." She couldn't. It would have killed her or destroyed her relationship with her mom. In hindsight, it did destroy her relationship with her mom. She never wanted that to happen. She'd been hoping to prevent that. But mostly she hadn't been thinking about anything but getting away. Maybe if she had, she would have put more thought into her choice of husband. But then again, everything happened for a reason, and she wouldn't be sitting where she was if it wasn't for that choice. "I agree—it wasn't the best reason to get married. But I liked Joe."

"You *liked* him?"

She shrugged. At the time, she thought she'd loved him, but looking back, it was clear to see she'd loved the idea of what he represented, which mostly was getting away.

"Okay. You've already told me about your ex." Ash leaned across the table. "But what does this have to do with your mom and you? I take it she didn't like you leaving?"

Heather shook her head. "Not even a little." She took another sip of wine and then another. "She said terrible things —about Joe mostly. But also to me. I know she didn't mean them. Well, she meant the things about Joe." She laughed. "But I know she was just hurt that I was leaving her. At least, I know that now. I didn't talk to her for a few years and then I felt guilty. Especially when it became clear that she'd been right about Joe and me."

"You couldn't fix things?"

"The only thing that would have made her happy was if I went home. But by then I'd had a taste of life on the outside." She used air quotes. "There was no way I was going back. Things with us have never been the same since. We mostly only communicate by email because that way I don't have to hear the disappointment in her voice—I just have to read between the lines."

"I think she's trying to fix things, Heather."

She stared at him, openmouthed. "What on earth would make you think that?"

He took his time answering, but when he finally spoke, his words pierced her heart. "Because she's here."

Chapter Fourteen

THE NEXT MORNING dawned bright and beautiful, the way they always did. Seeing the sun and feeling the heat on her face energized Heather. And she needed the energy after a restless night. It was as if her mother had invaded her thoughts and her dreams.

Thank goodness for Ash being at Casa del Sol, because even if he was right about her mother wanting to fix things between them, the idea of trying to bridge that gap was overwhelming for Heather. Besides that, her mother didn't indicate in any way that that might be the reason she was in Panama. She'd spent the evening complaining about how long the fight was, how muggy the air was, how hot the sun was, how *crazy* Bocas Town was, and how just in general, everything since she'd left home was terrible. Heather had to bite her tongue multiple times to keep from asking why she bothered to come if things were so awful.

But she didn't.

Because if Ash was right and underneath all the complaining and the tough exterior, her mother was trying to be vulnerable and open herself up to mending fences, she didn't want to slam the door before it was opened. Despite everything that had happened with her mom over the years and even the years before she'd left when Heather had felt trapped and smothered, she still loved her. And she was the only family Heather had.

She may not agree with her parenting style, but she didn't have to. She was her mom. Underneath it all, Heather was just a little girl who knew her mother loved her and wanted the best for her. That's why she'd made the choices she'd made.

Right or wrong.

Regardless, it would be way easier to try to bridge any gap if her mother had a better attitude. She'd suffered through the rest of the evening without saying anything she'd regret and when finally she suggested to her mom that they get a good night's sleep and regroup in the morning, Heather almost cried with joy when her mom agreed.

After guiding her mom back to her bungalow, she'd been hoping to have a chance to talk with Ash and maybe even finish what they'd started before her mother's interruption. It seemed like a million years ago that she'd been stranded in the mangroves. It had only been a few hours, but it might as well have been a lifetime ago because with her mother's arrival, Heather was taken right back to those same feelings of when she'd been a teenager, trapped in her mom's grip.

Only this time it was different because she'd had a taste of freedom. More than a taste…she'd had a life.

And it may not have been the life she'd dreamt of, but it was a start and she was finally ready for more.

And that's exactly what she was going to tell Ash.

Except when she returned, he was gone. It was probably for the best. It had been a long day and the conversation she wanted to have with him deserved a fresh start.

Which was exactly what she was hoping for that morning when she made her way down to *grande casa*. Camila was already there, cooking up something that smelled delicious. The coffee was on, and the sun was shining. It was the perfect day in paradise, and hope and happiness swelled inside her.

Heather took her coffee out to the dock and had just sat in one of the deck chairs when she heard the creak of the wooden boards behind her.

So much for a moment of solitude.

"Good morning, Heather."

"Mom. You're up early." Her mother was dressed surprisingly casual in khaki shorts, a light pink blouse untucked, and a gigantic straw hat that was almost comical in size. She stood and gestured to the chair next to her. "Do you want some coffee?"

To Heather's surprise, her mom nodded agreeably and sat next to her. Heather called to Camila and through a series of hand gestures, conveyed the message that she needed another cup.

"Did you sleep okay?" she asked as she sat back down.

"I did, thank you."

They were being exceedingly polite with each other but at least no one was upset. Still, it couldn't go on forever. When Camila brought out another mug of coffee and a tray of fresh papaya with a wedge of lime to squeeze over the fruit, they were given a reprieve from the small talk.

"This is delicious." Juices ran down her mom's chin as she spoke and picked up more fruit.

Heather nodded and took her own piece. "Everything tastes better in the tropics. Sweeter. Juicier. It makes it hard to believe that it's the same fruit we get back home in the grocery store."

Her mom paused and stared at her. "Do you still consider Idaho home?" There was hope in her question, and for a moment, Heather considered lying to her. But after a second, she shook her head.

"No. Not really."

"Heather." The disapproval was back in her mom's face, her lips pressed into a hard line. "You know you always have a home there. You didn't have to run away. And you certainly didn't have to stay away. You made the wrong choice with Joe," she continued. "But you don't have to stay away to prove a point. You don't have to be stubborn, you know."

She opened her mouth to reply, but closed it again.

She wasn't going to do it. She wasn't going to get dragged into her mother's trap. The trap that she'd never be able to get out of. Not this time. Heather stared out to the horizon and didn't respond.

"You don't have to like my choices, Mom. I'm okay with that."

Her mother cleared her throat and continued as if she hadn't heard her speak. "Now that Joe's out of the picture, why don't you come home with me?"

"Mom, I—"

"Even for a little bit. Just so you can—"

"Mom. I'm—"

"Don't say no. Just think—"

"Good morning, ladies."

Heather jumped up from her chair at the sound of Ash's voice saving her from what was quickly becoming a no-win situation. "Ash. Hi." She wanted to ask him where he'd disappeared to the night before. She wanted to kiss him and thank him for showing up at that exact moment. She wanted to do a lot of things. But just like when she was a child, her mother's presence held her back. She stopped a few feet away from him and tucked her hands in her back pocket. "Did you have a good night?"

He gave her a curious look but smiled. "I did." He turned his charm to her mother. "And Val, I trust you enjoyed your first night in paradise?"

Heather rolled her eyes when her mom giggled like a little girl. "I did. The bed was surprisingly comfortable and the water…"

"The sound of the waves is pretty soothing, isn't it?"

"It really is."

"You can see why Heather likes it here so much."

Just as quickly as the smile appeared on her mother's face, it was gone. "I don't see that," she said. "In fact, now that I'm here, I can see even more that Heather should come home where it's safe. This place is…it's savage. Do you know what I saw in that town?"

Heather actually had a pretty good idea of what she'd seen. Bocas Town wasn't for the faint of heart and it certainly wasn't any kind of place her mother should have been.

"There were drugs," her mom continued. "And half-naked people and—"

"I'm sure I know what you saw, Mom."

Her mother hopped out of her chair and glared at her as if she were twelve again. "You knew what I would see there and you still suggested I come here?"

Whoa. No. She hadn't.…she had. She had said the words, but she didn't mean them. Not really.

"I said you had to see *this* place to believe it, Mom. I didn't say anything about Bocas. And I certainly didn't mean that you should actually get on a plane and come here."

"Then why did you say it?"

"It was something to say." She could feel the anger and frustration rise inside her. She was starting to yell. She didn't want to yell, but she didn't know what else to do. If she didn't yell, she might just end up in tears and that would only give her mother more fuel. "I didn't want you to come."

The words landed as if Heather had reached out and slapped her across the face. She took a stumbling step backward.

Instinctively, Heather stepped forward, wanting to reach out, but her mother's next words stopped her. "You've always been so hateful toward me."

"What?"

"You have," she insisted. "All I've ever done is try to protect you and love you and—"

"Smother me." All the emotions bubbled up inside her. She couldn't have stopped herself if she'd tried. "You tried to trap me, Mom. You kept me from living. Sometimes I think it would have been easier to have just died, like Dad did."

She realized an instant too late that she'd gone too far but she couldn't find the words to fix what had just come out of her mouth.

It was Ash who spoke. She'd forgotten he was standing there until he felt his arm on hers. "Heather, Sherri needs to speak with you. Go up and visit with her, please. I'm going to take your mom on a little boat ride."

Heather only half heard what he said. She stared at her mother, who suddenly looked frail and small, standing on the dock with her huge hat flopping over her face.

"Heather?"

She turned blindly to Ash. When his face came into focus, she nodded.

"Can you do that for me? Go see Sherri?"

She nodded again.

"Go," he whispered. "I've got this."

She looked at her mom one more time. Regret filled her but she still couldn't find the words. So she turned and walked away.

———

Ash certainly didn't have any idea what he was going to do with Val or what exactly he was going to show her, but he needed to do something because watching a mother and daughter relationship self-destruct in front of his eyes was not an option.

It already may have been too late, but he needed to do something. He cared too much about Heather to sit back and let her ruin something that could still possibly be fixed. If there was even the slightest hint that it could be saved, he was going to try.

Even if it meant sending Heather up the hill before he'd had a chance to tell her the truth about Sherri. It wasn't an ideal situation, and Heather was going to be mad.

Oh yeah, she was going to be mad all right. But she'd forgive him. She'd understand.

She had to.

"Val?" He crossed the distance between them and reached out to touch her. She jumped back as if he'd startled her. "Are you okay?"

She didn't answer right away, but after a moment, she nodded.

"Why don't we spend a little time together today? I thought it might be nice to show you the island a bit, and then maybe you can see the beautiful side of Bocas, because it is so beautiful."

She nodded again. "I'd like that."

He gave her his most charming smile and led her back into *grande casa*. Before they went anywhere, they were going to have some of Camila's delicious frittata. Because Ash was pretty sure that what he was about to undertake was going to require stamina.

Camila fed them a delicious breakfast, and even packed a small basket of snacks when Ash explained what was going on. She may have moved on with Luis—a fact that Ash was glad for—but she still clearly had a soft spot for him. He gave her a kiss on the cheek, grabbed a cooler of water and led Val back down the dock to the boat.

"I don't much care for these little boats, Ash." Val stopped short at the end of the dock, clearly not very excited to get in.

He hopped down, tucked the basket and cooler away and held his hand out for Val. "I know you didn't look all that comfortable when you came over yesterday, but my boat is much better and we'll take it slow. If you hate it, we can come back. I promise."

She nodded and took his hand. "You do have a smooth way about you, young man. I can see why my daughter likes you."

He grinned. "You can, can you? And what makes you think she likes me at all?"

Beyond the fact that it got Val talking about her daughter in a positive way, it was a totally self-serving question. When it came to Heather—especially when it came to Heather liking him—he was all ears.

"When it comes to men, she really doesn't have much experience at all." Val sat on the cushion Ash had provided for her. She was facing him at the back of the boat. It was okay for the moment, but as soon as they started moving, he wanted her to turn around so she could see everything. "Her husband took advantage of that, you know?"

"Did he?"

"He did." Val pursed her lips together. "She was young and naive. So innocent." She shook her head, clearly remembering a younger, more innocent Heather. "He just wanted a young, pretty girl to be his companion when he moved to a destitute third world country. He got that with her."

"I'm sure that's not all there was to it."

"Oh yes. That was it. He used her."

Ash wasn't going to pretend to know all the details about Heather's marriage, but he was pretty certain there was more to it than that. She must have loved the man at some point if she was willing to move to Panama with him.

"But she was a grown woman who made a choice." Ash turned and started up the engine while they were chatting. "I mean, it's not like she was kidnapped."

"She might as well have been. Ash, she was just a baby when she left. She didn't know the first thing about the world. And he was her first boyfriend. I mean, I knew it would turn out the way it did. I should have tried harder to keep her safe. To keep her at home."

He patted the older woman's hand. "I'm sure you did the best you could, Val." He soothed her, because it was clear that it was the only thing to be done. "Whatever happened between Heather and her husband had nothing to do with you." She nodded, letting herself be comforted by him. "If it's okay with you," he changed the subject, "I'd love to show you a few things. Do you like beaches?"

She smiled. "It's been a long time since I've had my feet in the sand. I think I would like that very much."

"Perfect, because we have some of the most beautiful beaches in Panama, right here. Let's go."

"Sherri?" Heather knocked on the door, lightly at first and then stronger. She wasn't sure why she was hesitating. But something about the treehouse seemed very quiet and not quite right somehow. She hadn't given it much thought as she'd climbed the stairs leading her away from the bungalows and her mother. All she could focus on was getting away from that woman.

She drove her crazy.

Her mother must be fully out of her mind if she'd gotten on a plane and traveled for almost eighteen hours just to fight with her. *It was mind-boggling. She was crazy. She was controlling and delusional and...*

She was hers.

Heather shook her head. Ash was probably right. If she'd traveled all that way, there was only one reason for it. She wanted to make amends. She wanted to fix things. After all, they were the only family the other had.

She should be more understanding. It was just so hard.

With a sigh, Heather knocked on Sherri's door again. When there was still no answer, she tried the handle. She didn't know what to expect when she walked into the treehouse, and Ash certainly hadn't prepared her for anything. "Sherri? Are you here?"

"In here, dear." The voice came from across the room. It was dim, with the shutters closed up. The air was stale and... something wasn't right.

Heather stepped farther into the room and was finally able to make out what looked like a pile of blankets in the corner. The pile moved. "Heather. It's so good to see you. Come closer."

Something was not right. She crossed the room and dropped to her knees next to Sherri. "Are you sick? What's wrong?" She scanned the older woman as best she could with the pile of blankets heaped over her. "What's going on, Sherri?"

"He didn't tell you." It wasn't a question and there was a hint of laughter in the woman's voice.

"Who? Ash?" She shook her head. "No. He didn't tell me anything." Heather replayed all the conversations about Sherri they'd had. Ash told her nothing was wrong. He told her if there was a problem, he'd let her know. He'd *promised* her. "What's going on?"

Sherri clucked her tongue and shook her head. "I asked him not to tell you, so don't be mad."

Too late. She was absolutely going to have words with Ash when she got down the hill. He'd flat-out lied to her. But one thing at a time. "Sherri?" She reached under the blankets and grabbed her friend's hand. It was thin and boney and cold. Very cold.

"I'm sick, dear. I asked him not to tell you because I didn't want you to worry."

"I'm worried now."

"I can see that." She attempted a smile, but it didn't have Sherri's usual sparkle. "And that's what I didn't want. You had enough to worry about. After all, you were just getting your feet wet with Casa del Sol. Ash tells me you're doing an amazing job, by the way."

"Thank you. I—" Heather shook her head and refocused. "That's not important right now."

"On the contrary. It is very important. That's why I brought you here, Heather. I needed someone with heart and soul. Someone who would care about this place as much as I did. Someone I could trust to keep the spirit of the place alive."

"Why are you talking that way?"

"You are that person. You're perfect for this place and I think it's been perfect for you, too."

"Sherri, I—"

"Am I wrong?"

Heather shook her head again. "It's not that you're—"

"Am I wrong?"

She couldn't help but smile at the woman's persistence. "No," she said. "You're not wrong. I love it here and you're right. It's been just as good for me to be here."

Sherri nodded and closed her eyes. "I knew it would be. I knew it." She didn't say anything else, and she didn't open her eyes for a few moments. Just long enough that Heather started to get a little worried. She waited and was just about to give her a little shake when Sherri's eyes popped open again.

"I have cancer."

She stated it so simply and without preamble that it took Heather a moment to process the words.

"Cancer?"

"Yes. I didn't want to trouble you."

"With your cancer?"

That may have been the craziest thing she'd ever heard. *How on earth could she think she would be troubling Heather by being sick?* It was ludicrous.

"Exactly. I'm not going to go through this again. I've been through it a million times with Ash, and I think he finally understands now."

Would have been nice if he'd shared some of that information.

"What can I do to help?"

"Nothing."

That answer was not going to fly. Heather shook her head. "Sherri, I want to help."

"You are helping," she said. "You're taking care of Casa del Sol. That's helping."

"No." Heather paced the room. "It's not enough. I need to know what I can do. There must be something. Medicine, meals." She scanned the room. "Heck, I can do your laundry and get you fresh blankets."

"Heather." Sherri waited until she'd stopped pacing. "Sit. Please." She did as she was told and only then did Sherri start talking again. "I'm sick," she said. "Very sick. I don't know—"

"No." Heather shook her head. "Don't talk that way."

"At my age, when you've been through the things I've been through, you've earned the right to talk however you want."

Heather couldn't help but smile at her stern tone. She did have a point. "Sorry."

The older woman waved away her apology. "I didn't ask to speak to you because I'm sick."

No, of course not. Although it would have been nice if someone had given her the heads-up on Sherri's condition. Someone like Ash. *Why wouldn't he tell the truth about Sherri?* She should have known. *What if Sherri had needed something and she was the only one around? What if Sherri had needed something during the storm?* Hell, Heather hadn't even known they had cell phones and were talking to each other. There was a lot Heather didn't know, apparently, and if Sherri didn't look so sick and frail, she'd be angry at her, too. As it was, Heather's frustration was completely focused on Ash. They were definitely going to have words when she got back down there. For the moment, she focused on Sherri and whatever it was she needed to tell her.

"Did you want to talk to me about the business? I've been checking the reservations and responding to everyone," she said. "But I think we can do it a little more efficiently by listing Casa del Sol on a few websites like Airbnb. Have you heard of that one? It's amazing and so easy to use. Of course, we'd have to pay the site a percentage, but I think it will be worth it because of the exposure we'll get there." She got excited when she started talking about some of the ideas she had for Casa del Sol, and she started rattling off her other thoughts as well. "Right now we never seem to have full occupancy, and I'd like to try to change that going forward. We have rooms mostly for couples. And I think that's great, especially for people on honeymoons or anniversary trips. But you have that big shed off to the far side, and there's really nothing in it right now except some old boards."

"It was going to be an artist studio."

"Is that right?" Heather had never thought of that but now that Sherri mentioned it, a studio would be perfect, and it might even fit in with some of her expansion plans down the road. "I think that's perfect," she said. "But I bet we could find a better spot. Maybe even a little farther away from the bustle of the main buildings. Besides, I had a different idea for that building."

Sherri tilted her head, looking more amused than anything else.

"What if we used that building as more of a group bunk room? Kind of a hostel style of accommodation? That way we could appeal to singles, and small groups of friends as well, and could increase the numbers."

"I like it."

Heather couldn't help but beam at the approval. "I would need to help out Camila or maybe she could work a few more hours to help with cooking for a larger group. And of course, I'd need to sort out a more permanent solution for picking up guests from town."

"What about Ash?"

What about Ash? The truth was that she'd love it if Ash would help her with guests indefinitely. She wasn't going to pretend that it wouldn't be a lot of fun to carry on the way they had, both of them working together to run the B&B. But she couldn't ask that of him. Especially when she hadn't even had a chance to tell him how she felt about him. And after she did have that chance? He'd told her he would never let himself have a relationship again and even if yesterday, she was determined to tell him that she refused to accept that, she couldn't be sure how he would respond. She also couldn't make assumptions about him. Maybe it was the night of sleep to think things over, maybe it was her mother being there, maybe it was finding out how sick Sherri was. Whatever it was, Heather was definitely second-guessing things.

Yesterday, she might have told Sherri all that in search of some sage advice, but things were different now. She didn't need to burden the woman with her concerns and there was no way she was going to give her any cause for worry about her B&B. No way. As far as Sherri needed to know, Casa del Sol was in good hands with her, and Heather was perfectly capable of running it. All on her own if she needed to.

"I'm sure Ash can help out," she said, forcing a lightness into her voice. "But I don't want to assume that of him. I know it's not a job for him."

"It doesn't need to be a *job*, child. Ash loves Casa del Sol. But you're right."

"I am?"

Sherri nodded. "It's important not to tie Ash down. I just finished telling him that he needed to go."

"To *go*?" She tried not to sound panicked, but she couldn't help it. *Why the hell would Sherri be telling Ash to go away?* "Where would he go?"

"Toward his life, my dear." She said it so naturally, as if Heather should have known exactly what she was talking about. The confusion must have shown on her face and Sherri continued. "I'm not sure how much to say, but from the time he came to me four years ago, Ash hasn't been living. He's been on hold."

"On hold?" It made sense. A little bit anyway.

"He told you about his past."

Heather nodded.

"I'm glad he did. He's starting to open up again. I could see it from that very first night when you arrived on my dock. You bring him to life."

"So why would you tell him to go? I don't understand."

Sherri smiled and took Heather's hand. It looked as if the action drained her energy. "I don't know how to express this properly. I'm sorry if it's not making much sense." The corners of her eyes crinkled with a smile. "I'm afraid I confused Ash with my ramblings, too. Don't worry about a thing, child. You just keep doing what you've been doing and be true to your heart. But I get the feeling I don't need to tell you that."

"Oh no?"

Sherri squeezed her hand. "I see the change in you, too. You're finally living with your heart. If you keep doing that, you'll be okay."

Heather felt tears prick at the backs of her eyelids. "I feel like you're trying to say good-bye, Sherri. And I can't let you do that."

The older woman's laugh startled her. "Don't be so morbid," she said when she was able to get herself under control. "I'm sick. I'm not dying. It'll take a lot more than a little bit of cancer to take me out."

It was a relief to hear it, especially with the vehemence with which it was delivered. "You know what?" Heather laughed and shook her head. "I absolutely believe that. And I'm very glad to hear it. But why is it you wanted to talk to me? Why now? Was it because of my mother?"

Sherri looked surprised. "Your mother? No, but I think that's a story I might like to hear."

"No."

"Some other day."

Heather was thankful that Sherri knew when not to push her. She was a wise woman.

"I asked to see you because I wanted a chance to impart some of my wisdom on you. When you get to be my age, it's one of the few joys in life. Giving advice that may not be wanted."

Heather laughed again. "Oh, it's always appreciated, Sherri. Thank you."

She smiled and clucked her tongue. "You're a sweet girl. I also wanted you to know how much I love Ash. He's like a son to me." Heather nodded. She knew that. "He's afraid to love you, and I can see the same fear in you."

"Sherri, I—"

"No. This isn't up for debate. I just wanted to tell you that as much as I love Ash, I love you, too."

It was sweet and totally unexpected. "You don't know me like you know Ash."

"I don't need to. I love you both and my wish for both of you is to find it within yourselves to explore your greatest love. Does that make sense?"

"Not even a little bit."

"It will."

"I can't imagine how."

"I'm not getting involved any further than I already have. And I fear I've already gotten a little too involved. I don't like to meddle."

Heather's mind was spinning, trying to keep up. "I'm not sure I understand."

That was an understatement. Heather was absolutely certain she didn't understand. Sherri wasn't making any sense at all.

"Oh my dear. You will." She patted Heather's hand and smiled. "Now, how about a cup of tea?"

Heather spent another hour with Sherri, but they didn't talk anymore about her and Ash, a fact she was thankful for because she had no idea what she might say. It was hard to think that it had been less than twenty-four hours ago that she'd been so sure about her feelings both for her future self and for Ash and now there just seemed to be more questions than there were answers.

"I wish you would have told me you were sick, Sherri." They sat on the porch, in the shade of the trees, looking out toward the ocean below. Heather had fixed them both a cup of tea and had settled the other woman into her chair, with a blanket tucked around her legs despite the warm temperatures. "I don't like that you're up here all on your own. You should be down at *grande casa*, surrounded by people."

"Do you really think people like to be reminded of their own mortality when they're on vacation, child? My cancer would have been bad for business. Very bad." Sherri sipped at her tea. "And I don't want to be any bother. Besides, I like it up here. It's my special place up here in the trees."

Heather couldn't even begin to understand, but she also knew enough about Sherri to know that it wasn't her place to understand anything.

"I am glad you know now," Sherri said. "But not because I want you to worry. I would hate it if you spent even one second of your energy on that type of negativity. Your energy should be focused on love and all things good."

"I'm not twelve."

Sherri laughed. "No, child. You're not. But you're a young woman with your life ahead of you and that's reason enough to focus on the positive. Besides, nothing good ever came from dwelling in the dark, has it?"

Heather couldn't disagree with that.

"Besides, it sounds like I'll soon have an entire team of people to do the worrying for me," Sherri told her. "Ash talked me into letting him help me, whatever that means. I assume he already has plans in motion and my relative peace and quiet will be coming to an end soon enough. So I should enjoy it while I can. Has he started assembling his army yet?"

Army? Heather tried not to look confused. *Was she supposed to know about all of this, too?* Ash hadn't mentioned anything. Not that there had been any time. "Not that I know of." She tried to sound reassuring. "But if he told you he would be, I'm sure he's busy working on it now." It wasn't a total lie. If he was done with her mother, and he likely was—no one could last that long with the woman without going totally batty—then he was probably sorting out whatever arrangements he'd promised Sherri. "In fact, maybe I should go see if he needs any help."

She wasn't looking forward to seeing her mom, but she also knew it couldn't be put off forever. Especially considering they had new guests arriving the next morning. For better or worse, Heather needed to figure out what to do with her mother and with any luck, she'd be able to find a moment or two to be alone with Ash. The more time that passed without her saying anything about her feelings was just going to make it harder. Besides, even if she didn't understand it all, there was a good chance that Sherri was onto something when she'd been talking about love and light and life and whatever else she'd been saying. And one thing Heather knew for sure was that it was long past time that she said something. Not one more night would go by before she told Ash exactly what she felt. No matter what the results were.

"Well, what do you think? Is it the nicest beach you've ever seen?"

Ash promised Val the beach he was taking her to would be nicer than any beach she'd ever seen in her whole life. Once he discovered that she'd never been to a beach, he knew it would be an easy promise to keep.

"It's pretty nice."

"Pretty nice? It's amazing."

She looked up at him, and even from under the giant brim of her flopping hat, he could make out her smile. "It is. Thank you, Ash. I've never seen anything like this before."

The sand was fine, almost like icing sugar, and as they walked, Ash found a few beautiful seashells he'd picked out and handed to her. She held them all in her cupped hand as they walked.

"I don't believe you that you've never been to a beach before, Val. A real beach."

She stopped walking and dug her toes into the sand. "When we were first married, Heather's father and I went to the West Coast, but Seattle doesn't really have beaches. Well, not like this, anyway."

He shook his head. "No, they don't."

She was looking a little wilted in the hot sun, so he directed her gently to the shade of some palm trees at the edge of the sand where she could still enjoy the beach, but also get out of the sun for a bit. They sat on a low growing palm that made a perfect bench and Ash handed her a bottle of water. "Did you travel more with your husband after that trip?"

Her mouth pinched into a frown and for a minute Ash thought she might stop talking altogether.

"No," she said after a moment. "He died."

He knew that from what Heather had said, but he could see Val might open up a little. Maybe she *needed* to open up. "I'm so sorry to hear that."

"It was a long time ago." She shrugged, but he could see it still bothered her.

"Can I ask you, what happened?"

"Heather didn't tell you?"

Ash shook his head.

"I'm surprised." He waited. "I'm sure she told you I was a terrible mother."

"She didn't say that."

"Now I know you're lying." Val chuckled but there was no mirth in it. "I'm afraid I wasn't the mother Heather needed. But I did the best I could and I kept her safe. That was all I needed to do. Keep her safe."

"That's very important," he agreed. "I'd say you did that well."

"I couldn't keep Harold safe."

Ash wasn't sure he'd heard correctly. "Pardon?"

"I couldn't keep Harold safe," she repeated. "My husband. It was my only job as a wife and mother, to keep my family safe. And I failed."

He lifted the bottle of water to his lips, suddenly parched from the heat—or the familiar words being used in a totally different context. "I'm sure his death wasn't your fault. Sometimes terrible things happen." The irony of him using the exact same words that had been used on him for years wasn't lost on him, but Ash didn't focus on it.

"You're not telling me anything I haven't heard before," she said. "Everyone means well when they try to make you feel better, but they don't know." Val shook her head. "But the truth is, they just don't understand. I doubt you would either."

"Try me," he said. "I think you'd be surprised."

Val took her time, drank some water and deliberately put the cap back on the bottle before she spoke again. "It was his dream to see the world," she said. "He wanted to travel. Idaho was never big enough for him. Heather was just like him." Her lips turned up in a small smile, but then it was gone again. "I didn't share his wanderlust, but I loved him and I wanted him to be happy, so I agreed to a trip. Heather was only five. I thought she was too young to leave her with friends, but Harold insisted she was old enough and he wanted to celebrate our anniversary at one of those resorts in Mexico. You know the kind…drinks and food and…"

"An all-inclusive resort?"

She nodded. "Right. That."

"But you said you'd never been to a beach like this before."

"And it's true. You see, I didn't like the idea. But he talked me into it. He took care of everything. He booked the flights, took time off work, even had his mother come into town to babysit for us. But I just wasn't okay with it. I worried about leaving Heather. I couldn't sleep. I obsessed. I had nightmares that something terrible was going to happen and when it came time to go, I couldn't."

"You couldn't go?"

"You think I'm crazy, right?"

He kind of did, but he didn't say anything. Not yet. "What happened?"

"We didn't go. Harold was very calm about it. He didn't yell at me, or get mad. He got his money back. We lost a bit of the deposit, and I knew he was upset about that. Heck, he was probably upset with me about the whole thing. But he never said so. Ultimately he told me that if I wasn't comfortable with it, we'd celebrate at home and go on a trip another time. He knew how I worried about him and Heather. He loved me and wanted me to be happy."

"That's sweet."

Val shook her head. "No. It's not. Two days later, he was killed."

Ash was not expecting that. He tried to hide the shock on his face, but obviously didn't do a very good job. "But that can't possibly be your fault. An accident is terrible, but not in any way your fault."

Val nodded sadly and dug her toes into the sand. "Don't you see? If I hadn't have insisted we stay, he wouldn't have been on the highway that day, going to work. There was a car with a flat tire and he stopped to help. The truck driver didn't see them until it was too late. If we'd been in Mexico, he would have been safe."

Ash shook his head. "No. That doesn't make sense."

"I knew you wouldn't understand." Val stood and walked down toward the water again.

Ash packed up the cooler and quickly caught up with her again. "But that doesn't explain why you didn't want Heather to travel. It was staying home that killed your husband. Not that I think that had anything to do with it," he quickly added. "But like you said, if he'd been in Mexico with you, he wouldn't have been involved with the accident. So why are you so against traveling? Heather said you wouldn't let her go anywhere."

"It is my job as a wife and mother to keep them safe. If I could keep her close, I could protect her."

"You can't really believe that."

Val stopped walking and turned to Ash with such sadness on her face. He hardly knew the woman, but his heart ached for her and everything she'd lost in her life. "I don't," she said simply. "But I didn't know what else to do. I couldn't lose her, too." She dropped her head and Ash knew without looking closely that the woman was crying. "But all I did was push her away."

He couldn't disagree. He gave her a few minutes to cry her silent tears and then he took her by the arm and gave it a squeeze. "But there's a difference." She looked into his face, waiting for the advice he should have already taken himself. "Heather's not gone."

Chapter Fifteen

"SHE'S NOT BACK YET." Ash walked out of the kitchen where Camila was cooking up a grilled lobster salad for lunch. Alone. She hadn't seen Heather since she'd headed up the hill to Sherri's. "She should be back soon. Why don't you grab a book and relax in one of the hammocks for a while? I need to do a bit of research on the computer. Will you be okay for a bit?"

"Ash, I'm not an invalid. I'll be fine." She yawned. "Besides, I could use a nap and that hammock outside of my bungalow looked pretty inviting. Would you believe I've never been in a hammock either?"

He laughed. "As a matter of fact, I would. But today is the day to have your first hammock. So get to it."

She smiled and Ash couldn't help but think how much mother and daughter actually looked alike. Especially when they were happy. Maybe Casa del Sol could work its magic on Val, too. And hopefully the two of them could find their way back to each other.

As soon as Val grabbed a book from the shelf in the corner, and the mojito Ash made her, and headed back to her bungalow, Ash got to work at the computer. He was already behind in his research for helping Sherri and although it couldn't be helped, he wasn't going to miss another minute. Sheri's health was a priority and he knew as soon as Heather came back down, she was going to think so, too.

She was also going to be upset.

But maybe not as upset as she could be. Sure, he should have told her. But Sherri had asked him not to. And yes, he should have ignored that. But now that he had an actual plan to help, Heather would like that.

Oh yes. He could justify it in all kinds of ways. But it didn't matter; he was going to do as he said he would.

Without much to go on, Ash typed a few things into the Google search bar and filtered through the results. It surprised him how much he could find on natural treatments for cancer. Of course, there was just as much negative as positive, but that wasn't his job. He'd promised Sherri they would do it her way. And they would. At least for now.

It didn't take him long to find the contact information for nutritionists, cancer specialists, and even a man who specialized in healing through the mind with yoga and meditation. He composed a number of emails and made a list of phone numbers. He'd have to wait and call them when he got to town. The cell service could be sketchy at best so far from town and he didn't want to risk dropping such important phone calls. The emails were a good start, but what he really wanted was to talk to a few people personally and ideally secure them as staff.

He'd been hoping to avoid a trip into town, at least until he could line it up with a guest pickup for Heather. But the more he got into it, the more it looked as though he would need to go into town soon. Very soon. If he wanted to make things happen for Sherri, and line up a staff, let alone supplies and anything else she was going to need to fight and win her battle, he needed to get moving on it now.

Especially because everything he was thinking about doing was going to require money. Not that he didn't have a lot of it. He did. But it wasn't easy to access. Not in a place like Bocas Town. He kept a small supply of cash at the local bank but for what he wanted to do, he would probably have to make a trip to Panama City to unlock some major funds. He'd wait as long as possible to do that. And if there was a workaround, he'd take it.

When his list was made, he was just about to log off the computer when he decided to check his email on the off chance that he received a response already. To his shock, he did. And it was the one he wanted, too. Dr. Friesen, out of Arizona, who specialized in a holistic approach to cancer. Ash had been impressed with his website. *Very* impressed. Enough so that when he'd written the email, he'd mentioned that he would go to any means to have the doctor come to Panama as soon as possible. If he was the best, and he certainly looked to be, Ash wanted him on the team. As soon as possible.

Eagerly, he clicked open the email.

Mr. Anderson,

I'm sorry to hear about your friend, Sherri. She sounds like a lovely lady and from what you've described, she is an excellent candidate for my program. I don't do house calls very often, and I've never before been a 'doctor in residence,' as you put it. Sherri's type of leukemia is highly treatable; however, I am intrigued by her philosophy on treating herself. I would be happy to speak to you further and entertain the idea of visiting Sherri to see how I could possibly be of help in her situation. I am currently preparing to go on a small research trip and will be gone for the next few weeks. As I sensed some level of urgency in your correspondence, I thought I would offer the opportunity to talk to you as soon as possible and potentially shift my travel plans to include a visit to Panama to discuss the best course of action and further potential treatment plans.

If this is of interest to you, I would invite you to call me as soon as possible at the below listed number. If I do not hear from you within the next twelve hours, I will unfortunately be unable to accommodate your request.

Sincerely, Dr. Mike Friesen

"Sure sounds to me like he'd be willing to make a house call," Ash said aloud. "Everything is doable for a price." It was a lesson he'd learned years ago and although he hadn't had much use for money in Bocas, at least not the type of money he was used to dealing with, it was obviously a principle that stayed true.

Dr. Friesen was the guy he needed. No, he was the doctor Sherri *needed*. He needed to call right away. He'd change the man's entire travel plans if he needed to. Anything to get him to Panama and on Team Sherri as soon as humanly possible.

He pulled his cell phone out of his pocket and powered it on. From the moment Ash decided to leave his old life behind, ditching his old cell phone and the constant need to be in touch with the world had been one of his favorite things about leaving it all behind. His new phone existed mostly out of necessity to have a *home base*. Somewhere for his parents to reach him if there was an emergency, and of course for phone calls like the one he was about to make.

Ash plugged the phone in—it was almost never charged—and dialed the number.

No service.

"Dammit."

That was largely the problem with cell phones in Panama. He tried a different plug, closer to the water where maybe there was better reception.

Nothing.

There was no help for it. He'd have to go into town.

But Heather wasn't back yet. He didn't want to leave before Heather got back from Sherri's. He hadn't had a moment to talk to her about anything important. About Sherri, about them. *Them.* He shook his head. He didn't have time to think about how much had changed or how much more he still wanted it to change. There'd be time for that later.

He ran into the kitchen; Camila was still there.

"You haven't seen Heather yet, have you?" It was a stupid question, because he was sure she hadn't. Just as he thought, Camila shook her head. Ash glanced out the window toward the path that led to Sherri's. He could run up the stairs and find her. But there was no time. He needed to make the call.

"Dammit."

There was no help for it. He had to go. "Can you give her a message for me?"

"*Que?*"

"A message. Can you give Heather a message for me?"

Camila nodded, but didn't look at him. She pulled a cake out of the oven with a whistle. It was an impressive cake, and Ash told her so before returning to the task at hand. "You can give Heather a message for me? *Si?*"

"*Si.*"

The girl wasn't paying any attention to him and Ash probably would have thought it was funny given how into him she'd been a few months ago.

"*Muy bueno, si?*" She pointed at her cake, and Ash nodded again. "It is for my Luis. *Bueno?*"

He tried not to laugh. She was baking the cake for her boyfriend. No wonder she wasn't paying any attention to him. She was in love. "*Si,* Camila. Please just tell Heather I had to go to town—it's important. I'll bring her guests back with me. Okay?"

"*Si. Si.*"

Ash shook his head and left the kitchen. It was a simple

message. Heather would get it. He didn't have time to wait any longer. He needed to get there and make the call that could save Sherri's life. Heather would understand. Besides, he'd be back in the morning. With her guests. It was a win-win.

Without giving it anymore thought, he grabbed his cell phone and ran down the dock, hopped into the boat and took off toward town.

By the time Heather got down to *grande casa*, she was more than ready to see Ash. And give him crap for keeping Sherri's illness a secret from her for so long. But she wasn't mad. Not really. Mostly she was just looking forward to seeing him. Hopefully he'd been able to work his charm on her mother.

Her mother.

That wasn't something she was looking forward to dealing with. But talking to Sherri had also helped Heather realize something else. Life was short. Her mother may aggravate her, but she was the only mother Heather had. She was the only *family* she had. And Ash was right; there was obviously a reason for her traveling all the way to Panama and it wasn't likely to give her a hard time.

That was probably just an added benefit because didn't all mothers like to give their children a hard time?

Regardless. She could take it and she would. Because no matter what the reason was behind it, her mother was *there*. In Panama. And that was something.

"Hello?" She called into the empty room. After nearly all her time at Casa del Sol filled with guests and people all around, it was always so strange when it was empty and quiet. Considering she'd expected both Ash and her mother to be waiting for her, it felt especially quiet when she walked in and no one was there.

There was, however, a delicious smell coming out of the kitchen, so Heather followed her nose in there and found Camila icing a beautiful cake.

"Wow."

The woman turned and beamed. "*Bueno, sí?*"

"*Muy bueno.*" Heather agreed. "*Por que*...a cake?" She couldn't find the word she was looking for, so she settled on the English.

"For Luis. His birthday."

"Ah." Heather smiled. She didn't mind if the girl used the kitchen for some personal baking and she knew Sherri wouldn't have cared either. Especially if it was a birthday cake for her boyfriend. The girl was in love and it was nice to see. "Have you seen Ash? Or my mom?"

Camila nodded and went back to putting the finishing touches on her cake.

"Where are they?"

"Ash is gone?"

Heather spun to see her mother in the doorway behind her. She looked rumpled, rested and sun-kissed and totally unlike herself. She looked good. "You're back."

"Of course I'm back." Her mom straightened and attempted to smooth her blouse. "I've been back for hours. Ash fixed me a very nice drink and I've been in my hammock ever since. It was pure bliss."

She tried not to grin. "I can tell. What was in the drink?"

"I beg your pardon?"

It was the wrong thing to say. Her mother instantly got her back up. She should have known better than to try to joke with her. Especially with how they'd left things the last time they were in the same room together.

"That's not what I was trying to say, Mom," Heather tried again. "I was just thinking how relaxed you looked and I know if Ash fixed you a drink, well, it might have been a bit strong.

He has a habit of not measuring. Did you enjoy the hammock?"

Her mom looked as if she was going to say something harsh again, but instead she swallowed hard and nodded. "I did." A small smile started at the corners of her lips. "Did you know I'd never been on one before?"

"No way?"

"It's true." She paused to pet the dog, who stood at her side. "And it could have been tricky, too. But this guy helped me out. I kind of used him so I didn't swing off and into the water."

Heather's hand flew to her mouth in an effort to contain a giggle. "Thor stopped you from swinging into the water?"

"He did." She nodded quite seriously. "He stood there like a little wall. I thumped into him quite hard, too. But he didn't move." She patted Thor again. "You're a good dog, aren't you?" The dog turned his face up and licked her mother's hand, eating up the attention.

Heather couldn't help but laugh aloud. "He is a good dog." Maybe her time with Ash had done her some good? Or maybe it was the nap? Either way, they were both in better moods and Heather was going to take advantage of it. She was tired of fighting. "Are you hungry, Mom? I'm sure there's something to eat. We could find Ash and have a little late lunch."

"I am famished. Ash said something about a lobster salad before I went to lie down. Where is he?"

"I was going to ask you that same question."

Her mother's mouth dropped open. "Are you implying that I had a young man in my bungalow with me?"

"Oh, Mom! No. I would—" She stopped because her mother was laughing. Hard.

What was going on? Her mother was like a completely different person. She couldn't remember her mom ever goofing around with her like that before. Ash must have gotten through to her. She'd have to thank him later.

"Okay, okay. Are you done?"

Her mother nodded.

"Good. And you don't know where Ash is?"

Her mother shook her head, still obviously trying not to laugh. *Maybe her mother was drunk?* Maybe Ash had made her a *really* strong drink? She narrowed her eyes at her, and turned back to Camila, who was now pushing fresh blossoms into the icing on the cake. "Did Ash tell you where he was going?"

She shook her head but then quickly said, "*Si.*"

"He did?"

The girl turned, a worried look on her beautiful features. "He left."

Left? "Where did he go?"

"To town."

She was going to lose her patience if Camila didn't come out with exactly what he'd said. "Anything else?"

She nodded.

"What?" She tried not to sound frustrated, but she was pretty sure she failed. "What else did he say? Is he coming back?"

"Something important." Camila looked as though she was going to cry. "I'm so sorry, señorita. I didn't hear. I was…the cake…Luis…*lo sent mucho.*"

Heather closed her eyes and took a breath. It didn't matter. Except that she wanted to see him. But that wasn't a reason to get upset at Camila.

"Okay," she said after a moment. "So he went to town. Was he going to pick up the new guests?"

"New guests?"

Heather turned to her mother. "Yes. That's what we do here. We have guests."

"But you don't have any now."

"We have you."

Her mother's mouth opened and closed silently. Heather looked at Camila. "Do you know?"

The girl shook her head and Heather tried not to sigh. "Okay. I'll have to go get them tomorrow."

But she didn't have a boat. Ash would have taken the boat. How could he have left without telling her? Especially with guests coming.

Okay. Calm down, Heather. You can solve this, too. You're strong and capable and you don't need Ash to help you out with this stuff. Hadn't she just told Sherri that she wasn't going to be able to rely on Ash for her expansion plans? This was a good test of that. She wracked her brain and landed on a fantastic alternative. "Camila? Does Luis have a boat?"

The girl nodded with a smile. "*Sí*, señorita."

"Would he take us into town tomorrow?"

"Us?"

"Yes, us." She looked at her mom. "You don't want to come?" Secretly, Heather might have been hoping to find her mother a new place to stay, but she didn't say that out loud. Besides, there was room at Casa del Sol. She could stay.

"I have no interest in returning to that town," her mother said. "Besides, this place is much nicer and I've only started to discover it."

She wasn't sure about leaving her mother there on her own, but after a quick discussion with Camila and the girl's assurance that her mother could in fact stay with her and she'd show her how to cook some of the local dishes, the matter was settled and mother and daughter took their salads in hand and headed out to the covered deck to eat them.

Ash made it to town in record time. He tied up the boat and set off to find Mick at the Bitter End before making his call. The older man was exactly where Ash knew he'd be: behind the bar. He handed Ash a beer the moment he sat down.

"It's been awhile," Mick said. "You're keeping pretty busy out at Casa del Sol, huh? Or maybe I should say—"

"You probably shouldn't say anything." Ash laughed and took a swig of his beer. "Not if you and I want to stay friends, that is."

"Fair enough. You staying for a bit or just passing through?"

He'd thought about it on the boat ride over. He had two options. He could make his phone call, turn right around and go back to Casa del Sol where he wanted to spend the night. Or, he could make his phone call, and about a dozen others on his list, load up on some supplies, secure some finances, pick up Heather's new guests and spend the night at the Bitter End. He knew which one of the options he really wanted to do.

He also knew which one was the responsible one.

"I'll be here overnight," he told Mick. "Can I get a private room?"

"Private?" Mick wiggled his eyebrows. There'd been only one reason he'd wanted a private room in the past, and that was because he was planning to entertain a woman. Even then, he didn't always bother with it. After all, at a place like the Bitter End, there wasn't much in the way of privacy anyway. But that was the old Ash. That was the Ash before he'd met Heather. The Ash who was still running away from everything. The new Ash was different. And he wanted a private room for a very different reason.

Privacy.

"Definitely private." He wasn't about to encourage Mick's behavior. He may be an old friend, one of his only friends, but he also didn't feel like getting into a big conversation about everything. Not right then anyway. He had more important things to worry about first. "Do you have any?"

The man nodded. "Just so happens, I do." He turned and reached under a counter before producing a key. "You can have room five. I know it's your favorite. Right at the top of the stairs." Mick winked. "Easy access."

Ash tried not to shake his head. There would be no convincing Mick his reasons for a private room were pure. At least not right then. "Thanks, man." He took the key. "You spoil me."

Mick slid another beer across the counter. "I try."

"Thanks." Ash gathered up the key and the beer and slid off the stool. "I'll be back. I have some things to take care of before it gets too late."

Mick nodded, unconcerned with Ash's coming and goings. It wasn't anything he wasn't used to. Ever since coming to Bocas Town, Ash had been pretty transient. At one point, he had a little apartment in one of the buildings on one of the side streets, but it became more trouble than it was worth. Besides, it was too far from the main action of Bocas, where all the drinking, partying, and women were. It was just easier to live out of a backpack and the small locker he had in Mick's backroom, where he kept some clean T-shirts and shorts. He stopped at that locker before heading upstairs and cleared it out of clean clothes. The T-shirts were virtually untouched. He couldn't remember when he'd last worn one. But he'd have to when it came time to pick up members of Sherri's team. And they'd arrive, too. He knew it. His plan would work.

He made the first phone call as soon as he got up to room five. With his notebook in hand, Ash dialed the number Dr. Friesen had emailed him and waited. The phone rang three times before it finally picked up.

"Dr. Friesen?"

"You must be Ash Anderson. I've been expecting your call."

The two men exchanged pleasantries for a few minutes before Ash couldn't wait any longer. "You said in your email that you didn't make house calls, but you'd consider an exception."

"I did," the doctor said. "And I don't. But your argument was compelling."

Ash shook his head. "You mean, I have money."

"If you can pay for the service, I don't see why I shouldn't offer it." Ash had been in business too long to argue with that. "Besides, I'm intrigued by your friend's approach. You say she's fought cancer and won before?"

"She has. But perhaps she didn't win since it appears to be back."

"No one ever really wins the war, Ash. But you can win the battle. That's what I'm hoping to help you with."

"It can be done?" He wanted the answer to be yes. More than anything, Ash needed to save Sherri. He hadn't been able to save Carlie, but he *would* save Sherri. "Naturally, I mean? She won't use drugs. Well, she has some." He listed off the chemo drugs Sherri had procured for herself. "But she feels strongly about doing it without hospital intervention."

"Those are strong drugs. Combined with my natural treatments, she should have a chance. But I agree with you, it can't be done alone."

"And you'll come?"

There was silence on the other end of the line and for a moment, Ash was worried they'd been disconnected. Finally, Dr. Friesen spoke. "I will. I was supposed to travel to New York later today, but—"

"I'll send you the ticket. You should be able to get on the next flight to Panama City."

Dr. Friesen chuckled. "Persistent, aren't you?"

"She's important to me."

"I was going to say just that."

"It shouldn't be—wait. What?"

The other man laughed. "I'll come. Send the details to my email address and I'll get on the next flight."

Ash was silent for a moment in an effort to process exactly what was happening. "You will? I mean, you understand you're coming to the jungle? It's paradise, but…you understand it's not a hospital."

"I understand that. It's exactly the reason I'm interested. It's not a popular opinion in the medical community, but illness should be treated in a place of peace and tranquility. I'm very interested to meet your friend and learn about her philosophies. But you do have access to a clinic for supplies? I'll need you to prepare a few things."

Ash nodded and then said, "Of course." He flipped a page in his notebook and started taking notes as the doctor dictated a list of items he'd need to get. By the time he got off the phone, Ash was once again excited about the opportunity to help Sherri. Dr. Friesen was going to be just what they needed. He was sure of it. They'd decided together to wait until his arrival to decide on the rest of the team. But they had agreed they would need a team.

His next call was to the airline. It didn't take him long to organize a first-class ticket to Panama City, followed by a private plane to Bocas Town. There were two airlines that flew in, but they were notoriously hard to get seats on. Especially on short notice. Ash wasn't even going to take a chance. It was first class all the way. He needed Dr. Friesen at Casa del Sol as soon as possible. But it looked as though he'd have to settle for three days from now, which wasn't so bad. Everything was falling into place.

The last thing Heather wanted to do was jinx anything. But her afternoon with her mother had been surprisingly enjoyable. Maybe that was a stretch, but it hadn't been hard. It had been a long time since they'd been able to sit side by side and not have it end in a yelling match or tears. And even better, her mother hadn't mentioned anything about her coming home.

Her mother had spent the last few minutes telling her about the beach Ash had taken her to and how soft the sand was between her toes. She didn't bother telling her mom that she'd been to that beach and knew exactly what the sand felt like. She just sat back, sipped her drink and enjoyed the easy conversation between them. It was nice to hear her mom excited about something. Especially if that something didn't have anything to do with her or how she should move back where it was nice and *safe*.

Letting her guard down a little, Heather leaned back in the chair and stretched her arms overhead. With the heat of the afternoon gone, they'd moved their chairs out into the sun to soak up a few of the warm rays. It felt nice on her skin and warmed her from the outside in. "This has been nice, Mom."

"Nice?"

She turned and opened one eye. "Yes. This. You and me. It's been nice to hear about your day."

Her mother thought about it for a moment and finally smiled. "It has been nice." She looked out toward the ocean. "That Ash, he's sure something."

Not that she had any way to know, but her mother had just uttered the biggest understatement of the year. Ash was *definitely* something. Something she couldn't even begin to explain. But maybe that was the beauty of it. Maybe she didn't need to explain Ash or what was going on between them or any of it. Maybe she could just enjoy it and for the first time in her life, understand what love really felt like.

Heather was so lost in her thoughts about Ash, she didn't

realize her mother was staring at her, waiting for an answer to a question she hadn't heard. "Sorry," she mumbled. "What did you say?"

Her mother rolled her eyes. "I asked if it was serious."

"If what was serious?"

"Don't play coy, Heather. You're not good at it."

"No. Seriously. What's serious?"

Her mother straightened up in her chair and looked at Heather pointedly. "You and Ash. Are the two of you serious?"

Oh. Of course her mother would have gone there right away. She tried to think. They hadn't kissed or held hands in front of her. Or even looked at each other in any type of way that could be viewed as anything other than friends. *Had they?*

"Don't try to figure it out," her mother said, reading her mind. "I can just see these things, is all. Besides, you two don't hide it very well. You might as well have just told me."

Heather was so confused and she didn't bother trying to hide it. "What do you mean? We didn't advertise anything. We've been very discreet since you've—"

"So you admit it?"

Heather smacked her palm to her head. "I guess I do." She looked at her mom. "Okay. Yes. Ash and I are…well…I guess we're seeing each other."

Her mother clucked her tongue. "I already knew that. Is it serious? He's a nice young man. Very charming."

She didn't answer right away. It was hard to know whether her mother was setting her up for a trap, or whether she genuinely wanted to know about Heather and Ash. History would tell Heather that it was a trap, and she would use the information for her own benefit. Whatever that could be. But, that history was from a long time ago. Maybe things changed. Maybe her mom had changed.

She hoped so.

"I don't know," Heather finally answered honestly. "I was kind of hoping to have a minute to sort that out myself."

"I hope I'm not the reason you haven't had a chance to sort that out." *Could it be that her mother was actually being reasonable and understanding?* "I mean, you clearly had plenty of time to define your relationship before I showed up." *Nope.* Heather would have laughed at the irony, but her mother kept talking. "I don't think it's a good idea."

"Wait. What's not a good idea? You just finished telling me what a nice young man he is. And how charming he was."

"He is."

Heather sat up in her chair and stared at her mother. "What are you talking about then?"

"You just got out of a marriage, Heather. It's never a good idea to jump into anything when a marriage ends."

She opened her mouth, but the words just wouldn't come out. Which, as it turned out, was fine considering her mother wasn't done providing her unsolicited opinion.

"When a marriage ends, it's like a death, Heather."

As if she's suddenly an expert.

"You need time to grieve the end of the relationship. You need time to figure out who you are and what you really want out of life. You need at least a year."

"A year?" She managed to sputter out the words. "I need a *year?* One whole year to sort myself out and figure out who I am before I can enter into any type of relationship. That's the magic number?"

Her mom issued a long-suffering sigh. "It's not a precise number, Heather. Only a guideline. I think it typically takes about a year for a person to go through the process. But it's not fair to enter into a relationship before you're ready."

She sat back and shook her head. "I'm ready, Mom. I'm more than ready." Just saying the words aloud made her realize it in a way she never had before. She sat up again. "You know what? I've been ready for a long time. Long before my marriage with Joe officially ended. I'm not even mad at him for the way things went down because it was the out I needed."

"An out?"

"Yes, Mom. I've been unhappy for a long time. I just didn't know how to go about ending it. I guess I should thank Joe for having an affair and forcing the situation." *No. Maybe not.* "Okay, I won't thank him. But you get the point."

Her mother was silent for a few minutes. Finally, her voice was sad when she spoke. "I didn't realize you were so unhappy, Heather."

"Of course you didn't." She looked at her lap. "I never told you. I never told anyone, Mom. It wasn't something I talked about. And I knew if I said something, you'd just tell me to come home. You'd tell me how you always knew he was no good for me. And I didn't want to hear that."

"I wouldn't have—" Heather's pointed look cut her off. "Okay, I would have said that."

They both sat back in their chairs. The sun was starting to set, creating a vibrant palette of reds, oranges, and pinks streaking across the sky.

"Heather, do you know why I'm here?"

The question was so unexpected that she wasn't entirely sure she'd heard it correctly. Slowly, Heather turned to her mom. "No," she said after a moment. "I don't."

"Do you think it was easy for me to come here?"

She shook her head. "I know it wasn't."

"And I don't just mean the travel."

"I know, Mom."

"Do you know why I never wanted you to leave home, Heather?"

"To protect me."

Her mother nodded. They'd had the conversation before.

Many times. Or at least, some variation of it. Her mother was silent again for a few minutes. "I both failed and succeeded."

"What do you mean?"

"It's a hard thing for a mother, Heather. Maybe one day you'll understand." Her mom wouldn't look at her while she spoke, and Heather didn't force it. "After your dad died, I didn't want anything as much as I wanted you to stay safe. And with me. I don't think I ever told you that part before." Heather shook her head, but her mom didn't notice. "I wasn't only afraid of something happening to you; I was afraid of losing you."

"Mom, you would never—"

"But that's exactly what happened." She continued as if Heather hadn't said anything. "I lost you because I loved you too much. But you know what? You're safe. So I guess I did okay."

Heather reached over her chair and grabbed her mom's hand. A tear dropped from her eye. "Mom. You did great." She meant the words as she spoke and she realized she'd never before told her mother that before. "And you didn't lose me. I'm here. And you're right, I'm safe."

"That's all I ever wanted." There were tears in her mother's eyes when she turned. The light was starting to dim, but Heather could see them clearly. "And for you to be happy. It breaks my heart that you were unhappy all those years and you didn't say anything because you thought I wouldn't understand."

"I just couldn't go back. Not because I didn't love you," she added quickly. "But I needed to get out and see things. Experience some of the world. And I couldn't do that if I went home to you. At least I didn't think so. Does that make sense?"

Her mother chuckled and shook her head. "No. But it doesn't have to." She squeezed Heather's hand. "I'm glad I came."

"Me too, Mom. Me too."

Not all of their problems were going to be solved in one night. But they were off to a great start and that was more than Heather ever expected. They held hands and caught up on the last few years as the sun set below the horizon and the solar-powered lights on the dock flickered to life. And only when the first star appeared in the sky did they go inside and continue their conversation over dinner.

Chapter Sixteen

ASH HAD a cart full of groceries, bottled water, and other items he knew Heather would need at Casa del Sol and was headed back down the Main Street toward the Bitter End when Miguel caught up with him.

"*Hola,* Señor Ash!"

"Hey, buddy." He ruffled the kid's hair out of reflex. "It's been awhile." Ash felt bad that he hadn't been back in town much. And when he was back, it was usually for a pretty quick trip, without much time to find Miguel and get him to help out. He knew the kid was probably missing the extra pocket money he earned from Ash.

"*Sí.* It's late, señor." Miguel pointed to the full cart.

"It is." The sun was starting to get low in the sky and Ash still had to head to the clinic to stock up. If he got most of his supplies before retiring, he might be able to sleep in a little bit before picking up Heather's guests. They were scheduled to come in on the early flight, but a few extra minutes of sleep were always welcomed. His plan had been to find Sara over at the clinic once he was done with the groceries, because the clinic stayed open later than the store. His procrastination had nothing to do with the fact that he wasn't looking forward to seeing Sara again. Or…maybe it did. "I'm not going back tonight, Miguel. I'll head out in the morning. This stuff is going to Mick's tonight." The kid's eyes grew wide. "Would you take it for me?"

Of course, Miguel nodded eagerly. He'd never turn down the chance to earn a bit of money, which worked out well for Ash because if Miguel could take over the cart, he could head straight to the clinic and get it over with. Sara was going to be upset with him. He knew that. Hell, the woman had been upset with him from the moment he turned her down for a second date. Only she got a little madder every time she saw him. The situation might require a bit of finesse.

Yes. Putting it off wouldn't help. He should just get it over with.

"Great," he said to the kid. "You take this back for me and up to room five. Mick will let you in. Lock the door behind you and wait at the bar. Tell Mick the soda is on me."

Miguel's eyes lit up and he didn't have to be asked twice. He took the cart from Ash and happily skipped down the road, eager to claim his treat.

Ash laughed and pulled the T-shirt out of his back pocket where he'd tucked it. It got a little chilly in town when the sun went down. But more than that, he should probably cover up before seeing Sara. Not that it was going to help her be any less upset with him.

It only took him a few minutes to get to the clinic. He braced himself and headed through the front door. He waved at the familiar faces behind the desk and made his way into the back with familiarity. She stood at a small desk he knew acted as a nurse's station, filling out some type of form. She truly was an attractive woman and sweet, too. Maybe in another life they could have been good together. But she wasn't Heather.

And that's what it came down to. Ash hadn't been interested in seeing *any* woman beyond one date. Not until Heather. It wasn't Sara's fault. But it probably wouldn't be a good idea to tell her that. In fact, instead it might be a good idea to smooth things over a little bit.

He almost chickened out completely and left. It might be easier to secure supplies in Panama City and no doubt there'd be a better selection. But at that moment, Sara turned and saw him.

Her face reacted at once with a bright smile, but it faded quickly as her lips turned down into a frown. "Ash?"

He gave her his most charming smile and walked forward with his arms out. She let him hug her and he gave her a quick kiss on the cheek. "Sara, you look great. It's been awhile."

"Quite awhile." She tilted her head and narrowed her eyes. "Are you okay?"

"I'm fine. You're looking good."

"You said that." Sara stepped back and crossed her arms over her chest. The action had the desirable effect of stretching her scrubs tight. Not that he noticed. At least not the way he would have a few months earlier. *Things really had changed.*

"Only because I meant it," Ash said smoothly. He needed to stop letting her get to him and just focus on the end goal: getting supplies for Sherri. "I was hoping you could help me out again." He fished the list of supplies Dr. Friesen had dictated to him out of his pocket. "I need a few things for Sh— for Casa del Sol." He corrected himself quickly. It probably wasn't a good idea to make it public knowledge that Sherri was sick. At least not yet. He wasn't stupid. Once Dr. Friesen showed up, and the rest of the team started to arrive, Ash wouldn't be able to keep Sherri's illness a secret for very long. Besides that, he didn't think he should. But it wasn't for him to tell. Not yet.

Sara grabbed the list and scanned it quickly before she gave him a strange look. "What's all this for, Ash?"

"Just a few things Sherri wants to have on hand."

"On hand? She wants IV bags of saline on hand? In this quantity?" She shook her head. "I already gave her a ton of saline, never mind the narcotics she ordered from Panama City last time you were here. What are you guys doing out there? You're not starting your own medical clinic, are you?"

He laughed and hoped it sounded more natural than it felt. "Of course not." *Time to turn on the charm.* He took a step closer to her, reached out and tucked a stray hair behind her ear. She closed her eyes and blushed, just the way she always did. "Why would I do that when you have such a great thing going here?"

Ash felt bad flirting with Sara just to get his way, but it was for Sherri. He needed to keep remembering that. And ultimately, he wasn't hurting anyone. *Was he?*

"I suppose I could get you a few things," she said. "I mean, it's not too much and…"

"Of course I'll pay for them."

"Of course." She eyed him strangely. "And maybe we'll get that dinner after all."

There was no way out of it. If he said no, there was no way Sara would help him. And it would be totally innocent. It was for the greater good, after all. "Maybe not dinner," he said. "But I'm staying in town tonight, so what if we grabbed a drink at the Bitter End?"

As far as he was concerned, it seemed like a good compromise, and it was the best he could do. As expected, Sara smiled and nodded. "Sounds good. I'm off in a few hours. I'll meet you there?"

He flashed her another killer grin. "Looking forward to it. Now, about that list…"

"Are you sure you don't want to come with me, Mom?"

It was the third time Heather had asked her whether she wanted to make the trip into town, and although she didn't expect the answer to be different, she was kind of hoping it would be. She'd really enjoyed their chat the night before. For the first time in as long as she could remember, maybe ever, they hadn't fought. Not only that, they'd laughed. It would be good to continue the trend. But just as she had the last two times she'd asked, her mother shook her head firmly.

"I'm quite happy to stay here and learn some cooking techniques from Camila. Besides, I didn't like that town the first time I saw it. What makes you think it's improved any in the last few days?"

Heather had to laugh because she completely agreed with her mother's assessment of Bocas Town. "Okay, you can stay here. I won't be too long. I need to grab a few things at the store and then I'll bring our new guests back. You make sure you're on your best behavior when they get here, okay?"

Her mother looked affronted. "And why wouldn't I be?"

"Just…just don't treat me like your daughter, okay?"

That made her mother smile. "It'll be fine. You are sure you have enough room, though, right?"

They'd already been through it and Heather went over the guest bookings, even showing her mother in order to prove that they did indeed have the room. At least for a little bit, but her mother couldn't stay indefinitely anyway. It wouldn't be good for either of them if she did. "Don't worry, Mom. You're good. At least for a week, maybe two."

Heather grabbed her bag and slung it over her shoulder. "I should get going soon. Can you be sure to grab Ash if he comes back?"

If he comes back. It sounded so strange to say it out loud. Of course he would come back. She shouldn't even be thinking otherwise. Of course, she never would have expected him to leave without letting her know or leaving a note or anything at all except a broken message from Camila. She'd thought about calling him on the cell phone she'd recently discovered he had, but of course she had no clue what the number was. Short of walking back up to the treehouse and asking Sherri, she had no way to get it either. And she didn't need Sherri worrying, or worse, thinking she was a crazy obsessed woman. Ash was a grown man and he didn't report to her. Hell, they hadn't even defined their relationship. Not that it would make a difference, but maybe it would make her feel as if she should have some right to know his comings and goings.

She was getting ahead of herself, though. She needed to focus on one thing at a time. And right now, it was getting to town by herself for the first time, picking up her guests, and making sure their vacation started on the best note possible. Which meant she couldn't be late.

"Okay," she said. "I'm all set."

Her mother walked her down to the dock, where Luis waited with his boat. Her mom even untied the bow line for her once she got settled. Heather tried not to worry, or think about Ash while they drove slowly away from the dock. She had to focus on Casa del Sol. Now, more than ever, Sherri needed her to do a good job and she wasn't going to let her down. There'd be time enough to figure things out with Ash later. Because even if he'd pulled a disappearing act, Heather couldn't imagine her feelings doing the same.

In hindsight, having drinks with Sara was a bad idea. Not that Ash felt he had any other choice at the time. But what he was hoping would be a simple drink, maybe two, before he excused himself had turned into a round of shots, followed by another, followed by the music being turned up and the whole bar dancing all night. He hadn't drunk so much in years. Not since he'd first come to Bocas del Toro. But it felt like a celebration that Dr. Friesen was on his way to Panama, even if no one else knew what he was celebrating, and then it just became easier to deal with Sara the more he'd had to drink.

He'd managed to avoid any dances with Sara, at least for the most part. Things got a little fuzzy at one point in the evening, but that was when Ash had the wherewithal to know it was time to retire.

He had a vague memory of stumbling up the stairs to room five before flopping onto the bed and passing out. He woke up at one point in the night to use the bathroom and chug a bottle of water before he climbed back into bed next to Heather's sleeping form. Ash had a fleeting thought that it couldn't be Heather sleeping next to him as he faded back into sleep, but then his eyes closed and he fell back into the deep, hard sleep of the intoxicated.

It wasn't until the sun shone through the blinds and hit him on the face that Ash's eyes fluttered open again. He groaned and held his head. There was a reason he didn't drink like that anymore, and the morning after was a large part of that reason. He rolled over to stretch and stared directly at the bare back of a sleeping woman.

A woman?

Shit!

The memory of the night before when he'd woken to go to the bathroom flooded back. He'd crawled back into the small bed with Heather. At least that's what his tired, drunken brain told him. But it wasn't Heather. No. Of course it wasn't. Because Heather was back at Casa del Sol.

Shit. Sara. It had to be Sara. But he wouldn't...no. Of course not. He'd never.

He'd been pretty drunk, but not *that* drunk. He would never do anything like that. Not when Heather was...well, just because of Heather. He wouldn't. But he needed to get out of there.

Ash tried to slip backward out of the bed without waking Sara, but no sooner did he have one foot on the floor then she stirred and rolled over. "Good morning, handsome."

"Hey." He reached down and grabbed for his shorts, slipping them on quickly. *Why exactly was he naked?* "Why are you… what are you…we didn't…"

Sara sat up, only partly holding onto the sheet that wasn't doing a very good job covering her naked breasts. "You don't remember last night?"

"Of course I do." He didn't and they both knew it. "It's just that so much happened and then…"

"You were pretty out of it."

"Sara. Tell me nothing happened."

Her grin was wicked. "I can tell you anything you want."

Ash shook his head and ran a hand through his hair before trying again. "Nothing happened between us."

"Are you telling me or asking me?"

"Dammit, Sara." He paced across the room and grabbed a T-shirt from his pile. "You're not helping."

"That's not what you said last night."

He shot her a look. "You were very helpful with the supplies," he said after a moment. "Thank you. Now put this on. You have to leave."

Ash tossed the T-shirt at her but she let it fall on her lap. She crossed her arms and the sheet slipped farther. "I don't think this is a very nice way to treat me after I—"

"After you helped me? Yes. That was great. Thank you. But nothing happened between us. Right?"

She didn't answer right away and the frenzy within him started to build. *He would not betray Heather. He wouldn't.* It didn't matter that they weren't official. As far as Ash was concerned, they were and he was not going to destroy that. Not with Sara. Not with anyone.

"Right?" he asked again.

This time she nodded. "Right." Sara grabbed the shirt and pulled it over her head. "Why are you so worked up about it? I honestly didn't expect that this was how the morning would go. Not at all." She flipped her hair over her shoulder and stuck her bottom lip out. "You don't have to play so hard to get, you know?"

"I'm not playing. I'm kind of seeing someone."

"You're seeing someone?" Sara stepped from the bed and stretched her arms overhead, causing the shirt to slide up dangerously short. Ash looked away, not even tempted. "That's fresh."

He shook his head; he didn't have time to engage in this. Although he did feel bad if she'd somehow gotten the wrong idea, he couldn't spend his entire morning trying to make her understand that it was all a misunderstanding. He had to pick up the new guests and get the boat loaded and get back. To Heather.

Chapter Seventeen

"*GRACIAS, LUIS.*" He helped her out of the boat and handed up her bag. "I won't be long. I just need to get a few things and I can meet you at the Bitter End."

"*Sí,* señorita." The young man nodded and smiled, the smile that was almost always on his face these days. It must be love. Both he and Camila had the same smile. It made Heather happy inside. It also made her wonder. Did she have that same smile? Ash certainly made her happy. In so many ways.

She could do without him taking off with her boat unannounced, though.

Speaking of her boat…as if she'd conjured it, there it was. Tied up at the far end of the dock was, in fact, her boat. Which meant Ash was in Bocas Town. Not that there were many other places for him to go. Her curiosity flared again but it would have to wait. She had business to attend to.

Heather picked her way down the broken dock before she glanced at her watch. She was earlier than expected. Luis had made good time in his boat that had a larger engine than her own. She hadn't expected to be there so quickly, but it worked out well because she'd have time to say hi to Mick and maybe he'd have some coffee on. She hadn't been back to see him except for one other time after that first day she'd arrived in Bocas. It was past time for a visit. The fact that he might know where Ash was only played partly in her decision.

Just as she'd expected, the front door was open. Security was pretty much nonexistent in Bocas Town. A fact she was slowly getting used to. So early in the morning, the place was pretty quiet, and Heather started to make her way down the hall but she was stopped by voices.

Ash's voice.

She backtracked. The voices came from upstairs. A feeling of dread washed through her, making her fingers numb, but she couldn't turn back. Her mind instantly played through a million scenarios. Each of them worse than the next one. She put a foot on the stairs and froze.

You're being ridiculous, Heather.

She was. She was being stupid. If Ash was upstairs, it was probably because he'd gone into town for some reason, and it was too late to get back. Mick would have given him a room and that was probably it. Nothing more sinister than that. It was likely quite simple. Still, she needed to know. Besides, it's not as though she could ignore the fact that he was there. Especially not since he had her boat.

Having reasoned it to herself, Heather took the rest of the stairs two at a time and followed the voices to the room at the top of the stairs.

"Put some clothes on." It was Ash's voice.

"I think I like what I'm wearing just fine."

Heather's stomach dropped at the sound of a woman's voice. *No. No. He wouldn't.*

But he had said that he'd vowed never to have a relationship again. *Maybe that's what this was?* Maybe she'd just been naive thinking that she could change things for him.

No. She'd been naive.

"Ash…" The woman's voice was pleading and nauseating for Heather to listen to. And she wasn't about to stand there and listen to another word. But she was going to get her boat back. Anger rose up inside her and she flung the door open.

If there had been any doubt about what she thought she'd see when the door opened, it vanished. The door slammed against the wall and Ash spun around. The look on his face went from anger to shock to concern. All in a flash.

"Heather."

She opened her mouth, but no words came out, so she shook her head and bit her bottom lip. Hard.

"It's not what it looks like."

Heather laughed then because it was about the most cliché thing he could have said. The sound came out as a cross between a choke and a cough. He reached for her, but she shook her head, warning him off. She didn't think she'd be able to survive his touch. The betrayal was fresh and raw and… damn it hurt to see him standing in a bedroom, the bedsheets rumpled, with a beautiful half-naked woman next to him.

It hurt all right.

A lot.

She couldn't stand there for one more second. With the image burned in her mind, Heather turned and ran down the steps.

"Heather!"

He started to run after her, but Sara stopped him.

"I wouldn't do that."

He turned and stared at the woman. "What?"

"She obviously doesn't want to talk to you right now. She's mad."

"No shit."

"She won't hear anything you have to say right now. You should wait."

"Wait? Why the hell would I wait?"

He was done listening to her. He grabbed his things from the table and was ready to chase after her, when Sara said, "She had a reason to turn and run, Ash. What was it?"

"What are you talking about?"

Sara stood with her arms crossed over her chest, looking bitchier than Ash ever remembered her looking. *Was it possible she'd always been a bitch, and he'd just never seen it?*

"Women don't just run off like that without a reason. If you're *sort of seeing* her." She used her fingers for air quotes. "Don't you think she would have stuck around to hear what you had to say? Don't you think she would have believed you when you told her it wasn't what it looked like? Nice line, by the way. Very original."

Yes. Maybe she'd always been a bitch and Ash just hadn't seen it before. But she did have a point. *Why would Heather just take off without listening to his explanation?*

He knew exactly why.

Because he'd told her that he'd vowed never to have another relationship. And now he was demonstrating that.

"Dammit."

"No shit."

"I love her." The words surprised him because he hadn't even allowed himself to think the words yet. He knew he cared about her. A lot. He knew he wanted to try a relationship with her. He knew she was the first woman since Carlie to make him feel anything. He knew all of that. And now, he knew he loved her. A smile crossed his face despite the situation. Saying it out loud felt good. So good.

"Why do I get the feeling you've never told her that before?"

He'd forgotten she was still there. He stared at her, unable to think of anything worth saying.

Her sigh was long and loud. "Seriously. Why are you still here? Go tell *her*."

He shook his head and bit back the urge to scream before he took one more look at her and left her behind to find Heather.

She couldn't think clearly.

Ash.

A woman.

In a bedroom.

Together.

The image kept flashing through her head as if it was on neon lights and she couldn't turn it off. *Is that why he'd gone off without telling her? To meet up with a woman? And ruin everything they had together.*

No. They didn't have anything together. He told her. He'd warned her. He wouldn't let himself be in love again. But that didn't mean he could stop her from falling in love. And she had. *Oh, she had and now…*

"Heather?"

She heard her name as she pushed out the front door of the Bitter End and stood on the porch. But she didn't turn around. She stood on the steps and looked down the street. *What was she supposed to do? Where was she supposed to go?*

She couldn't think straight and she needed to pull it together. Fast.

"*Chica.*" Mick appeared behind her. "I thought that was— whoa. Are you okay?"

She started to nod but shook her head instead. "No. I'm not okay. I need to go. I need…" She turned to look at Mick and got an idea. "I need the key to the engine lock on my boat. Do you—"

"Ash left the keys behind the bar last night. Let me grab them for you."

She nodded. That would be good. If she could get the keys and get her boat back, that was a good first step. Ash didn't need to be with her. He didn't need to pretend anymore. That was fine. She didn't need him. She could get her guests and get them back to Casa del Sol without him. But he had no right to take her boat.

She paced on the street in front of the hostel, letting her thoughts clear. She was no closer to understanding anything when she heard her name again. This time it wasn't Mick's voice. She turned slowly to see Ash in the door, the keys to the engine lock in his hand.

"Mick told me you were looking for these." He took a step down, but Heather crossed her arms and he stopped. "Heather, let me explain what you just saw."

"There's no need." She kept her voice as calm as she could, to the point where she knew she sounded cold and detached. She didn't care. She couldn't. She needed space. Or it would hurt too much to do what she was going to have to do.

"There is." Ash took the steps down to the street and stood in front of her. "Nothing happened with Sara. Nothing."

"Sara." Somehow it made it worse to know her name.

"I went to bed last night and she just...she...well, she climbed into bed with me." He must know it sounded bad because Ash closed his eyes and squeezed the bridge of his nose. "I'm not interested in her. It's not like that."

"It doesn't matter."

"It does!"

"No, Ash. It doesn't. You told me you would never love again." Heather had to focus to get the words out, but she needed to say them. She needed to hear it as much as he did.

"And now you've demonstrated that. If you were trying to make the point, you did. Now if you'd please give me the keys, I have guests to pick up. Because you didn't think of that either, did you? While you were running off into town to scratch an itch, you left me stranded when I have a business to run. I assume you'll be able to find your own way back, or…wherever it is that you go when you're not at Casa del Sol. But I don't think—"

"Stop."

She shook her head.

"No, Heather. Stop." He gripped her upper arms, and forced her to look at him. "You need to listen to me."

She shook her head again, harder, before she focused on his eyes. "No. I don't." She could feel the crack in her heart as she spoke, but she had to get it out. "It was nothing. We were just fooling around and I know it wasn't anything serious. It's fine."

"That's not true."

"You tried to tell me, and I wouldn't listen. But I get it now. I know who you are, Ash. I get it."

He dropped his hands, his face twisted into a mask of hurt, but she couldn't let herself care. "Here." Ash held the keys out and she took them.

There was something final in his surrender and that might have been the part that hurt the most, but she took the keys and tucked them into her bag. With one more look and her heart breaking into a thousand pieces, she turned and walked down the street to the airport and her guests. She still had a job to do.

He let her go. Every fiber in his body yearned to go after her, pull her into his arms and kiss her until she listened to him. He needed to make her understand. Force her if necessary. But it wasn't the right time because she was right—he'd said those things. He'd told her he would never let himself love again.

He'd been wrong.

Very wrong.

And he'd prove it to her, too.

Because as he watched her walk away, Ash knew one thing with complete certainty: he loved Heather Holt. And he wasn't going to lose her.

Chapter Eighteen

HEATHER WAS thankful for the distraction of picking her guests up from the airport. To her relief, the plane was on time. She sat and waited while the passengers disembarked. Mostly backpacker types, but there was a mix of resort vacationers as well. There were more and more all-inclusive resorts popping up around Bocas, attracting an upper-scale clientele. The mixture of people was almost comical, but Heather was not in the mood for laughing. She watched carefully, and picked out the foursome she assumed to be her new guests.

There were two men and two women, but they weren't couples. The email hadn't given her a lot of details, except that they worked together and had a short work break to enjoy some downtime. She waited until they grabbed their backpacks and duffel bags from the baggage area before she approached them.

"Hi and welcome to Bocas del Toro." She forced a smile she certainly didn't feel and introduced herself to the group.

"Mason Wells." The bigger, darker man held out his hand and shook with a strength that didn't surprise her, given the muscles on the man. "This is Eric, the beautiful Layla, and the equally beautiful Phoebe."

Heather said her hellos, greeting each of them before setting off for the dock. They were an easy bunch, and agreeable to walking the short distance down the road to where she'd left Luis and the boats. Heather had already decided to ask Luis to pick up a few supplies for her and she'd take her own boat back with the guests. Ash could figure out some other way to get around. It couldn't be her problem.

She wanted to get away as soon as she could and if she could avoid Ash in the process, all the better. Her plan was slightly derailed when she got back to the dock to find Luis, and the young boy she recognized as the kid who was with Ash the day she met him. Luis's boat was loaded with what looked like all the groceries she needed, plus some items from the clinic. *Supplies for Sherri.* Of course. She likely needed something and she hadn't even thought to ask. She was way too wrapped up in her own drama. That would have to change. At once.

"Señorita. Are you ready?"

"What's all this, Luis?"

He looked to the boy, who answered. "Señor Ash asked me to bring this for you."

Ash.

She bit her tongue to keep from asking where Ash was. She didn't want to know.

"He said you'd take the boat back, señorita." The boy looked so eager to please, she couldn't be mad at him. It wasn't his fault that the man he worked for had taken her heart and stomped on it. She gave him the biggest smile she could manage. "Thank you…"

"Miguel."

"Thank you, Miguel." Heather reached into her pocket and handed the boy a few dollars, but he shook his head.

"No, señorita. *Estoy buen.*"

She withdrew the money. Of course Ash would have taken care of him, but as Miguel was busy helping her guests into the boat and loading their bags safely in the bow, Heather slipped the bills into the boy's bag. Luis gave her a wink and the simple act helped lift her spirits a little bit.

"All done, señorita." Miguel beamed at her from the dock when the last of the bags was loaded.

"*Gracias*, Miguel."

"Are you guys ready?" Heather turned to her guests, who were excitedly chatting among themselves. All but one. An extremely beautiful young woman. Her long, dark hair was twisted up into a messy bun. Her oversized mirrored sunglasses covered half of her face, but Heather could still tell the woman had the type of easy beauty of a movie star. She sat off to the side of the boat, gazing out across the water and the buildings that lined the shore, while the other woman and two men joked and laughed.

They were all good-looking in that beyond gorgeous movie star way. They had the easy, carefree mannerisms Heather imagined celebrities must have. But where the brunette seemed a little more breakable somehow, the others looked a bit tougher, all of them sporting smooth, sleek muscles, even the blonde.

The brunette, Phoebe, looked at her and smiled. "I think we have everything."

"Are you sure you got all your bathing suits in that bag?" The bigger of the two men, Mason, teased her and she blushed.

"Just one," she said. "And my script."

Script? "Are you guys working on a play?"

"Not since high school." The other man laughed. "We're working on the new Dean Harrison movie."

"A movie?" Heather quickly checked the engine line and started up the boat. Miguel threw her the bow line and she started to move slowly away from the dock. "That's really cool. I'm sorry for asking, but…are you—"

"Movie stars?" The blonde, Layla, saved her from herself. "No. We're stunt doubles. Well, all of us except Phoebe Flynn. This is her first film. She's the lead."

"Well, not the lead." Phoebe, obviously uncomfortable with the attention, blushed and shook her head. "I'm just the female—"

"Lead," Mason finished for her. "It's okay. You're going to be huge after this and you won't want to hang out with us anymore." He looked at Heather. "Remember the name— Phoebe Flynn. She's going to be huge."

It didn't look to Heather as though she was totally comfortable hanging with them as it was, but she didn't say anything. It was likely the girl was just shy. She was clearly uncomfortable with attention, which made her career choice an interesting one. "Well, I think it's cool," she said. "We haven't had any celebrities or movie people at Casa del Sol. At least not while I've been in charge. I'm excited to have you stay with us."

"We're excited to be here. It's always an unexpected bonus when we get to take a little break." Eric spoke up. He was leaner than his friend, but clearly extremely fit. He had a scruff of facial hair. *In a different light, he might be confused with—*

"Are you Dean Harrison's stunt double?" she asked, making the connection.

"Guilty." His smile was bright with a hint of cockiness. Heather instantly liked him.

"Very cool." Heather had never been the fan-girl type, but it was pretty cool to have celebrities of a sort staying with her. "Where are you filming that you were able to come down for a bit?"

"This is kind of a cool film because it's mostly being filmed on site instead of a studio. My favorite kind of shoot," Eric said.

"Because Panama is *way* more beautiful than LA," Layla chimed in.

"It's true," Eric agreed. "We're filming mostly in the San Blas Islands and our home base is a little marina a few hours outside of Panama City."

Heather felt a strange tug of familiarity. "Shelter Bay?"

"You've heard of it?"

"Have I ever." She smiled. But the mention of her old home didn't cause any sore feelings, the way it might have a month ago. A lot had changed. *She* had changed. "So how did you hear of Casa del Sol? I haven't had a chance to get it up on the Airbnb site yet."

"Archer told us." Layla all but swooned when she said Archer's name. The mountain man had that effect on women. "He's so great," she told Heather. "He has this boat and we're using it for some of the shots."

"The *Cassiopeia*."

"You know it?"

"I do." Heather tried to hide her grin. "It's Cass's boat. His girlfriend. You must have met her, too."

Layla's face fell, twisting into a frown. "Yup."

"Cass is great." It was Phoebe who spoke up. "She's just so sweet and her boat is…it would be nice to live on a boat, don't you think?"

"Phoebs, you just wait till this flick comes out. You'll have enough money to buy us all a boat."

"And if you play your cards right, I'll let you all come visit." Phoebe laughed. It was the first time Heather had seen her open up with the group and joke. Judging by the way the rest of them ran with it, Heather guessed it didn't happen all that often.

She urged the boat faster as they left Bocas Town behind, but she didn't open up the throttle to full speed, choosing instead to get to know her new guests a little bit.

They turned out to be fun, friendly, and super interesting to talk to. And they had the added benefit of distracting Heather from the ache in her chest and the realization that when she got back to Casa del Sol, Ash wouldn't be there.

———

By the time Heather got to the dock, Luis had already arrived and was unloading the supplies. Camila—and surprisingly, her mother—helped him.

She tied up the boat quickly and before she could even get to the dock to help her guests, they were already jumping up, excited to get their vacation started. "Welcome to Casa del Sol!" She spread her arms. "Make yourselves at home. I'll go mix up a jug of drinks and then we can get you all settled into your rooms."

"No hurry, Heather." Layla stripped her tank top off to reveal a tight, toned body in a string bikini. "I've been dying to get in the water."

"Have you now?" Mason pulled his T-shirt off to reveal an impressive eight-pack of rippling abs, and before anyone could say anything, grabbed Layla's hand and pulled her with him into the ocean.

With her new guests happily entertained, Heather grabbed their bags and headed into *grande casa*. Her mother was behind the bar, mixing something in a large pitcher. "Mom, you don't have to—"

"Nonsense. Camila showed me the garden out back. Did you know there's bushes and bushes of mint out there?"

Heather smiled. "I did."

"I thought I could help you out. You've been gone so long and—" She stopped herself and looked around. "Where's Ash?"

Heather felt something in her gut twist and she bit her bottom lip. "I assume he stayed in town."

"You found him then? What was he doing in town? Camila said something about picking up something or other, but I have no idea what she's saying half the time. I was thinking of learning Spanish."

Heather's head spun, trying to keep up with her mother's train of thought. It was as if she'd left one version of her mom and returned to a completely different, more relaxed version. Of course, Panama did seem to have that effect on people.

"You're going to learn Spanish in a week or two?" Heather moved around the bar and grabbed a few glasses and a tray to stack everything on. "You are going home, right?"

They'd had a good evening and mended a lot of bridges in the last twenty-four hours, but it was going to take a lot more than one night to mend them all.

Her mother waved a hand. "Of course I'm going home. Eventually. But right now you need me here. So I'll stay."

It was an argument she wasn't going to have. She didn't have the energy. Besides, maybe she'd be able to use the help with Ash gone.

With Ash gone.

She just assumed he'd be gone now that they'd...what? Broken up? There wasn't really another word for what happened between them. Even if they hadn't technically been dating, it was a breakup.

"You didn't answer me, Heather."

She'd totally forgotten her mother was still standing there. "What?"

"Did you find Ash?"

She nodded.

"Where is he then? I wanted to ask him about showing me another beach. He told me about another place where he could find sand dollars in the shallows. Wouldn't that be amazing? Sand dollars. I don't think I've ever seen a sand dollar before. Have you? You must have. Living here for so long and all. I thought maybe I could—"

"Mom!"

Heather instantly felt bad when her mother's face fell. She'd never seen her mom so animated and excited about anything and she didn't want to stifle that, but at the same time she absolutely couldn't handle listening to her mom for one more minute.

"Sorry, Mom. I didn't mean to snap at you. It's been a long day. Do you think maybe you could take our new guests those drinks you just made? I think you're going to like them. They're all working on a movie."

"A movie?" Heather knew that would catch her mother's interest. "Like movie stars?"

She nodded. "And stunt doubles. Cool, huh?"

"I would say so." Her mom grabbed the tray, put the jug on it and moved around the bar before she stopped and looked back at Heather. "Are you okay, sweetie? You look...sad."

"I am sad." She answered honestly because she just didn't have the energy for anything else. "But I'll be okay." She nodded. "Yes. I'll be okay."

Her mother's smile was so genuine and familiar, Heather felt it in her heart. "You will be okay, Heather. If there's one thing I know about my daughter, it's that she's a strong woman. It may have taken you a little bit of time to get there, but you know who you are and what you need. Whatever's making you sad, you *will* be okay."

Heather bit her lip to keep from blubbering. It was the sweetest thing her mother had ever said to her. "Thanks, Mom."

Her mother nodded. "And in the meantime, if you want to talk, I'll be rubbing noses with our celebrity guests."

"Elbows, Mom. You'll be rubbing elbows."

She winked. "Maybe those, too."

Heather chuckled and shook her head, as her mother walked out to the dock. Only a few days in Panama, and the change in the woman was incredible. *Maybe it was the place? Maybe it was being in Panama, and more specifically, Casa del Sol that changed people?*

She couldn't be sure. But she did know her mother was right. Heather *did* know who she was and what she needed. She *would* be okay.

But she couldn't help but think that she'd be even more okay with Ash standing next to her.

Chapter Nineteen

HE'D GIVEN Heather the day. But that was all Ash was prepared to give her because every minute that he wasn't with her, she was off somewhere thinking the worst of him. He'd tried to give her some space, but he was over it. He needed to see her, to talk to her, to *make* her understand that not only was what she saw a major misunderstanding, it was not in any way representative of who he was or what he wanted.

What he wanted was Heather.

He was in love with Heather.

Madly. Desperately.

It was inconceivable to him that he'd ever have the capacity to love after Carlie, but now, more than ever, he was so certain that's exactly what it was he was feeling with Heather. It was different than it had been with Carlie. Much different.

And maybe that's why he hadn't recognized it at first. But it was definitely love. His chest hurt when he thought about her; his entire body yearned to be with her. To hold her. To hear her laugh. To kiss her.

With Carlie, it was different. He was young and that didn't make it any less valid, but now that he was older and maybe more importantly, had lived through everything he lived through, love with Heather felt different.

Maybe it was different, but it was so real that he was going to burst if he didn't get the chance to tell her how much he loved her. And soon. Because he was positive Mick was getting sick of hearing about it.

After loading the supplies for Casa del Sol in Luis's boat and paying Miguel to help Heather with her guests and make sure she got off okay, he'd spent the rest of the day walking around town, trying to figure out what he was going to do to show Heather how sorry he was for not recognizing what was directly in front of his face sooner. About two hours earlier, he'd come up with the perfect plan. Now he just needed to wait.

"I swear to God, Ash. Staring at me like that is not going to make anything happen any faster." Mick polished a glass and put it on the shelf behind him. "Frankly, I can't believe you pulled this off for today as it is. Nothing ever moves this fast in Bocas."

"I got lucky, I guess." The truth was, as soon as Ash came up with his plan, he was not prepared to wait another minute to execute it. Or at least, as it turned out, a full day. Most of the supplies were found in town at the shops, but it was the new boat that was proving to be a bit more of a problem. Mick made a few calls for him, and he somehow found a boat at one of the new resorts that the manager was willing to sell him. But not until the end of the week.

Unacceptable.

Ash got on the phone and made a deal with the manager that he couldn't refuse. The deal included delivery to Bocas Town, which was what Ash had been waiting for, rather impatiently, for the last hour.

"Seriously," Mick said. "How did you manage it? He was

asking too much for that boat, if you ask me. Did you talk him down?"

Ash shrugged. "Something like that."

It was nothing like that. In fact, he'd paid extra to have the boat delivered ASAP but he didn't need Mick to know that. Not yet. He still wasn't in a hurry for everyone to know that despite his modest lifestyle, in reality, Ash was a millionaire with more money than he'd ever be able to spend, despite his generous annual donations.

"I guess I got lucky," he said. "But I'd feel a whole lot luckier if he'd hurry up. I have to get going if I'm going to pull this off."

The truth was, he wasn't sure he'd be able to pull it off at all, but he was going to try his best.

He pushed back from the bar where he'd been chugging bottles of water and paced the length of the bar, keeping his gaze on the docks. "There." He stopped and dashed back to the bar, where he fetched his box of supplies. "He's here. Thanks, Mick."

"Good luck to ya, man." He smiled. "And don't screw it up."

"I don't plan to."

The new boat moved a whole lot faster than he was used to, and in no time, Ash neared Casa del Sol. He slowed as he approached, aware that Heather would see him. He didn't know how she'd react, but he was fairly sure it wouldn't be very positive. She wouldn't make a scene in front of her guests, though, that much he could be sure of.

Regardless, he didn't plan to pull up to the main dock. He navigated the boat toward the thick trees at the edge of Sherri's property. There was an old dock, or at least what was left of it, hidden in the trees. It wasn't ideal, but Ash didn't want to disturb Heather. Not yet. Not until he was set up.

He tied the boat to the wooden pillars and ran an extra line to a tree on the shore. It was an expensive boat; he didn't want to take any chances.

He gathered his stuff and picked his way through the trees until he got to the large storage shed. Or, the building Sherri had once wanted to turn into an artist's studio. As long as Ash could remember, it had been used for storage, mostly because no one had ever turned it into more. He'd always thought it was a bit of a waste of space, but now that he wanted to use it, he was glad it was empty.

The building was unlocked, so he pushed open the door with his back and went inside. There wasn't much inside, but he spent the next thirty minutes clearing aside the old chairs and crates. He opened the shutters to expose the room to the ocean and let the fresh air in. He spread out his supplies, tested the electricity and plugged in the lights he'd brought with him.

When the shed was organized as much as possible, he grabbed the rest of the supplies and set out toward *grande casa*, hoping to find Luis before anyone else. Just as planned, the man must have been watching for him, because Ash had barely taken a few steps toward the building, when Luis appeared.

"*Hola.*"

"*Hola, mi amigo.*" They shook hands and Ash thanked him again for bringing everything back for him and delivering it up the stairs to Sherri's place.

"Now, you're still okay to help me with this part?" Ash handed him the box he'd brought. "Remember—not until the sun goes down. Everything should be there. Just paddle it out to the platform and set it up. It should be easy enough to figure out."

"*Sí*, señor." Luis grinned. "I have my share of experience with romance, too, you know?"

"I know it, Luis. I know it. Thank you again."

He waved away his gratitude. "Good luck, *mi amigo*."

"*Gracias*." *I'll need it.*

———

Heather did her best to go through the motions for the rest of the day. It was made easier by the fact that her guests were a lot of fun and didn't seem to need much entertaining. They were happy to hang out and relax. They'd found the storage room full of inflatables and had spent the better part of the afternoon floating on the ocean, drinking mojitos and enjoying the sun.

Camila had cooked up a delicious feast and they'd all gathered around the table to celebrate their first night at Casa del Sol. She wasn't much in the mood for celebrating, and had never been so thankful for her mother, whose presence was surprisingly a huge help. She never thought the day would come when she would be able to say that, but more and more, Heather was starting to expect anything but the expected.

She sat in the back corner, watching as Mason fired up his iPod and started dancing. Soon, everyone was dancing, even Phoebe, who'd come out of her shell a bit more as the day progressed. Even Luis and Camila had stuck around and were demonstrating their Spanish dance moves. Heather's mother had played hard to get, but Eric only had to ask once before getting her up on the dance floor, too. No one bothered to ask Heather to join in, a fact she was more than grateful for as she didn't think her spirit could handle it. It was one thing to play happy hostess as your heart was breaking; it was a completely different thing to join in the festivities. All she really wanted to do was make her escape and go to bed so the day could be over.

After a few songs, Luis and Camila disappeared into the

kitchen—likely Camila was preparing a dessert or another round of delicious munchies of some kind. Her mother broke away from the dance party and joined her on the couch. "I haven't moved like that in years." She flopped down next to Heather and smacked her thigh. "You should get out there, sweetie. It'll make you feel better."

"I feel fine."

"You're a bad liar."

Heather didn't bother to respond. "I just feel like sitting out tonight."

Her mother eyed her suspiciously but fortunately didn't say anything.

"I wonder how long they're going to—"

"Señorita Heather!" Luis appeared in front of her, looking panicked enough that Heather sat up.

"What is it? Is everything okay?"

"No, señorita." He shook his head. "There's a situation in the storage shed."

"The storage shed?" She looked around. "Weren't you just in the kitchen with Camila?"

"No, señorita. The shed. You must go."

Heather looked between Luis and her mother.

"Go," her mother said. "I'll make sure everyone has whatever they need and I think Camila is going to serve those yummy cookies we made earlier."

She looked back at Luis. "A situation?" He nodded. "Okay." She sighed. "Let's go."

"Oh no, señorita. You go. I'll be right behind you."

She shook her head, but didn't bother objecting. It was likely some type of superstition or something. Or more likely, Luis needed to go get a kiss from Camila before venturing out into the dark. Either way, she didn't have any such requirements. Heather grabbed a flashlight from the shelf by the door and set out the back door. The pathways were marked with solar lights, and as usual, Thor was right behind her. If there was any type of situation that she required backup for, she'd have to rely on the dog.

There was a full moon, which made the traveling easier, and Heather was able to avoid tripping over too many roots and rocks as the path became a bit rougher. If Sherri agreed to her plan of turning the shed into a hostel type of bungalow, she'd have to improve the path for guests. Maybe put a few more solar lights in.

Her pace slowed as she approached the building. Everything looked fine from the outside, but there did appear to be a faint glow coming from inside. Maybe Luis left one of the lights on when he was out there. It didn't even occur to ask him why he was out in the shed, or what he was doing. It hadn't seemed important. But as soon as Heather opened the door and stepped inside, it all became clear. And she almost turned right around and walked out.

Twinkle lights had been strung around the room. In the middle of the floor was a large blanket with a vase of flowers in the center. Next to the flowers was a folded piece of paper with her name on it.

She stood in the doorway, battling with herself, trying to decide whether she should just turn around and walk back to *grande casa*, or whether she should bother with reading the note that was so obviously left by Ash.

It had to be Ash.

Finally, curiosity won. She flicked the flashlight off and walked across the floor to the note.

Heather,
I'm sorry you're upset. Please give me a chance to explain.

. . .

She shook her head and held the note down by her leg. *What was there to explain?* She'd found him in a compromising position with another woman. There was no way to explain being half dressed in a bedroom with a woman. It could only mean one thing.

Or maybe not.

With a sigh, she lifted the note again and kept reading.

The truth is, I was involved with Sara at one point, before I met you.

Reading that hurt more than she'd expected it to, which was completely ridiculous. Everyone had a past.

There's nothing between us. There hasn't been for a long time. Last night, I drank too much and I didn't know she was in my bed with me until this morning. Shortly before you walked in. It was her idea, and I made sure she knew in no uncertain terms that it was unacceptable. I know it looked bad. I'm sorry. I hope you know I would never do anything to hurt you. You must know that. Deep down.

She did. Reading his words, Heather knew it was true. Ash wouldn't hurt her. Not like that. Not intentionally.

There's more. Please follow the trail of shells.

For the first time, Heather looked up and saw the trail of tiny seashells leading across the floor, to the porch. She followed them but the trail ended at the water's edge. When she looked up, the sight took her breath away and despite herself, she giggled.

Out in the water, under a beautiful blanket of stars, was the swim platform lined with candles, flickering in the gentle breeze.

"What on earth?" Heather looked all around, certain Ash was going to appear out of the shadows, but there was nothing. Besides the candles, the platform was empty. "This is ridiculous."

Ridiculous or not, she was intrigued. Very intrigued.

"Why not?"

She'd come this far, and what he'd written in his note made sense. Maybe it wasn't his fault. Maybe there was more to it. She might as well find out. Thankful that she always had a bathing suit on under her tank top and cut-offs, she stripped to her bathing suit and dove in. After all, there was nothing else to lose.

When Heather surfaced, the bioluminescence shimmered all around her. Just as it had the first time, the sight of the neon blue water took her breath away. She'd forgotten all about the magic of the water and for a few moments, she reveled in it.

With gentle breaststrokes, she moved toward the swim platform and climbed up the ladder, which had been returned to its position in the water after the storm. She knew he wasn't up there, but still, she was disappointed not to see Ash standing there waiting for her. Instead, there was a towel and beside it, another note.

She picked her way through the candle border, careful not to drip on any of them and extinguish them. She picked up the towel, wrapped it around her even though the night was warm, and sat down with the note in her hand.

Her heart was hopeful when she opened the paper, but still guarded. She didn't know what to expect. Although nothing about the day or evening had been expected up until that point, so what did it matter?

There were only two words written on the paper.

Turn around.

She did.

Ash stood on the ladder of the platform, dripping wet. His bare chest glistened with flecks of electric blue from the lingering bioluminescence. Her breath hitched. But not because he looked like a water god from the sea, but because her heart pounded out of her chest. She struggled to stand, but somehow got twisted in the oversized towel.

"No. Sit." He held out a hand and climbed the last few steps to the platform.

"Ash, I—"

"Please just let me say what I need to say."

She closed her mouth.

"I need you to hear me. And really listen to me, okay?"

She nodded.

He took a breath. "I know what you saw this morning hurt you and that was never my intention." She squeezed her eyes for a second before she opened them again. Hurt was an understatement. "I need you to believe me that there's nothing between Sara and me. I thought I was clear with her before, but apparently not. That's been remedied. What happened today will never happen again."

She nodded, because there was nothing else to say.

"Do you believe me? Nothing happened, Heather. I need you to believe me."

"I do."

"You do?"

"I do." As she said the words, she found she believed them. Seeing Ash standing there with another woman shocked her. It hurt her. But listening to him, seeing his face as he explained it, she did believe him. But that didn't fix everything.

"I'm glad you believe me." He let out a breath, and visibly relaxed, but not all the way. "I've been thinking about what you said. About how I told you I would never love again."

Her heart clenched in her chest, hearing him speak the words out loud again.

"I was wrong, Heather. I think I already knew I was wrong when I told you that. In fact, I *know* I was wrong because when I told you about Carlie and my past, it was just that. My past. But what I didn't realize was that I'd already fallen in love with you."

His mouth kept moving, and more words came out, but Heather wasn't listening. There was an intense buzzing in her head, with his words on replay. *I'd already fallen in love with you.*

"Wait." She interrupted him. "What did you say?"

"I was talking about how I was wrong."

"Right." She stood and the towel dropped in a puddle at her feet. "Before that. About how—"

"I love you?"

She nodded.

"I do." He smiled. "I'm not even totally sure when it happened, but all I know is that I love you so much, Heather. When you ran away from me today, I knew I'd do anything it took to make you understand about what you saw and more than that..." He stepped over the candles and closed some of the distance between them. "I needed to make you understand that it doesn't matter what I said before because I was wrong. I *can* love again and I do. I know you feel the same way." He shook his head. "No, I *hope* you feel the same way."

He took two more steps until he was directly in front of her and took her hands in his own. "Tell me, Heather." She looked directly into his eyes. The candles and the moonlight lit them perfectly, so she could see everything he was feeling and she knew he could see the same. "Tell me you love me."

"I love you." The words were soft at first, as if they were hard to say, but the moment they were out of her mouth, she had to say them again. "I love you." And again. "I love you." This time she laughed, because it just felt so right.

"You do?"

She nodded.

Ash bent and kissed her forehead. "Good."

"Good?"

"Good," he said with a laugh of his own. "Because I was all out of ideas on how to convince you."

Heather reached up and pulled his head down to hers so she could kiss him properly. He tasted of spice and salt and everything Ash. His arms came around her bare back, holding her tight as their lips explored each other. They kissed as if it had been months since they'd had the taste of each other. And when finally they came apart, Heather said, "I think you just said it all."

Chapter Twenty

THEY'D STAYED THAT WAY, wrapped in each other's arms on the platform until the candles burnt down. Later, once they'd swum back to shore, he didn't waste any time getting her out of her wet bikini and into his arms, where he could feel her bare breasts pressed up against his chest.

Earlier on the street, when she'd walked away from him, Ash wasn't sure he'd ever have her in his arms again, and the feeling had threatened to overwhelm him with the intensity of it. Now, with Heather exactly where she belonged, he was determined to make sure she knew how much he loved her. In every way.

He swept her wet hair to the side and gripped it with one hand, exposing her neck so he could kiss and nibble his way down between her breasts. His breath hitched in his throat as he kissed the swell of her perfect breasts. "You are so beautiful," he whispered between kisses.

Her gentle groans were the only response he needed.

Both hands slid down her body until they cupped her ass; he lifted her easily until her legs wrapped around his waist. He kissed her full on the mouth then. A possessive, hungry kiss that didn't even begin to express his need for her.

With her wrapped around him, Ash walked slowly to the blanket he'd laid in the middle of the room and gently lowered her to the floor, where he could give her the attention she deserved.

Her wet hair was spread out beneath her in a wild tangle that just made her that much more irresistible. "Heather, I... God. I just…"

"Ash?" She reached up and stroked his face. "Less talk." And pulled him down to her again.

He didn't need to be asked twice. His kiss was harder, more demanding and she responded with the same need. When he reached one hand between them, to the cleft between her legs, she was hot and wet and more than ready for him. Although he would have liked to have taken his time with her, there would be plenty of opportunity for that later. For now, he needed her and there was no doubt in his mind that she needed him just as badly.

When he entered her, she gasped and locked her legs around him, holding him in place. He pulled away from her kiss, just far enough so he could look her in the eyes and they could watch each other as they both took their pleasure and quenched the flames inside.

Later, lying with Heather in his arms, letting the tropical winds wash over their heated bodies, Ash couldn't remember a time he'd ever been happier. There had been good times, but never one quite so perfect when the world was just *right*.

He stroked the back of her head, and her now almost dry hair, gently working the tangled strands with his fingertips.

"Ash?"

"Mmm?"

"Please don't keep anything from me again, okay?"

He knew without asking she was talking about Sherri. Ash scooted back just enough that she could turn in his arms and look at him. "I wanted to tell you."

"I know she asked you not to."

"But I should have."

"It's a gray area," she admitted.

"But when I went to town," he said, "I wanted to. I waited for you, but...it was just a big misunderstanding. All of it was, really. I'm sorry." He kissed her nose. "I won't keep anything from you again."

She smiled and he knew it was okay. "She's going to be okay, you know?"

A question flashed in her eyes, so he told her about the last conversation he'd had with Sherri and all about Dr. Friesen, and why he was in Bocas Town in the first place, and the hope he had for their friend. When he was finished explaining everything, in the interest of not keeping anything from her again, he added one more detail. "You might have guessed by now that I have a bit of money tucked away."

"A bit?"

"Okay. Quite a bit. After everything happened with Carlie, I sold my business and most of my shares. Let's just say that... no matter what happens, I'll be okay. In fact...I had an idea that I think you might be interested in."

"What's that?"

"Before we go there, I just want to make sure that we're good. Everything that happened with Sara, you know it was nothing, right? Like nothing happened? I didn't even know she was there and—"

She held a finger to his lips, silencing him. "I know. Ash, it's okay. I was just in shock, I think, and seeing her there with you, like that..." She shook her head, not wanting to replay the image. "It hurt. But not as much as realizing, or thinking that I was realizing, that you meant what you said about not being able to love again." Before he could interrupt, she kept talking. "But I know now. I heard you. I believe you. And I love you, too."

He kissed her then and she didn't think she'd ever get enough of him. There was something different in their kisses now that they'd declared their love for each other. An honesty, a rawness that wasn't there before. It made her heart sing.

"Now, tell me. What's this idea of yours?"

Epilogue

THREE WEEKS LATER...

Ash stood on the deck outside *grande casa* and took it all in. In three short weeks, everything had changed so much, and yet, looking at it, everything was exactly the same. After sorting things out with Heather, their love had grown so quickly and with such strength, it took him aback at times. But in a good way. Ash hadn't known it was possible to love someone so much and with such depth. He had to shake his head when he thought about all those years he'd convinced himself that he'd never love again. He should have told himself he'd never love the way he loved Carlie again.

This love with Heather was different. And he was thankful every day that he woke up next to her that he'd come to his senses and realized what he had before letting it all disappear for good.

That night, lying in the shed that he'd transformed into their own private *love den*—as they'd started jokingly referring to it—Ash laid out his idea for Heather in all its rawness. He'd only come to the thought earlier that day, but the more he sat on it, and percolated it, the more it made sense. And with Heather in his arms that night, he felt as though he could do anything. He wanted to buy Casa del Sol from Sherri. But only if Heather was on board. It had to be something they'd do together. Or not at all.

Ash hadn't even been able to finish his thought before Heather was literally jumping up and down yelling her approval and sharing all her own ideas for the place. He had no idea that she had so many ambitious plans for Casa del Sol as well, but it shouldn't have been a surprise. She'd loved the place just as much as he had from the moment she set foot on the dock. That was easy to see.

He was only slightly worried that Sherri wouldn't want to sell it to him. But he needn't have been concerned because the next morning, after staying up until the sun came up, excitedly talking over their ideas and making love, both Ash and Heather had gone up to see Sherri.

Part of him thought she might resist the move, but the moment Ash explained that they wanted to run the place together, with Sherri as long as she wanted to stay, his old friend burst into tears.

"Nothing would make me happier than to see you two here, together."

"And you can focus on getting better." Heather squeezed her arm. It was a priority for both of them—for Sherri to get better—and her health status dominated many of their conversations. But things seemed to be moving in the right direction, according to Dr. Friesen. Once he'd arrived, he'd wasted no time setting things up and making sure Sherri's treatment was dialed in. He remained optimistic that they'd be able to knock her cancer into remission in no time and had even convinced Sherri to accompany him to Panama City when the time was right so she could receive the proper scans to make sure the cancer was being treated properly.

Ash had never been more grateful for making that phone call to Dr. Friesen. With Sherri happy and more than willing to sell him the property, things moved quickly. Ash called a lawyer friend he knew in Panama City and he arranged for a more than fair sum of money to be transferred to Sherri. He also made sure both his *and* Heather's names were put on the deed. Casa del Sol was both of theirs. Equally.

And just like that, Casa del Sol was theirs and besides falling asleep and waking up with Heather in his arms, nothing had ever felt so right.

"Hey, babe." As if he'd conjured her, Heather came up behind him and slipped her arms around his waist. He turned so he could pull her into a proper kiss. "That was nice." She winked at him. "What are you looking at?"

Ash turned back toward the water, keeping his arm around her. "Just all of this. Are you ready for this?"

"For you? Or for this?"

He squeezed her close. "All of it. The crew arrives tomorrow." With Heather's plans to expand their *love den* into a hostel style of accommodation, they also decided to build a few more bungalows. Including two up in the trees for those who wanted a more secluded stay. They were both excited to get their hands dirty with the work, but neither of them were experts in construction, let alone construction in the jungle, so they'd hired a crew to help them out with the work.

"It's going to be exciting," she agreed. "But tonight, it's just us. Finally."

Ash laughed because Val had extended her stay twice, but was finally headed back on the boat and set to fly out. As much as Heather protested her mother's extended stay, secretly Ash was certain she loved it. And he had, too. Not only had mother and daughter been able to finally repair their relationship, it had taken on a completely new life. Panama agreed with Val and once she met Sherri, she spent more and more time up in the treehouse, looking after not only their patient, but also the crew of doctors and caregivers who had started to arrive. She'd declared herself a bit of a *house mom*, saying it gave her purpose to look after someone again.

"I think I'm going to miss your mom."

"Oh, don't you worry about that." Val joined them on the dock. "I'm not going anywhere for very long."

Heather spun around. "What do you mean? I thought you were leaving today."

"Simmer down, sweetheart. I'm heading to Shelter Bay today, as planned. I'm looking forward to meeting these friends of yours and of course seeing the movie crew. Phoebe told me she'd be able to introduce me to Dean Harrison. Can you believe that? Maybe I'll have him sign my tote bag. That would be something, wouldn't it?"

"It certainly would, Val."

"But then you're going to go to the San Blas Islands, right, Mom? To visit Sherri's friend, Josie? You'll be gone at least a month, right?"

Val laughed. "If I didn't know any better, I would think you're trying to get rid of me."

"Not at all." Ash smiled at her. "But it will be a bit of a construction zone around here for a few weeks. It'll be a good time for you to go on vacation. And we haven't talked about when you might be ready to go back to the States."

"About that. I was thinking—"

"No."

"Don't say no when you haven't heard my idea, dear. It's rude."

"You're going to say that you're not going home." It would have been Ash's guess, too. "You want to stay in Panama."

It wasn't a good time to have the type of conversation Ash

knew was coming. Especially because he had another, more important conversation he wanted to have. One that had involved a quick trip to Panama City a few days earlier.

He stepped between the women. "Why don't we have this discussion when Val gets back from her trip to San Blas?"

"I think we should shut this down—"

"Babe," he interrupted her. "Let's table this one, okay? There was something I wanted to ask you before Val has to leave."

She tipped her head in question.

Ash took a deep breath, reached into his pocket and got down on one knee. Behind him, he heard Val shriek but he ignored her and focused on the one woman in the world who held his heart. "Heather, ever since I met you on the steps of the Bitter End, I haven't been able to take my eyes off you. You have captured my heart in a way no one else ever has. Every day I wake up and think I must still be dreaming because you're in my arms. And baby, I don't ever want to wake up from this dream. I love you. Will you make my life complete and be my wife?"

His hands shook, but he held the ring out to her. A single diamond nestled into a setting surrounded by the blue sapphires that reminded Ash of the phytoplankton on their first swim together. The moment he saw the ring, he knew it was perfect.

She didn't answer. She couldn't because tears flowed down her face. Finally, she nodded, put her hand to her mouth and nodded again. "Yes. Of course. I can't imagine any other future."

The moment Ash slipped the ring on her hand and sealed her agreement with a kiss, Val let out a whoop. Together, they turned and invited Heather's mom into the hug as well.

"Well, it doesn't look like I'm going anywhere for a while after all," Val said. "After all…we have a wedding to plan!"

I hope you enjoyed your visit to Paradise! But the adventures aren't over, yet! There's a movie to be filmed and Phoebe Flynn is the reluctant star. She's staring in the hottest movie of the year, but it's the chemistry between her and her sexy co-star that really heats up the big screen!
Hidden in the Sand is next! Read an exclusive excerpt next!

And if you want even more romance...click HERE for an exclusive FREE novella that isn't available anywhere else!

Hidden in the Sand

Enjoy this excerpt from Hidden in the Sand, the next in the Destination Paradise Series.

His pulse thundered in his ears and he worked hard to control his breathing.

In. Out. In. Out.

Dean Harrison knew he had less than thirty seconds before he would be discovered behind the tarp-covered barrels. Thirty seconds before the bullets would start to fly and he would start running.

Fast.

He forced himself to focus on the count in his head.

Ten…nine…eight…

A blast from somewhere farther off in the boatyard shook the barrels he was hiding behind.

"Shit." It was early. Or his count was off. *Dammit.* He hated it when he was off.

Not that there was anything he could do about it now. With another curse under his breath, Dean squeezed the revolver in his hand a little bit tighter, and took off running through the boatyard. Just as he expected, the yelling started and the deafening sounds of guns firing rang all around him. Adrenaline fueled him and narrowed his vision, blocking out everything but the obstacles in front of him. He jumped and dodged just the way he'd planned and visualized in his head for the last few days.

An explosion sounded directly in front of him, and he jumped to the right, just barely avoiding the blast. He landed hard on his shoulder; a hot, sharp pain shot up his neck as he rolled in the dirt.

Shit.

But still Dean didn't stop. He jumped to his feet and once again started to run through the boats that were propped up on blocks and stands. The cargo net, and the crane it hung from, was only ten yards away. Dean knew if he could get there, jump on, and swing over the dump truck that, once he was on the other side, they couldn't stop him.

He pushed himself harder. He was almost there. *Just a few more—*

"Cut!"

The word ripped through him, and reflexively, Dean's body slowed right as he reached the cargo net, his fingers wrapped through the netting.

"Cut!" the director yelled again. "Everyone, cut!"

Reluctantly, Dean let his hand slip down. His head dropped and he silently cursed the situation before he turned around. "Come on, Wes. I was almost there."

Wes Reacher jumped down from the platform where he'd been watching the progress of the scene and joined Dean on the ground. "You know you're not doing that scene, Dean." The director patted him on the back, sending a fresh shot of pain from his shoulder into his neck. Wes didn't miss the flinch. "My point exactly. You landed hard back there."

Dean handed the prop gun still in his hand to an intern

who'd run over to collect it, and used his free hand to massage his shoulder as he rotated it. "It's nothing. I'm fine."

Wes gave him a sidelong glance, but didn't push it. He knew better. They'd worked together before. In fact, *Run From the Sun* was the fourth Max Silver movie they'd shot together. Wes knew exactly how far he could push Dean. And vice versa. As big of a movie star that Dean Harrison was, Wes Reacher was just as big of a director. The fact that they'd worked together for so many projects had been mutually beneficial.

"Go to medical and get it checked out. I can't afford the downtime if you screwed your arm up."

Dean swallowed a growl. He was fine. He just landed funny, that was all. And if Wes would just give in and let him do his own stunts, he'd have even more training in how to fall properly and things like this wouldn't happen. It was an argument they'd had more times than he could count. Still, Dean wasn't going to give up. He hated not doing his own stunts. And he hated even more being told he couldn't do something.

Dean stopped walking and turned to his director and friend. "Wes, seriously, man. I think it's time that I did at least—"

"I can't talk about this now. We have exactly ten minutes to set up for the next scene and you know just as well as I do that time is money." Wes started walking again.

Dean swallowed hard, bit back a reply and caught up with the director. He wasn't a demanding star. Never had been. But he was starting to get tired of being treated as if he were going to break if he did the slightest thing. The Max Silver movies were the hottest thriller franchise in decades. And sure, they revolved completely around his character, which meant if something did happen to him, shooting would come to a halt. But they were also action-packed thrill rides and dammit, Dean wanted to be part of that ride. And, as the star, was he not entitled to make a few demands?

"Okay," Wes conceded, as if he knew exactly what argument Dean was going to try next. "We'll get you involved in some of the stunts."

Dean grabbed his friend by the arm so he stopped and finally turned to look at him. He needed the director to look him in the eye and say that. "Seriously?"

Wes nodded, although somewhat reluctantly. "Yes. There's the boat chase scene that could work. You swim, right?"

Dean nodded.

"Okay. We'll work with your double, Eric, on it and I'll have him show you a few things so you don't kill yourself."

Dean worked hard to control the smile that was blooming across his face.

"I mean it, Dean. Do *not* kill yourself."

He lost the battle and let his grin take over as he slapped Wes on the back. "I promise," he said as he turned to head to his trailer. "No dying."

"No dying!" Wes called after him. "And for God's sake, go get that arm looked at before your next scene."

Phoebe Flynn stood off to the side, in what she hoped was an inconspicuous spot. She knew she probably shouldn't be on set when it wasn't time for her call, but *Run From the Sun* was her first major film. Hell, it was her first film at all. She wasn't a movie star. She wasn't an actress. And she definitely wasn't Silver Starlet material. She was completely out of her depth, and if she didn't figure it out soon, everyone was going to see what a fraud she was.

She watched the scene in front of her play out. Dean was a pro. He moved quickly and without hesitation through the set. Phoebe could see the way he controlled his face, perfectly in character as he ran through the boatyard, occasionally looking over his shoulder just the way Max Silver would. He made it look effortless, the way he turned into his character. She'd heard stories about Dean Harrison on set, and the others who she'd been hanging out with since arriving in Panama had filled her in on what it was like to work with him.

A total pro.

Intimidating.

Humbling.

And her new friends were largely all the stunt doubles, so they didn't actually exchange lines with Dean. *What would it be like playing his leading lady? What would it be like to—*

No.

Phoebe would only work herself up further if she let herself think about shooting the sexy scenes that were coming up. Sure, Dean Harrison's movies were famous for being fast paced, intense action movies, but that wasn't their only defining feature. For as much action as they contained, they also were chock-full of steamy scenes. Like everyone else in the world, Phoebe had watched them all. She'd known exactly what she was getting herself in to when she'd accepted the role of Misty Falls, the female lead.

It was a decision that had made enough sense in the moment. But now that she was actually here, on set in Panama, it was starting to feel different. Very different.

The director yelled cut and just like that, the boatyard filled with people, all with a job to strike the set and prepare for the next shot. With all the chaos, controlled as it was, Phoebe took her chance to slip away and go for a walk.

Since arriving, her time had mostly been occupied with wardrobe fittings, running lines, and a multitude of other things to prepare for the actual shooting of the film. She'd been lucky when some of the stunt doubles had invited her to join them for a quick getaway in Bocas del Toro, a few hours away at a jungle-themed bed-and-breakfast type of hotel. It was a perfect little holiday to help her break the ice with some of her castmates, who all tended to think she was really stand-offish, or stuck up. She wasn't either of those things, just shy and completely terrified that she was about to make an epic mess of things the next day when she shot her very first scene with Dean Harrison.

She wasn't a complete newbie, though. Phoebe had already shot a few scenes back in LA in the studio, a fact she was grateful for because at least she was able to warm up a little bit before being thrown to the sharks.

Leaving the boatyard and the movie chaos behind her, she made her way toward the breakwater that kept the rough ocean seas from the harbor and the boats moored in the bay. The ocean breeze whipped all around her and pulled her long, dark hair from the loose ponytail she'd tied it back in. It had been almost two weeks since she'd arrived, and still Phoebe was having trouble getting used to the muggy heat of Panama. It sat on her like a weighted blanket when she was inland. But the moment she got near the water, where the breeze washed over her, she felt lighter.

The breakwater was one of her favorite places because from that vantage point, she could look out to sea and see the massive container ships anchored out in the deep water, waiting for their turn to go through the Panama Canal system. Despite the waves that crashed up on the rocks below her, the anchored ships hardly seemed to move. Occasionally, a sailing yacht or power yacht would go by, and they'd look like a toy boat next to the container ships. She'd never seen anything like it.

Of course, she hadn't traveled far from her small town in Montana, either. Except for a few trips when she was a kid, Phoebe hadn't really been anywhere before she was *discovered* at the mall serving frozen yogurt. She laughed every time she thought about that day when Lorilee, her now agent, had ordered a scoop of the strawberry before demanding to know who represented her. As if that were a thing in the middle of nowhere, Montana.

It wasn't.

When Lorilee finally accepted that Phoebe was not in fact *represented* by anyone, whatever that meant, she had insisted on having a meeting with her when she was done with her shift. Preferably before she was done. Finally, Phoebe had to agree so she could serve the other customers in line. Of course, she didn't expect anything to come of the meeting, and no one was more surprised than Phoebe when Lorilee had insisted that she sign her to the agency because she had the *perfect role* for her.

That had been a little over three months ago. Everything had happened so fast, she'd barely had a chance to catch her breath. Let alone think about what any of it meant.

Her cell phone chirped in her pocket. It was Kristen, the assistant who'd been assigned to her for the duration of the film.

"Where are you? Mr. Harrison wants to meet you."

Mr. Harrison. Dean Harrison.

Phoebe's stomach flipped.

She'd have to do it sooner or later. After all, Dean Harrison *was* the star of the movie. And her character's love interest.

She exhaled slowly.

The fact that he had a reputation for seducing his leading ladies didn't mean anything.

No.

Just because he'd been romantically involved with every single one of his costars didn't mean the same thing was going to happen to her.

Phoebe squared her shoulders and tipped her head back, letting the breeze wash over her.

No. None of those things meant anything. Nor did it mean

anything that Dean Harrison was drop-dead gorgeous with sexy, dark eyes and a smile that made it hard to breathe.

Nope. Didn't matter.

Maybe those other actresses fell for his smooth operator act. But that didn't mean she would. If anything, it only made her more determined not to.

She took a deep breath before typing in her response to Kristen. She was on her way.

Chapter Two

He watched her walk out on the breakwater. Her hair blew behind her in the wind. She wore a simple tank top and cut-off jean shorts. But even from a distance, Dean could tell she was beautiful.

Of course she was beautiful.

She'd been cast as his leading lady.

An unknown who would become a star.

The way they all did.

Every single one of his leading ladies had been plucked from obscurity and literally catapulted into stardom. It had become part of the Max Silver franchise. Just as much part of things as the heart-pounding action scenes and the steamy sexy scenes, the world also waited anxiously to see who the next Silver Starlet would be. Revealing her was almost as important as the movie premiere.

Almost.

Dean was still the star who pulled in the viewers. It was just an added bonus that he always ended up dating his leading lady by the time filming wrapped. A bonus that was almost always carefully executed by Bruce Warner, his manager.

It was also the part Dean was starting to hate the most, and he'd resolved not to date this female lead. No matter what.

He watched as Phoebe held her arms out into the wind, completely unaware that her life was about to change. She looked so innocent, so free. And so real. Like a real person, not the fake, over-plucked and over-polished women who tended to dominate his social circles.

His phone rang in his back pocket. Without even glancing at the caller ID, he knew who it was. Bruce had a sixth sense.

"What's up?"

"Give me good news, Harrison."

Dean shook his head and lifted his arm to run a hand through his hair before the pain in his shoulder reminded him he was supposed to report to medical. "Dammit," he muttered under his breath and shook out his arm.

"What's that?" Bruce never missed a thing. "Are you referring to a certain star you're supposed to be getting to know, or the accident you had on set today?"

Dean swallowed back a sigh. The man truly knew everything. It was beyond annoying. "It wasn't an accident," he said, ignoring the comment about Phoebe. "I just landed a little strange in a roll. No big deal. Probably just a bruise. It'll be fine by tomorrow. Wes finally agreed to—"

"A stunt," Bruce interrupted him. "I heard."

"Shit. How do you hear everything? I swear, you know things before I do."

"I do." Dean could picture the man on the other end with his trademark shit-eating grin. "That's why you pay me the big bucks, Deano. It's my job to know things before you even *think* them."

Dean laughed. "Oh yeah?" He turned and once again locked his eyes on Phoebe in the distance. "What am I thinking now?"

"Easy one. You're thinking of a way to tell me that you're not going to make a move on that sexy beast of a woman who is your newest costar, which is absolutely crazy since she's very likely the hottest one you've ever had. I mean, Jess Jenkins was pretty cute, but no tits to speak of, am I right? But Phoebe? Damn. I saw her casting photos. That girl has curves in *all* the right places. You should be sending cookie bouquets or some shit to the casting directors for finding her for you. Am I right?"

"Yes," Dean answered before he realized what he was agreeing to. "No," he added quickly. "You're not right. I mean, yes. She's gorgeous. Of course. But no, I'm not sending a thank you-gram or whatever to anyone because you were also right about the other thing. I'm not dating her, Bruce. I'm done with that crap. It's not—"

"It *is* friggin' brilliant, is what it is. You know as well as I do that the public eats it up and they expect it, Deano. And hey, don't forget whose idea it was in the first place."

Dean sighed. Bruce used it as an argument every time. But it wasn't as if Dean had meant to start something when he'd dated his first costar, Emma Dennis. That had happened naturally. And no matter what anyone thought, it hadn't been constructed. It was real. Even if it wasn't meant to be.

And then his next costar, Ashlyn Bay. He'd genuinely liked her. It wasn't until after the premiere when she broke it off that Dean had realized he'd been played. Ashlyn wasn't dumb; she'd seen what dating him had done for Emma's career. And by the third movie, when Bruce suggested he play nice with Jess Jenkins, he'd gone along with it. Because why not? He just hadn't expected to feel so dirty afterward. It wasn't who he was. He wasn't that type of guy. He wasn't interested in playing with people's feelings or using them. Even if they didn't think twice about doing it to him.

"No, Bruce." He was putting his foot down. He wasn't going to play that game anymore. It was why he'd waited so long to even meet Phoebe Flynn. Normally he liked to meet everyone early on and have a cast meeting. Filming was always more fun if the cast felt like a family. But he was more than aware of the expectation on him to hook up with Phoebe. It seemed easier to keep a distance from everyone this time around.

"Don't make me get on a plane," Bruce said. "You know I don't like the humidity. Besides, I've already reached out. Her assistant is going to set something up for...right now."

"Bruce, I—"

His objections fell on deaf ears. Bruce had already hung up.

Kristen was waiting for Phoebe at the Dockside Inn, the main building of Shelter Bay Marina. It was still a working marina during the filming, with boat crews and yachters coming and going. The movie crew had more or less taken over the premises and the combination was an interesting mix of people mingling together all the time. It actually relaxed Phoebe having *non-movie* people around, too. Made things more normal somehow. If that was a thing.

"I didn't think I had a call until tomorrow," Phoebe said when she got close enough to her assistant, who she'd very quickly come to depend on. Not only was Kristen the most capable and organized person Phoebe had ever met, who knew the movie industry in and out, she was also a genuinely nice person. It hadn't taken long for Phoebe to think of her as a friend. "I assumed I'd meet him then."

She actually hadn't assumed anything. But she had hoped that there wouldn't be any awkward meeting with Dean Harrison.

"You don't," Kristen said as they walked up to the deck of the Dockside. "But I got a message from his assistant that he'd like to meet you before then. And you know—"

"I know." Phoebe cut her off. "You can't say no to Dean Harrison." She tried not to roll her eyes, but judging by Kristen's smile, she wasn't very successful. She didn't know whether she'd ever get used to the *game* of everything.

"You got it." Kristen squeezed her arm. "But it won't be so bad. I promise. He's actually a really nice guy and—"

"Phoebe! Over here!"

Both women spun to see Mason Wells, one of the stunt doubles Phoebe had become friendly with, standing on the other side of the open-air deck restaurant with a bucket in his hand. Phoebe raised her arm in a wave and started to walk toward him.

"Don't do it, Pheebs. He's it!" Layla, her stunt double, appeared next to her with a cup of water in her hand. Her hair hung wet and dripping down her back.

"What the—"

"Water fight!" Layla turned and, before Phoebe could react, threw the glass of water at her.

Phoebe shrieked. A sound that immediately turned to laughter as—pending meeting forgotten—she ran after Layla, grabbing a jug of water off a nearby empty table as she went. It didn't take long to catch up to the other woman, and she dumped the water over her head with a splash and a laugh.

"You are so dead," Layla playfully threatened before dissolving into giggles.

"You're both in trouble!" They turned to see Mason approaching. His bulging arms lifted the huge bucket with ease.

Phoebe and Layla exchanged a look, eyes wide. It was a massive bucket.

"Fend for yourself," Layla called and took off down the deck.

"Where are you..." Phoebe started to call after her, but Mason was approaching quickly. Sitting around waiting to accept her fate didn't seem like a solid plan, and with only one other direction to run in, she scanned the deck. There were only a few tables with actual customers. There was one table, just behind the pillar, with only one person sitting at it. If she was quick, she could get to the empty chair next to the man who had his back to her and use him as a shield. No way would Mason throw water on a *civilian*. It was her only chance.

"No way, Mason!" Phoebe laughed as she darted through the tables toward her target. "Not today." She landed with a thud in the empty chair and, out of breath and giggling, dropped her head to her chest in an effort to pull herself together.

"Excuse me?" Her table mate cleared his throat.

"Sorry." She glanced behind her, but could no longer see Mason and his bucket of water. "I'm just hiding from my friend." She turned to introduce herself. "I hope it's—"

Dean Harrison.

His sexy, dark eyes sparkled with humor and instantly, it was hard to breathe.

"Dean? I mean…Mr. Harrison." What *was* she supposed to call him? *Shit.* "I'm sorry. I thought—"

Her words were lost in a tidal wave of water that flooded over her, plastering her hair to her face and soaking her to the skin.

Above her, she could hear Mason celebrate his victory with a shout. "Got ya! I—oh shit. Dean?"

He sputtered and coughed as an incredible amount of water rushed over him. One second, he'd been looking into the most dazzling blue eyes and the next, he was trying not to drown on dry land.

What. The. Actual. Fuck?

"Got ya! I—oh shit. Dean?"

Dean managed to wipe away enough water from his eyes to look in the direction of the voice above him. "Mason?" He could see the other man trying hard not to laugh. It was a battle he was mostly losing.

"Dean," Mason sputtered. "I'm so sorry, man. I was trying to get Phoebe and when she sat down here, I just assumed you were Eric. I mean…"

"We look alike," Dean finished for him. They did look alike. Eric was Dean's stunt double and from the back…well, he could see how Mason could have made the mistake.

"Exactly! And man, you got caught up in an epic water fight." Mason looked over Dean's head and covered his mouth with one of his big meaty hands as he burst into laughter. "Phoebe, oh shit. You are—"

"Drenched." Next to him, his costar stood up and pulled her long, dark hair from her face and wrung it out.

Dean tried and failed to notice the way her tank top stuck to her curves. Dammit, Bruce was right. The girl had curves in all the right places.

No.

He chastised himself. No matter what Bruce—or the public —wanted, he was not getting involved with Phoebe Flynn. No matter what.

"Nice one, Mason." Phoebe shook her head, but she didn't look mad. In fact, her smile lit up her face and she was positively gorgeous. "I thought I was home free," she continued. "I completely underestimated your desire to soak innocent people." She laughed and looked down at Dean. "Sorry, Mr. …"

"Dean." He extended his hand. "Call me Dean. Please. It's nice to meet you, Phoebe. Even under the rather wet conditions."

"Damn." Mason looked between them. "You two hadn't

even met yet?" He wiggled his eyebrows and Dean resisted the urge to glare at him.

He knew exactly what Mason was thinking. It was the same thing as virtually everyone else on set. But no. He wasn't going to hook up with his costar. Not this time.

"We haven't." He flashed Phoebe a grin. "But we were just about to."

"It's nice to meet you, Dean. I'm—" The smile on Phoebe's face dipped a little as she took his hand. She froze for a moment before continuing. "I'm sorry I got you caught up in this." Her smile returned as she pulled her hand away from his.

Dean instantly felt the loss of her touch.

"I'm sure you weren't expecting this when you sat down."

"I wasn't." He laughed in an effort to keep things light. Mostly so he didn't focus on the way his body had reacted to the simple touch of her skin on his. "Thanks for that, Mason."

The big man saluted comically and backed away. "I think maybe I'm needed on set or maybe…well, anywhere but here. I'm out, guys. Have fun." He took his bucket and with a few huge strides, he was gone, leaving Dean and Phoebe, both completely soaked, alone.

"Maybe we should reschedule our meeting?" Phoebe picked at her clothes.

He watched as she glanced over her shoulder at a blonde woman in a ponytail, standing at the edge of a restaurant. She held a clipboard and a cell phone. Phoebe's assistant.

"Later? After we've dried off, maybe?" Phoebe added as she turned around again.

Dean knew there would be no later. His schedule almost always accounted for, down to the minute. If Bruce had cleared a few minutes for him to meet with her now, it was likely the only chance he'd have for a while. And more importantly, he didn't want to reschedule. Now that he was in her presence, he didn't want to be away from her. She had a strange magnetic pull about her. It was innocent, as though she had no idea that she had that power. Likely she didn't. Whatever it was, Dean liked it.

"Nonsense," he said. "If your schedule looks anything like mine, we won't get another chance until we meet on set. And I always think it's a good idea to get to know someone before I kiss them, don't you?" Her face morphed, and at once she looked mortified. Dean instantly regretted his words. "Not that we're going to kiss…I just meant…"

"I know what you meant." Phoebe had recovered, the playful smile back in place on her face. "And I agree. But I don't think that's our scene tomorrow." She winked at him, and his entire body reacted at the simple action.

"Okay." Dean cleared his throat. "I'll tell you what. I'm going to grab us each a drink and then maybe we can go sit in the sun and dry off. Sound good?"

She nodded.

"Beer okay?"

She nodded again, and before she could change her mind, Dean went to grab the drinks.

Read the rest of **Hidden in the Sand,** now!

About the Author

Elena Aitken is a USA Today Bestselling Author of more than forty romance and women's fiction novels. The mother of 'grown up' twins, Elena now lives with her very own mountain man in the heart of the very mountains she writes about. She can often be found with her toes in the lake and a glass of wine in her hand, dreaming up her next book and working on her own happily ever after.

To learn more about Elena:
www.elenaaitken.com
elena@elenaaitken.com